Tara Moss is the author of the best-selling acclaimed novels *Fetish, Split, Covet,* *Countess.* Her novels have been published in seventeen countries in eleven languages, and have been nominated for both the Davitt and the Ned Kelly crime writing awards.

Born in Victoria, British Columbia, Moss is a dual Australian/Canadian citizen. When not writing her next novel she enjoys reading voraciously, spending time with her pet python, Thing, collecting morbid memento mori and Victoriana, serving as a UNICEF Goodwill Ambassador and ambassador for the Royal Institute for Deaf and Blind Children, and presenting shows on Foxtel's Crime & Investigation and 13th Street channels. She is married to Australian poet and philosopher Dr Berndt Sellheim with whom she has a daughter. Visit her on the web at www.taramoss.com and pandoraenglish.com.

Also by Tara Moss

*The Blood Countess*

A
PANDORA
ENGLISH
NOVEL

# TARA MOSS

## The Spider Goddess

MACMILLAN
Pan Macmillan Australia

First published 2011 in Macmillan by Pan Macmillan Australia Pty Limited
1 Market Street, Sydney

National Library of Australia
Cataloguing-in-Publication data:

Moss, Tara.
The spider goddess / Tara Moss.
9781742610030 (pbk.)
A823.3

Author photograph: Elizabeth Allnutt
Typeset in 12/18 pt Baskerville by Midland Typesetters, Australia
Printed in Australia by McPherson's Printing Group

Papers used by Pan Macmillan Australia Pty Ltd are natural, recyclable
products made from wood grown in sustainable forests. The manufacturing processes
conform to the environmental regulations of the country of origin.

*For Sapphira Jane*

# CHAPTER ONE

I looked at the fashion model and reassured myself she wasn't dead.

She was a stunning blonde, heavily made up, and she sat in the centre of a large, white-walled and brightly lit studio that smelled of fresh paint and cosmetics, and faintly of burning lights. She had something of the skinniness, the eerily perfect skin. Maybe it was something in the eyes that made me wonder? But no . . . The sun was up. She was definitely alive, I decided.

It was the second time I'd come to that conclusion in as many hours.

'Get what's-her-name to hurry up and bring that coffee over here.'

The photographer spoke, breaking me from my analysis. He was a lithe and aloof man, dressed in fashionable jeans and a skin-tight T-shirt. He was so skinny I'd wondered about him, too.

He was speaking to me. *What's-her-name.* Well, technically he hadn't spoken *to* me, but spoken to his assistant *about* me. All day, neither of them had really acknowledged my existence, let alone spoken directly to me, but this was not a particularly new experience.

My name's Pandora English. I'm not rich, famous or powerful, and, as I've discovered, people don't tend to talk to you in New York unless you are one of those three things. I'm from a small, unfashionable place called Gretchenville (population 3999 with my recent, unprecedented departure). When I was growing up I never imagined I would end up in New York, let alone on a photo shoot for a fashion magazine – the kind of magazine I'd spent years perusing as a girl.

So here I was watching my first real fashion shoot. And, to my surprise, it wasn't all that exciting. Go figure.

I found I was less interested in the designer fashion and expensive makeup and all the things I'd coveted in my unglamorous hometown, and more in whether the people around me were human. My recent experiences in New York had made me wonder about such things. In the past few months, a whole lot had changed for me. I'd moved from my small town, got my first job in publishing, been on my first real date, and met some undead folks. The latter had been particularly eye-opening. Life and death, and the states in between, were a whole lot more complicated than I ever could have imagined. And considering what my late father had called my 'overactive imagination', that was really saying something.

'Hello? Coffee?' The photographer spoke in a quick, impatient voice.

I walked up to him, balancing the tray of hot drinks I'd been sent to fetch from a cafe on the cold SoHo street outside.

'Um, here is your coffee,' I said and smiled nervously, holding out the tray.

The assistant only turned his head my way momentarily, he was too busy holding up a big silver reflective disc at an uncomfortable angle. The photographer was back to clicking the shutter of his camera busily.

Again, I looked over at the model he was photographing in the apex of lights. There were so many lights pointed at her that I wasn't sure how she kept her eyes open. Every couple of seconds she changed her expression ever so slightly – from sultry to pouting, and then back to sultry again. The process seemed kind of mechanical. It wasn't how it looked in the magazines.

I looked down at my hands. They were bare and they looked a tad blue. It was winter in New York and it had been literally freezing outside. My tightly wrapped wool scarf had fallen free of one shoulder, exposing my cold neck, which took happily to the heat of the overblown lights around me. I looked forward to a sip of the nice hot tea I'd ordered for myself. A hand reached out and snatched one of the coffees. It was the photographer. He took a sip and frowned. 'Is this a *non*-fat latte?' he demanded to no one in particular, though I was standing right there.

If there is one thing I have learned about the fashion industry in the past two months, it is that no one drinks full fat milk. Also, they have some perplexing issue with carbohydrates, which, as far as I know, are in most foods anyway. They seem to believe that full fat milk and carbohydrates are the big bad. If only they knew about the big bad things I knew about.

'Yes, it is non-fat,' I confirmed, and resisted reminding him of my name. It wasn't that hard to remember, after all, considering it happened to be the same name as the magazine paying his bill. This shoot was for *Pandora*, the glossy fashion mag I worked for.

How I came to be hired by *Pandora* magazine is an odd story. I came to New York at the invitation of my great-aunt Celia, and, well . . . she's kind of different. She has an uncanny knack for knowing things – like when there is an opening for an assistant at a fashion magazine, and just what I should wear to get the job. Don't ask me how. She just knows things. It's something that runs in the family, I'm discovering.

'Just one more shot,' the photographer said, after a sip of coffee.

At this, the model cast her eyes to the ground and raised an eyebrow. I was the only one who saw her expression, or detected her resigned sigh. I knew why she was impatient. We'd heard that line from the photographer at least three times in the past hour, and the fetching of fresh coffee didn't really denote an end to the shoot, either. The sun would be going down soon and I probably wasn't the only one eager to get home to a warm bath and a hot meal. The model would doubtless be feeling the same, only in a slightly more transformed way, as she was wearing something called a 'transformative knit'.

When I'd landed in New York, vampire chic was all the rage – a little too much the rage, if you ask me. Next season is apparently all about 'transformative knits'. Knitwear is the new black. Especially black knitwear, I guess.

The flawless model before me was swathed in knitwear,

and layered with brightly coloured enamel jewellery, some of the pieces quite large. The tight-fitting knitwear garments apparently 'subtly shape the figure'. Which was interesting, because they had chosen a model with a perfectly proportioned figure in no danger of needing any kind of shaping or transforming. The fashion world was a very strange place.

'Peppermint. Great,' the photographer's assistant muttered, and snatched my tea from the tray.

'Oh, that's actually mine —' I began, but he was already across the room with it. I gave a little resigned sigh of my own.

The photographer took another sip of his drink and cast a glance towards a large computer screen he had set up on a wheeled cart. He was shooting on a digital camera, and the images he'd taken were blown up on the monitor. He squinted at the screen, and muttered something to his assistant, who scrolled through some images. A little square zoomed in to magnify parts of the image, and the assistant manipulated it to fall on the model's face, making each miniscule pore and slick of makeup jump out in jarring high definition. Then, with a couple of clicks, he smoothed a wrinkle I hadn't even noticed she had. Incredible.

'Let's change. All this black is too . . . black. We need some colour for the cover shot. What about the Sandy Chow samples? Did they arrive?'

'No,' the stylist said. She was loitering around the screen as well, staring at the magnified images as if they held the key to the meaning of life. 'They've had some mega-crisis. We only have the Smith & Co, Helmsworth, Mal and this stuff. The Victor Mal has some colour panels.'

'Too eighties,' the photographer said.

'Could I have my coffee please?' The model's voice had a slight whine. 'The extra large?' Clearly she wasn't happy to be working overtime.

I stepped further into the circle of lights to pass her the over-sized drink. 'Here you go. I'm sure the shoot is nearly over,' I said quietly as a form of encouragement, but her frown stayed firmly in place. Mind you, she looked pretty good with a pout. Perhaps that was why she used it so often.

I stepped away with the empty tray, and seconds later there was a small cry.

'Ohhhh!'

The fashion model scurried backwards across the floor on her hands and the balls of her feet, her face contorted in shock. Had she burned her lip on her coffee? No. The drink remained untouched on the floor of the studio. *Strange.*

'A spider!' someone yelled from behind me.

I spotted the animal and nearly dropped the tray I was holding. It was a spider, true enough. But it was not just any spider. It was a very large, fat and hairy spider.

I stood transfixed, as it seemed, did the rest of the studio. I'd heard that Manhattan had cockroaches the size of rats and rats the size of cats, but spiders the size of . . . *that?*

'Is that a . . . tarantula?' I asked. *In New York? In the winter?* 'No. It can't be. Maybe a wolf spider? Or . . .'

'I'm outta here,' the model cried and shot to her feet. She pulled off the clingy knit top and ran across the studio towards the tiny changing area in only a bra and black capri pants. In record time she was out of the rest of her wardrobe. I'd never seen someone undress so fast. The makeup artist was standing on a chair, mumbling something unintelligible. The model ignored her. She changed quickly into her own street clothes and made for the exit at high speed.

The door slammed behind her.

'Um, is there a pet shop nearby or anything?' I asked, but no one was really listening. The photographer and his assistant were backed up against the wall of the studio, and the wardrobe stylist was retreating slowly across the room, holding a sweater like a matador. They were all struck mute by the large spider moving slowly across the stark white floor. It was plump and hairy and as big as my palm. It paused and shifted sideways, then stopped again. Maybe it liked the lights?

'I'll get it,' I finally said. I bent down and gently placed the cardboard coffee tray on the floor. Moving slowly, I took the model's oversized cup and poured the liquid out on to the floor. (No one would care about the mess, I figured.) Holding the empty styrofoam cup, I crept forward slowly. 'Come here little buddy . . .' I called out to the spider in a sing-song voice.

'Kill it!' the photographer shrieked in a high voice.

'No, I'll just . . .' I began.

And there it was in front of me, less than a foot away. I felt its eight tiny black eyes on me and I felt something else, too. This spider was *aware* of me. Not just aware of the changes in light and movement, and the presence of a person approaching, but aware of *me*. It seemed ridiculous, but I felt some kind of strange connection with the spider. Not a friendly connection, per se, but a connection. And my gut felt funny – a bit cold like it sometimes did.

I often have what you might call odd 'feelings'. Sometimes I know things I have no normal or scientifically explainable way of knowing. When I was growing up my father had always reprimanded me for my 'overactive imagination' when I'd suggested I could foresee things, intuit truths, sense the magical or speak to the departed. Until recently I'd assumed he was right but my great-aunt told me that this is a 'gift' of mine. She claims I am 'genetically predisposed to extrasensory perception and sensitivity to the supernatural', and that my mother was similarly gifted, and her mother before her. It's a gift of the Lucasta women. And I was the Seventh. Whatever that meant. It was news to me.

I still don't completely understand the feelings I get, and I am not confident about distinguishing them from normal feelings, but there it is. Great-Aunt Celia thinks my feelings are something I should listen to.

So, I had a weird feeling about this big spider and, as it stared at me with its eight little beady eyes, it seemed perhaps the feeling was mutual. 'Now just stay still, okay, pal?' I managed. I waited for it to rear up aggressively and bare its fangs, but it just sat there, staring at me. I brought the cup close, and it shifted sideways slightly. 'Easy now . . .' And just like that, I placed the big cup over it at an angle and scooped it inside with the discarded cardboard tray. I kept one hand on top of the container, as any spider that size could easily flip over the styrofoam and scurry off. Soon I had a flat piece of cardboard covering the opening. 'Give me some of that tape, please,' I said, and the photographer's assistant reanimated before my eyes. He threw me a roll of black gaffer tape, still keeping his distance.

'Don't let it out . . .' he squeaked.

'It's just a spider,' I said. 'It's not dangerous.'

I guessed that it was indeed a tarantula. I'd never seen a real one up close, but I'd read about them in my late mother's many books back home. Tarantulas looked impressive and had big fangs that could give a pretty good bite, but their venom was meant for much smaller prey, and was not deadly to humans. Tarantulas were usually found in tropical and subtropical climates. So this one must have escaped from a pet shop or private collection somewhere nearby and wandered in looking for shelter or heat. Our little staring contest had left quite an impression on me, but I supposed a stray tarantula was likely to make an impression on anyone.

'It's not going anywhere,' I assured the room and held up the cup sideways so the spider wasn't bunched up at the bottom. I felt its legs scratching at the styrofoam as it moved from side to side. I'd taped the cardboard across the top. It would hold.

There was an audible, collective sigh.

'Oh my god!' I heard the makeup artist say as she got down from her chair.

I stood in the centre of the studio for a while holding the cup, and waiting for instructions, but no one spoke.

'So,' I finally said. 'Does this mean the shoot is over?'

I stepped out into the cool darkness of the SoHo street with my leather satchel over my shoulder and my scarf pulled tight around my neck. In my right hand I held a coffee cup with a live tarantula in it; not quite the souvenir I expected from my first photo shoot. The studio wasn't very far from the office of *Pandora* magazine, so I knew the area without having to reference my creased map of New York. I would take the subway at Spring Street and get home to my great-aunt's place. That hot bath could not come too soon.

I took a couple of steps on to the pavement and noticed that someone was waiting for me.

A long black car was parked at the kerb and a formidably tall man stood before it like a bodyguard, his feet shoulder-width apart, his hands neatly folded. The sun had just set, yet he still wore dark sunglasses and, though the sidewalk was chaotic with pedestrians, he seemed eerily serene and motionless among them. If he was breathing, I couldn't tell.

'Hello, Vlad,' I said. I did not expect a response. This was my Great-Aunt Celia's chauffeur. He never spoke, or if he did, he didn't speak around me. I hadn't asked for his services, and yet here he was. My great-aunt must have sent him. She did that sometimes.

*Guess I won't be taking the subway.*

Vlad smoothly opened the door for me and I slid into the back seat of the car, placed my satchel at my feet, and the cup in my lap. 'Thank you,' I said.

We soon began the drive uptown, hitting traffic on Madison Avenue. We crawled past the Guggenheim Museum at a walking pace and, after driving through the Upper East Side, we took the route through Central Park that I always enjoyed. In this monumental city of concrete and steel, it still impressed and surprised me to find the magnificent green of Central Park waiting. And then the little-used single lane road wound its way through the shadows and disappeared into a tunnel filled with fog – the tunnel that led to Spektor, the Manhattan suburb that didn't appear on any map.

The car slowed and Vlad pulled up to the kerb at the front of my great-aunt's large Victorian mansion at Number One Addams Avenue. Dr Edmund Barrett, the infamous scientist and psychical researcher, built the mansion in the 1880s and it took up most of a small city block at the heart of Spektor. I'd never seen a building like it. It seemed narrow and stretched up, with a series of stone arches, turrets and spikes pointing to the sky. It was five storeys tall, with heavily embellished window arches placed in twos and threes across the front. A perceptive person would notice that the windows on the middle floors were boarded up from the inside. The building remained impressive despite the slightly abandoned air that all of Spektor seemed to share. It possessed an eerie beauty.

Vlad opened the door for me and I stepped into the wintry dusk. The mist on the street was faint compared with the thick wall of fog we'd driven through in the tunnel.

'Thank you, Vlad,' I said, and strode up to the iron gates of the building with my tummy rumbling. I put my key in the heavy front door and turned the lock. 'Okay, open up,' I mumbled under my breath, and the enormous door permitted me to enter. I slid inside and felt the familiar tomb-like coolness of the air in the high-ceilinged lobby. The heavy door closed behind me with a small puff of dust, and with the flick of a switch the dark space came to life under the blinking illumination of a very old chandelier.

'Oh, now. Look at that,' I muttered and shook my head.

High above me, the large chandelier was askew again. Last week, I'd made an attempt to fix it, but already the old fixture was back to its former position. Cobwebs had even begun to re-form between the dusty crystals. I shook my head again. Despite the apparent futility of it, I wanted to clean the place up again for my great-aunt. She did so much for me, the least I could do was dust a few cobwebs.

The lobby was decorated with majestic tilework and gilded wall sconces, now both in a state of disrepair. A circular staircase snaked up towards the sealed wooden door of a mezzanine floor, and an old lift sat in a cage of elaborate ironwork, including spiked fleurs-de-lis – one of which was missing. Not a month ago I'd used that missing fleur-de-lis to stab a vampire . . . sorry, Sanguine (vampire is a very negative term, apparently), hence my new-found paranoia about the undead. My staking attempt had been a literal and metaphorical mess, however. In direct contrast to the rules of all the novels I'd ever read, my undead aggressor *survived* the staking, and I'd had to scrub the lobby floor of blood until it was clean enough to perform heart surgery on. Which is almost what I'd done, come to think of it. Despite all that, the lobby looked just how I'd first seen it when I'd arrived in Spektor almost two months before – a bit like a crypt, yet, in its way, a magnificent space.

But now was not the time to dwell.

After dark I had friends within these walls, but also enemies. Some of my . . . well, *housemates*, were not terribly pleased with my presence. Especially since the staking incident. With that in mind, I removed a rice bag from my satchel and held it in my hand, ready for use. Those enemies of mine were much more affected by what was in that bag than by any karate move I might produce. Or my new-found tarantula, for that matter.

I hurried across the tiles.

'S-s-h-r-a-a-a-ak . . .'

I paused for only a moment. I'd often heard sounds like that, as if the building was settling. But I'd never heard a building settle quite like this one. By some trick of acoustics, the strange noise sounded like it came from *beneath* the floor. With little delay, I traversed the lobby, jumped in the old rattling lift, and began my ascent to the penthouse. I silently watched the other floors pass, keeping an eye out for movement on the landings.

When I arrived home to Great-Aunt Celia's penthouse I knocked on the midnight blue doors before I entered. This was one of her rules. After a moment I used my key to let myself in. 'Hi, Great-Aunt Celia. I'm home,' I called out. I hung up my coat on the mirrored Edwardian hatstand, and slipped off my flat shoes.

Celia was the reason I was in New York. She was my mother's mother's sister and one of only two living relatives I had. (The other was my Aunt Georgia in Gretchenville – my late father's older sister, and I'd lived with her for eight years after my parents were killed.) I'd never met Celia before I moved to New York, but I had gratefully accepted her offer to have me stay. Who wouldn't trade Gretchenville for Manhattan? Leaving my stifling little hometown was an exciting and much needed change. At the time, of course, I'd had no idea just how much of a change it would be.

Great-Aunt Celia's elegant penthouse was quite unlike any other place I'd seen. The floors were polished wood and the domed ceilings were crowned with a sparkling chandelier at the highest point. The large main lounge room, which I now looked upon, was lined with rows of impressive bookcases filled with tomes to make an antiquarian weep with envy. Glass-fronted sideboards housed curious artefacts, objets d'art, exotic plants and antiques – a Venus flytrap, a carved tusk, a fertility statue, a tiny art deco nymph, fading photographs and art prints, and strange butterflies and moths displayed in small glass domes. Everything seemed both beautiful and intriguing. In keeping with the era of the mansion, the penthouse rooms were elegantly appointed with polished and carved furniture from Victorian and Edwardian times, mixed with some art deco touches. Yet, unlike the rest of the building, there were no cobwebs, no wear and tear, no dust. Celia's rooms were immaculate. Tonight the curtains were open over the tall, arched windows, letting in the faint bluish light of a waxing gibbous moon. The famous Manhattan skyline was visible in the distance through a faint fog, the Empire State Building a black silhouette speckled by lit windows.

It still astounded me to know I was really in New York, the city I'd always dreamed of.

'Darling, how was the photo shoot?' came the familiar voice.

My great-aunt was in her usual spot, reclining under the halo of her reading lamp in the little alcove to one side of her palatial lounge room. Her shoes were off and her feet were up on the hassock, ankles crossed elegantly. I could see the thin casing of her black silk stockings, and the little seam across her manicured toes. Great-Aunt Celia was an impeccably stylish woman, as one would expect of a former designer to the Hollywood stars. Lined up next to her chair was a pair of fluffy heeled slippers decorated with ostrich feathers. This was one great-aunt who would never, *ever* own pressure stockings and sensible shoes.

Celia placed a long feather in the pages of her book to mark her place, and rested it on the wide arm of her leather chair. She shifted and faced me. She was, as always, a vision of pale 1940s glamour – high cheekbones, arched brows, alabaster skin and red lips, her dark hair set in movie-star waves beneath an omnipresent black widow's veil that fell delicately to her chin. She had a slim, hourglass figure built for the couture of her day and tonight she wore a black silk dress with a waist-cinching leather belt. Decades after the death of her photographer husband, Roger, the widow's veil seemed an eccentric habit. It suited her, I thought. The thin mesh only partially obscured her peculiarly youthful beauty – peculiar because she was, in fact, at least eighty years old.

There was much I didn't know about my great-aunt.

'Now, what have you got there?' she said, eyeing the styrofoam cup. 'It's not like you to bring home a takeaway coffee.'

Celia was a staunch tea drinker.

'Oh, it's not coffee.' I felt the creature inside the cup shift. 'It's kind of a weird story actually . . .'

'A weird story? I always have time for one of those,' my great-aunt quipped, and smiled from beneath her veil. She took her silk stocking clad feet off the hassock, inviting me to sit with her.

I left my satchel at the door and popped the bag of rice back inside. I wouldn't need it now that I was safely ensconced in Celia's penthouse. The others who lived here were not invited into the penthouse, and could not enter.

'It was the strangest thing, Great-Aunt Celia,' I explained as I perched on the edge of the hassock. 'The knitwear shoot was going on forever, and I'd just been sent on yet another coffee run, and when I got back there was this spider in the middle of the studio. The model bolted immediately, and no one else did a thing. You should have seen the photographer and his assistant, completely frozen with fear. The makeup artist was on a chair . . .'

The corners of Celia's mouth turned up slightly.

'It's a tarantula, I think. Quite odd considering tarantulas aren't native to the area,' I said.

'Odd indeed,' she agreed.

'Well, I just emptied this cup and popped the spider inside,' I said. 'I couldn't leave it there and I didn't know what else to do. So, here I am with a tarantula, or whatever it is.'

'Were you not afraid?' she asked me.

I frowned. 'I guess not. I've never seen a big spider like that before but I'd read about tarantulas and I just . . . acted on instinct.'

This seemed to please Celia. 'Good. You should trust your instincts more.' She nodded to herself. 'And how was the shoot? Did you take note of which knitwear labels they were using?'

'I didn't think to check,' I said, trying to remember the names. Perhaps Celia would be displeased that I wasn't as interested in designs as she was, despite the fact that I was attempting to start my writing career at a fashion magazine. Some fashionista I was.

'That's okay, darling. So . . .' She grinned slightly. 'What would you like to do with it? You haven't brought it home for dinner or something like that?'

I gaped. 'The spider?'

'Fried tarantula is a delicacy in Cambodia. It's apparently quite delicious, though I've never tried it.' She paused, watching the blood drain from my face, and then leaned forward to pat my knee. 'But I am only pulling your leg, darling. Of course we won't eat it.'

I took a moment to recover from her wicked sense of humour.

'I don't know what to do with it,' I said. 'I just couldn't leave it there. They were going to kill it, and that wasn't right. And I can't leave it on the street outside. It's winter. It will freeze to death.' I paused. 'Tomorrow I'm going to look up pet shops in SoHo. It must have escaped from one of them.'

'You do have a great deal of compassion, Pandora. I can't think of a lot of young women who would care what happened to a spider on the winter streets of New York, so long as . . .' She looked at the cup in my lap. 'So long as they didn't have to hold it,' she finished.

'My mother said that spiders are misunderstood.'

'Indeed they are.' She paused. 'We'll put it in a jar for now, if you like. And maybe Harold will be able to get us a nice spider cage, or whatever such creatures are meant to be housed in.'

Harold owned the nearby grocer in Spektor. He was an odd fellow – very nice, but peculiar. 'A vivarium is what people keep them in, I think. But I don't think I'll have the spider long enough to need one.'

I'd heard that people kept tarantulas as pets, but honestly I couldn't imagine why. It wasn't quite the same as having a dog or cat.

There was a noise and we both looked up. 'Oh, there you are,' Celia said. Right on cue, Celia's cat had arrived. She was named after a Norse goddess who was often depicted in a glorious chariot pulled by cats. She was pure white – an albino – with eyes the colour of pink opals. Sometimes she liked to sneak into my room at night for a cuddle. Strangely, though, this evening she stopped several feet away from me and sat with her ears back.

'Hi, Freyja. Hi, kitty,' I said in a sing-song voice.

She let out a low feline growl.

'I don't think she likes your new friend,' Celia remarked.

*Friend?* I thought of that odd moment on the studio floor – the moment of connection. It wasn't friendly contact. It was something else. Some sense of recognition, perhaps? I had no idea what it might mean, or if it was indeed only my imagination, but I tried to trust my gut feeling the way Celia had been teaching me.

My great-aunt leaned forward. 'Do you think it knew who you were? That it was trying to tell you something?'

I blinked. 'The spider, you mean? That's crazy.'

She smiled. 'Yes, of course it is. Crazy.'

# CHAPTER
# TWO

I was in my long, delicate white nightgown, standing on a grassy hilltop. A breeze blew against me, bringing goose pimples to my arms. I'd thought it was night, but above me was a radiant blue sky. The sun felt warm and gentle, and I tilted my face up to receive its rays. I closed my eyes and breathed in. The air smelled of wild flowers.

I did not know this place, but it was beautiful.

I searched the horizon, and in the distance saw a man on horseback riding towards me. He rode a pure white stallion, and I made out his dress as he approached – leather riding boots and a sharply tailored uniform of blue, the frockcoat long and fitted across his broad shoulders and slim waist. He wore a sword in a scabbard on his hip, and a cap on his head.

He pulled up his magnificent horse at my side. It neighed and panted, standing tall. Its muscles shivered and I smiled. It was the most beautiful beast I'd ever seen. I wanted to reach out and touch it.

'Miss Pandora,' the man said in a formal tone.

I looked up. The man was handsome and familiar. *Lieutenant Luke*, I tried to reply, but the words would not come.

He reached down to take my hand. 'Join me,' he said in a deep, masculine voice, his bright blue eyes seeming to glow with a strange intensity. I did not hesitate, yet as I reached out to accept his hand I found that I could not touch him. His hand, though it looked like it was right there, was somehow untouchable; my own moved through it.

*What's happening?* I tried to ask, but found that I could not speak.

I felt a rumble under my bare feet. Something was coming. Something terrible. The ground shook. I retracted my hand, as did he, and my gaze fell to the crest of the hill. We both felt it. We both heard it – the grunts and curious moans, the hundreds of running feet.

*What's happening?*

And then we saw.

Corpses. Thousands of reanimated corpses ran towards us, mouths open, tongues lolling, their eyes blazing red. Some had no arms, some no head, but still they propelled themselves up the hill towards us with remarkable, unnatural speed. *Revenants. Zombies.*

I reached again for Luke but, to my horror, my hand went right through his again. It was *me*, I realised. *I was the ghost.* I couldn't touch him because I wasn't real. He couldn't take me away from all this.

Luke's white horse moved restlessly, inching sideways and throwing its head up and down. 'Easy now . . .'

The ghoulish creatures were nearly upon us. I stumbled backwards as the magnificent white stallion reared up, and Luke unsheathed his shining sword.

'Luke!' I finally managed to yell, my voice returned to me. *'Luke!'*

But he was gone.

Some sound or sense woke me from my nightmare.

I ran a hand over my clammy face and opened my heavy eyes. I was in the four-poster bed in my room at Great-Aunt Celia's. It was a beautiful room with a high ceiling, and everything in it seemed wonderfully old and ornate. Even in the low light I could make out the mirror on the oak dresser, and the tall antique wardrobe next to it. My dress for the next day – for later this morning, in fact – hung from the front of the wardrobe, waiting for sunrise. It was another outfit Celia had designed in the forties, this one black, with an elaborate gold belt and a white collar. I could also make out the sloping Victorian writing desk under one of the two tall, arched windows that faced on to Addams Avenue outside. One of the windows was open just a crack, as usual, to let air in. The curtains were only partially closed, just as I'd left them. They swayed slightly in the night breeze. Even in my sleepy state, I could see that everything was in its place. I was safe. There were no rushing hordes of rotting revenants. Not yet, anyway.

'Miss Pandora?'

I wondered if I was still dreaming. I blinked and looked around me.

'Miss Pandora. I heard you cry out.' My eyes rested on a white, nebulous form materialising near my bed.

*Lieutenant Luke.*

He appeared at the foot of my bed, wearing a dark blue cap emblazoned with a pair of crossed gold swords, his long frockcoat neatly fitted on his masculine form, the polished buttons done up to the neck. The coat fitted his broad shoulders impeccably and tapered at his slim waist, cinched with a leather belt. He was dressed as he had been in the dream, just as he always was – in the Union soldier's uniform of the Civil War. A war in which he'd fought and died.

I'd first met Lieutenant Luke in my bedroom at Great-Aunt Celia's two months ago. I'd only just arrived and he'd given me quite a shock at the time. I thought that some crazed New Yorker had broken in to burgle the place or do me harm. It was funny now to think of it – Luke had been trapped as a spectre in this house for decades, I was the interloper here.

Since moving in with Great-Aunt Celia one of the many things I had learned about was the existence of ghosts. Well . . . I'll admit I'd had a few rather enormous hints while I was growing up. Even when I was young I could sense the dead, but my parents had strongly disapproved of my fanciful tales. After I foresaw the death of the local butcher when I was just a little girl – and then told several people that I'd conversed with him after the accident that killed him – people stopped coming around to our house. (Except a few tiresome child psychologists. *They* came around.) And although I was reasonably smart and not unattractive, I had the 'weird kid' tag tattooed to my forehead after that. I was never going to be popular in school. And I suppose it didn't help when my mother and father died in an accident in Egypt, where my mother had been working on an archaeological site. I was eleven at the time. I was at my Aunt Georgia's house when the news came, and there I stayed. Georgia is the maths teacher in Gretchenville. It's not a popular subject, and she is not a particularly popular teacher. So it was books instead of boys for me, and that was my life up until recently. A life spent with my head in novels and fashion magazines. (Everyone was so popular and so glamorous in those magazines. I wanted *that* life.) Now here I was living in a suburb of Manhattan that didn't appear on maps, and conversing with a handsome ghost.

Shows you how much those child psychologists know.

Naturally though it had taken me awhile to come to terms with these aspects of my new life in Spektor. Lieutenant Luke certainly helped in that regard. Truthfully, Luke was . . . Well, he was rather dreamy.

'Are you okay, Miss Pandora?' he asked, looking as diligent as ever. He was clenching his magnificent jaw – a jaw that always brought to mind an anvil, for some reason. Luke was twenty-five, or had been when he'd died in 1861 at the start of the Civil War. He had a lean, tanned, clean-shaven face with the sort of sideburns that were popular in his day, and sandy hair worn a bit long around the collar. He also had the brightest blue eyes I'd ever seen. They seemed at times to even glow slightly in the dark.

Luke moved slowly from the foot of my bed to stand just next to me. Some lingering feelings from my dream were still upon me and I felt an urge to reach up and kiss him.

'Sorry, Luke. I was only dreaming,' I said. 'I didn't mean to alarm you.'

'I thought you might be hurt,' he replied, concerned.

'I'm fine.'

I had mentioned to Luke once that I didn't like him turning up in my room unannounced. Although it was always wonderful to see him, there was an immediacy and intimacy to his materialising unexpectedly in my bedroom that was confronting for me, especially considering the nature of my dreams, many of which involved him. Now I sensed that he was unsure about appearing without being called upon. Which was, of course, just what I'd done by calling out for him in my dream.

'I'm glad you're here,' I assured him, and did a terrible job of trying to disguise my excitement. I enjoyed being with Lieutenant Luke; forget that, I *savoured* it. Never mind that he died one hundred and fifty years ago and didn't even exist to other people. I missed him when too many nights passed without a visit. But what could one do about a ghost crush? Not very much.

'Have a seat,' I said, patting the bed.

He sat on the edge of the mattress more softly than any living man his size could manage. 'You brought a strange spider home,' he commented.

'Yes.' It was now in a large glass jar with a punctured lid, sitting on one of the shelves in Celia's lounge room. I'd used the tin lid of a smaller jar as a makeshift water dish. 'You noticed that?'

He nodded.

'I'm not sure if it is safe to have it here, Pandora.'

I smiled. 'It's fine, really. It's harmless.'

It was a peculiar creature, though. I had a feeling the tarantula was following me with its cluster of alien-like eyes every time I passed through the lounge room, and I found that no matter which way I turned the jar, it shifted around to stare back at me. Did spiders normally do that?

'Besides, tomorrow I'm going to try to find out where it came from,' I continued. 'The poor thing probably escaped from a pet shop or something. In any event, I'll find somewhere for it. It's just here temporarily.'

He didn't seem reassured by any of what I said.

'I've read about tarantulas,' I told him. I'd read about many exotic things in my mother's books. 'The North American tarantulas aren't actually that poisonous, they just look big and scary. They usually eat insects.' I knew that tarantulas had a paralysing agent in their venom, and that they injected a powerful enzyme into their prey in order to eat them. It was kind of gruesome to imagine a spider liquefying the insides of their prey, then sucking them dry and casting away the husk.

'I'm not sure it's a good idea to keep it here,' he repeated, but I stubbornly dismissed his warning.

'It's not for long.' I rolled on to my side and smiled at him, propping myself up on one elbow. 'Can we talk?' I asked. 'I have some questions.'

At that moment, Freyja headbutted the partially closed door of my bedroom open. She walked straight in and leapt up on my bed, purring and settling between Luke and I with a distinctly feline sense of entitlement that was both endearing and amusingly arrogant. She appeared to gaze at Lieutenant Luke, who sat near me, silent and protective. I was sure she could see him. Her owner, Celia, could not.

'If you want, I'll tell you what I can,' he replied. 'But then you must sleep.'

I looked at the bedside clock and saw that it was only one o'clock. I had to get up for work around seven. I was already beginning to feel the pull of sleep. 'You know, there are so many things I don't understand. Where do you go when you aren't . . . here?'

'I can't tell you that, Pandora. There are . . .' he paused, 'rules about what I can and can't tell you.'

'What rules exactly?'

'There are some things the dead can't tell the living.'

Luke had told me this before. The dead were prevented from telling certain truths to the living, which was one of the reasons so many ghost sightings involved precisely that − a sighting and no dialogue. To have a verbal relationship with a spirit, as I did, was unusual. Celia said it was one of my special gifts. But despite our special relationship, Luke could not explain everything I wanted to know. It didn't stop me from trying, though.

'Can you tell me if there is a heaven or hell?' I asked.

'You have some big questions tonight,' he said. I smiled again. 'I've never seen any evidence of the kind of heaven or hell people used to discuss in my day. The horned devil. The pitchfork. The men in white robes, with bright haloes. There are places where spirits go, but . . .'

'No "pearly gates"?'

'Not that I've seen. You're getting tired now. We should make sure you get some sleep —'

'And you don't know where you were between the time you died and when you found yourself here in Spektor?' I asked quickly. The building had been erected in 1888, some time after his death.

'That is a curious thing to consider, Miss Pandora. I just found myself here after a time. I don't even remember the exact moment when I arrived. I must have been in some kind of limbo before that. I'm not sure for how long.'

Ghosts didn't have a sense of time, I'd discovered.

'I remember Dr Barrett and his wife, but . . .'

'You do?' Celia had told me something of them and their tragic deaths. 'Oh, tell me about them. What were they like? What kind of experiments was he conducting here?'

But Luke sat up quite suddenly, as if hearing or sensing something I could not.

'What is it?' I asked. 'Did you hear something?'

'Wait here,' he said, as if I could have followed him as he stepped past the four-poster bed and *through* the wall, disappearing from view. It always made me uneasy when he did that. When we were together, he made a point of walking through *open* doors, instead of closed ones, and he even sometimes took the lift with me, though I knew he could pass through the levels of the mansion with little effort, as he was probably doing now.

I waited in my bed, feeling the strangeness of the hour and wondering how long it would be before my dead Civil War friend returned. I did need to get some sleep before work. But maybe I should get up and take a look?

Perhaps two minutes passed before I heard Luke's voice, and felt a cool mist descend. 'There is someone downstairs who shouldn't be here,' he said, materialising. 'You need to see.'

'Oh.' This was a first. I swung my legs out of the bed, and my bare toes touched the cold floor. Luke turned to allow me some privacy as I threw back the covers and emerged in my white nightie. I grabbed my winter coat and put it on over my gown while I slipped my feet into my soft house slippers.

'Okay,' I said, and he turned.

'We must hurry.'

He took me by the hand and, unlike my dream, his hand felt nearly as real and solid as any I'd felt – an illusion we sometimes managed. He led me gently, but quickly, towards the bedroom door, remembering as always to open the door for me before passing through. We walked through the lounge room and arrived at the front door.

'Do we have to go downstairs, or . . .?' I began, but it was clear there was too much urgency to worry about precautions, like rice. We stepped out of the doors of the penthouse and Luke led me to the rail.

'She was just . . . there, in the lobby,' he said, and pointed.

'Who was there?'

'I'm not sure. I hoped you might know.'

We stood for a moment looking down through the building. The elevator wasn't at the penthouse level where I'd left it. Someone had used it.

'Whoever the lady was, she did not belong here. I have seen her coming and going lately,' he said, obviously concerned. 'The lady should not be here.'

'She's a mortal? Is that what you mean?'

He nodded. 'Yes.'

There weren't a lot of us in Spektor. 'What do you think she was doing here?' I asked.

'I think someone might be using her. She seemed to be in a kind of trance . . .'

'Oh,' I said. That sounded ominous.

I wondered who it could have been.

# CHAPTER THREE

When I emerged on Tuesday morning the main street of Spektor was lifeless.

I was growing used to the peculiar quiet of the suburb, and even to the fog that clung to the buildings with its faint odour of old books and mothballs. At one end of Addams Avenue, in the direction I was headed, the smell became a little more intense.

*Harold's Grocer.*

In some ways Harold's Grocer was your typical corner store. In other, significant ways, it was not. For one, it's supposedly *always* open, night or day. Harold also claimed he could get anything for anyone in Spektor. I wondered if my request today would push that theory.

'Hi Harold,' I called out, as I pushed the door open. A bell chimed to announce my arrival.

The store was a bit musty, and the shelves were stocked with old grocery goods. Harold had detergents and soaps, tins of vegetables, sauces, and boxes of cereal and rice, but I didn't recognise the brands nor their somewhat antediluvian labels. I always had the feeling those boxes and tins had been there an awfully long time. He had an old, humming glass-fronted fridge that he kept stocked with things I regularly picked up: milk, cheese and soda; and he kept a fresh stock of my favourite crackers. But those tins on the shelves could probably walk out on their own, I thought. Harold had a cool, old-fashioned sign out front (declaring, simply enough, 'Harold's Grocer'), and his cash register was a collector's dream. It was a big metal register with round keys that sat on metal stalks like an old typewriter, and big white number tabs that popped up to show the total. The most impressive thing about the shop, however, was Harold himself.

'Well hello there, Pandora English.'

Harold emerged from the back, trailing dust like a moulting dog might trail hairs. He was a short man, and he always dressed in the same plaid shirt, tucked into high work pants, his oversized belly bulging above the belt. The thin tufts of hair on his head swayed back and forth like green sea kelp, and his jolly cheeks were the colour of Granny Smith apples. He was, it must be said, the most green person I'd ever seen. The whites of his eyes were yellow. His viridescent appearance had taken some getting used to, but it was hard not to like him as he was always so agreeable.

'Hi, Harold. It's good to see you. Are you keeping well?'

'I'm a little green around the gills,' he joked. It was a joke he made often. I smiled every time.

'I have a request,' I told him.

'Ms Celia let me know that you need a little house for your spider friend,' Harold said before I could continue.

'Oh. She spoke to you last night? Well, I don't know if it

is a spider *friend*, but . . . No, I don't think I need a vivarium. I'll only have it for another day. I was just going to order some food for it. Some crickets?'

'Ms Celia said you did need a vivarium. But, quite right, she didn't use the term friend,' he remarked.

Celia always made sure anything I bought at Harold's was put on her tab, but buying a vivarium for a stray tarantula hardly seemed fair. 'I suppose the spider has to be in decent housing until I find some place for it to go,' I said, pondering the situation. 'That small jar is a little inhumane, I guess.' Celia tended to be right about things. 'Well, I'll probably only need it for a few days. A week at most. Can you get something like that? It shouldn't be fancy. Just a cheap one will do.'

'I've already put the order in. Should come in tonight.'

My eyes widened. 'Really? That was fast.'

'That's what I do,' Harold said, and smiled. 'Now just to be sure . . . It isn't the Goliath, is it?'

'Pardon?'

'Well, Ms Celia – a great lady, Ms Celia – she mentioned you thought it was a tarantula. But there is one kind of South American tarantula called a Goliath Birdeater that would need a much bigger vivarium. *Theraphosa blondi*, it's called. It's supposed to be the largest natural spider in the world. I looked it up.'

'Oh, goodness no. This is just a regular-sized tarantula. I caught it in an extra large coffee cup.'

Harold chuckled softly and his belly moved up and down. 'Oh, I see. That's good then.'

'How big is the Goliath?'

'About a foot across.'

*No, I would not have been game to pick that up in a coffee cup.* 'Oh, no. This is nothing like that. Just a little tarantula. I'll need a bit of food for it, though, just enough for a few days until I find its home,' I said. 'Do you think you can get a few crickets?'

'I take it you aren't afraid of creepy-crawlies then, Pandora?'

'No spider has ever done anything to me.' That was the truth. My late mother, the archaeologist, had told me that in some cultures spiders were thought to have weaved the very universe itself. We'd never killed spiders in our home, not like Aunt Georgia did. She smacked them with her cooking magazines, whether they were venomous or not.

'No cricket has ever done anything to me, either,' I added. 'But I guess a spider has to eat, so . . .'

He nodded. 'You are one interesting young lady, Pandora. One vivarium and some crickets, coming right up. By the way, that's a nice dress you're wearing today.'

'Oh, thanks,' I said, blushing a little. I pulled back the camel-coloured winter coat Celia had given me and gave a little twirl so that the hem of the dress underneath flicked up around my knees. 'Celia made it.' It was the black one with the elaborate, twisted gold belt and starched white collar. I was awfully lucky that her wardrobe fitted me. Celia claimed the Lucasta women were always the same size, right down to the shoes. I was a Lucasta through and through, she often said. I would have been Pandora Lucasta instead of Pandora English if the naming of children were not so unswervingly patriarchal, she also told me.

'That Ms Celia is one great lady,' Harold remarked again, and sighed.

He often said things like that about my great-aunt, more to himself than to me. I was beginning to think he might be enamoured with her.

'Well, bye, Harold,' I said and made my way out. 'I'll come by after work.'

'See you tonight. I'm always open,' he said, as the door shut behind me with the chime of the bell.

I reached Spring Street station a touch early, and made my way up to street level in a jovial mood. I felt upbeat, considering my lack of sleep. A visit from Luke could do that.

South of Houston, or SoHo, was an area once known as 'Hell's Hundred Acres', but now it was gentrified and even trendy, with beautiful warehouse conversions, high-end designer boutiques, studios and cool cafes. A lot of artists lived in the area. It was the suburb where the photo shoot had taken place the day before, and it was also where I was beginning my career as a writer at *Pandora* magazine. True, I wasn't actually doing any writing – I'd been hired as an assistant – but it was a job and New York was a hard place to get a foot in the door. It beat waiting tables, and I really loved coming to SoHo each day.

I arrived a few minutes early and was gawking at the Venus flytrap plants and strange taxidermy lined up in the window of the EVOLUTION shop at 120 Spring Street, when I felt someone sidle up next to me. I tensed.

'I so want that skull.'

I relaxed. It was only Morticia, the receptionist from *Pandora*. I think her name is pretty funny, though I've never told her so. It's no more weird than Pandora, after all. Despite her name, she bore no resemblance to the *Addams Family* matriarch, except for her pale skin. In fact, she more closely resembled Olive Oyl, Popeye's cartoon love interest . . . If Olive Oyl were into Tim Burton. A breeze flipped her shaggy, faux red hair over her eyes and she tucked a section back behind her ear. She gave me a lopsided smile and I bid her good morning.

'Which skull?' I asked. As well as the Venus flytraps and taxidermy in the window, the shop was filled with skulls and skeletons, both human and animal. It was an odd shop. I often found myself staring in the window.

'See the case there on the left, up on the wall?' She pointed. I cupped my hands around my face and peered through the window. There were five human skulls lined up in an immaculate glass case on one wall. The middle skull was extraordinary to behold. It had been elaborately decorated with carved silver embellishments – silver teeth, ears and nose, and a headband of tiny silver skulls. There was a gemstone in position over the 'third eye' and the eye sockets themselves were big silver discs with luminous black stones for pupils. 'That's where they keep the real stuff,' Morticia explained. 'Not the medical models, but the real thing. I want that one in the middle.'

I could see the price on it. 'Expensive,' I commented.

'It's not that . . . well, actually it *is* that, but even if I had a spare six grand, it would be illegal for them to sell it to me.'

I'd heard that. It was illegal to sell body parts of any kind. The rule seemed to apply to anything that was derived from a human, with the exception of hair. I'd seen delicate Victorian heirlooms – necklaces and bracelets – made of the tightly braided hair of someone's long-departed loved ones. Creepy perhaps, but beautiful.

'This shop has a licence to sell though,' Morticia said. 'They can sell the real skeletons as well as those plastic medical models, but they can only sell the real stuff if it's for medical research.'

'You've really looked into this,' I said.

'I know. I'm weird,' she replied quietly.

I shook my head. 'No, no. I don't think you're weird at all, Morticia.'

We were both the same age – nineteen – and so far we hadn't seen each other outside the office or the walk to the subway, but I was trying to think of ways to hang out with her more. The other part of my life – the part with ghosts and mysterious happenings – had been occupying me a fair bit. We stepped away from the window, opened the entrance next door at 120b and climbed the staircase, passing signs for photographers and PR companies. When we reached our floor with the simple but stylish little sign for *Pandora* magazine, we pushed our way inside the brightly lit office and saw that we were some of the first ones in. That wasn't a bad thing.

I did a quick, anxious scan of the large, open-plan warehouse conversion that made up the office. It was always hard to tell if my boss, Skye, was in, because she was the only one who had her own contained office. Her door was closed. I couldn't see her or the deputy editor, Pepper. I figured it was probably safe.

'Nah, she's not in yet,' Morticia told me, and I relaxed a touch. Skye DeVille was the editor of *Pandora* magazine and not the most easygoing boss in the world, to put it mildly. She evidently thought she was the love child of Anna Wintour and Medusa.

I plonked my leather satchel at my feet, undid Celia's beautiful winter coat and sat down on the edge of the wide reception desk. Morticia positioned herself at her desk, turned her computer on and whipped off her black coat. She brought an equally black fingernail to her lips and pulled a face. 'You look a bit tired. Are you okay?'

From this woman such comments were innocent and genuine. I couldn't be offended. There was something quite weird, though, about coming to work tired so often and not being able to tell anyone why I had underslept. Perhaps they all assumed I had some kind of wild night-life? After all, I could hardly mention that I had been up late with a handsome, deceased friend. Or that I'd had to get up early to order a little something from my local 'green' grocer.

*My life is so very peculiar.*

'Yeah, I'm fine. Sometimes I stay up late.'

'You're always reading,' she commented. That was true. Although my voracious appetite for books had slowed recently thanks to the rather more peculiar and pressing goings-on of my life in Spektor.

'I've been meaning to ask what happened with that guy

you were seeing a while back? The roses guy? You two still seeing each other?' Morticia asked me.

The roses guy. I'd come to work one morning to discover a rather generous bouquet of roses on my desk. It had left quite an impression on Morticia, and, at the time, on me. I remembered the strange feeling I'd had when we'd first met by chance in the elevator at his work. The way I was jolted by a vision of my hand sliding up his bare chest. The way I'd fallen right into a feeling of his kiss, his hard body, some sensual moment between us which had not yet happened. And then, just like that, I was back to reality, standing in the elevator with him, at that stage a stranger. I'd been embarrassed, though of course he could not have known what I'd felt.

I often thought of him. *Jay Rockwell.* We had a little hiccup in our relationship a month earlier. The hiccup was that he couldn't remember me. It could be far worse. He'd fallen into the hands of a group of vicious villains (my fault, naturally) and I'd truly feared him dead. I couldn't find him for days afterwards. What I'd discovered, however, was that rather than being killed, he'd suffered a rather inconvenient bit of amnesia. We'd only managed two dates, but he showed no evidence of remembering either. Finding that out had been rather an embarrassing exercise. That's not a phone call I'd like to blunder through again. And now there were no emails from him. No roses sent to the office. Nothing. I'd even got my own mobile phone since the encounter, but now that I had a number, he didn't even know that he wanted to call it.

I had a strong feeling we would connect again. But what did I know?

'We're not seeing each other at the moment,' I told her.

'Shame.'

I shrugged.

'How was the shoot yesterday?' she asked.

'I've never been on a shoot before. It's kind of . . .'

I thought of the day I'd spent in the studio, watching the blonde model get made up and photographed, yawning between takes. They'd pinned the clothes at her waist to make them look better on her, and photoshopped her imperfections before she'd even left the studio. I wasn't sure how to describe the experience.

'Not how it looks in the photos, huh?' Morticia said.

'Exactly. The really weird thing, though, was that a spider got into the studio somehow, and everyone sort of freaked out.'

'Really?' Her pencilled brows shot up.

'It was basically the end of the shoot, so it didn't really matter. But it was definitely weird. And it was a *big* spider. Not a local, I don't think.'

'My brother used to have a spider,' she mused. 'They aren't that scary, really.'

'This one is a tarantula, I think. I'm going to have to find a pet shop or something to take it to, because I can't keep it.' I planned to use the office Internet to check the Yellow Pages for pet shops in SoHo. The spider was sure to have escaped from one of those. Someone had to be looking for that big fella – or big lady? Surely there weren't tons of tarantulas in Manhattan?

'You *have* the spider?' Morticia said, shocked.

'Not with me. Imagine what Skye would say!'

It would be rather fun to put the tarantula on her desk though, just to see the look on her face. But no, I couldn't do that.

'I have it at home,' I explained. 'They were going to kill it.'

Morticia shook her head. 'Wow. So you saved it?' She put her feet up on the desk. She did this whenever our bosses weren't around. She seemed to wear Doc Martens every day, with striped leggings. Today was no exception. I liked that she dressed how she wanted to, despite working at the front desk of a fashion magazine. Granted, it wasn't exactly *Vogue*, but . . .

I heard the door and Morticia glanced over my shoulder. 'Oh, here's Pepper,' she whispered, and took her Docs back off the desk in a flash. I stood up.

The deputy editor was in, looking sober, fashionably dressed and whippet thin as ever. At the moment she wore her hair in a severe, bleached blonde short ponytail. Her carefully ripped jeans, paired with a silk top and fur coat, were probably worth more than everything I owned. I nodded to her by way of greeting and took my cue to hoof it to the back of the office to my little cubicle outside Skye's office. I heard Morticia utter a polite greeting and, in usual form, Pepper ignored it.

Morticia and I were the second-class citizens of *Pandora* – that much I'd learned fast. After the events of the past month, it felt rather ironic that Pepper and Skye treated me like a lowly peasant. But never mind . . .

I put my satchel down on my desk, threw my coat over the chair and settled in. Absent-mindedly, I opened the top drawer of the desk and looked at a small, partially torn photograph I kept inside, just where I'd found it when I first got the job and had cleaned out the desk. It was a photograph of a young woman with blonde, wavy hair, worn just above the shoulder. She stood next to an older woman. They had similar hairstyles, the same smile, the same wide blue eyes and round faces. This was my predecessor. She'd been twenty when she went missing, and I knew she wasn't ever coming back – not to *Pandora* magazine, anyway. I knew where she was and what had happened to her. But I couldn't tell anyone. Not even the woman in the photograph – her mother.

*Secrets. So many secrets.*

The phone rang up the front, and Morticia answered in her usual chirpy voice. After a moment the phone on my desk lit up, and tore me from my dark thoughts. 'Skye DeVille's office, how may I help you?' I answered.

'It's Mark Winston.'

The photographer. I recalled his childish shriek at the sight of the spider, and my lips curled up into a little grin.

'How may I help you, Mr Winston?'

'Is Skye in?'

'She's not available right now,' I said, looking at the time on the big round wall clock. It was 9.40 am.

'Well, I'll have the proofs ready by this afternoon,' he said.

'I'll let Ms DeVille know.'

'And tell her the Chow samples never arrived, so we only shot the Helmsworth, Smith & Co, Arachne and Victor Mal.'

And that was it. He hung up.

I took note of the call, and tried to ignore his rudeness.

It was two hours later when I looked up and saw Skye marching through the office. I'd spent a criminal amount of time surfing the web for local pet shops, and had come up with a sure-fire answer for my spider's origins. There was an exotic pet shop two doors down from the studio where the knitwear shoot had been. I hoped to check it out at lunchtime.

'Good morning, Skye,' I said as she breezed past in a long, tan fringed winter coat and heeled boots, with a silk scarf tied around her neck. Skye was petite, dark, formidably groomed and about ten years my senior. She never had one single slick black hair out of place on her head, and everything she wore, no matter the style, seemed to be a form of chic body armour on her. I wondered if she could deflect laser beams.

She certainly had no trouble deflecting me. My polite greeting was ignored. She returned a minute later with her hand out, and I quickly placed her messages into her palm before she retreated into her office and shut the door behind her without a word.

*Yes, she is a pleasure to work for,* I told myself.

I sat back down and continued to wade through the computer's inbox, sorting her correspondence from wannabe designers and second-rate advertisers. It had taken me a while to figure out which people were which, because initially I didn't really know who was who in New York design, but I was getting the hang of it.

The door flew open, and I spun in my chair.

'You! Where are the Chanel samples?' Skye screeched.

My eyes widened and my heart did a little jump. 'The what?' I was caught totally off guard.

'The Chanel tattoo samples that were on my desk yesterday. Where are they?'

'Tattoos? Chanel do tattoos?' I was gobsmacked.

She gave me a withering look. 'Pepper!' she yelled, and the entire office leapt to uneasy attention at her call. Skye didn't usually have these outbursts. Not when we weren't close to deadline.

The wispy deputy editor strode straight over and gave me a withering look of her own.

'The Chanel tattoos are missing. Do you have them?' Skye asked her.

Pepper shook her head in response.

I stood, and felt a bit small next to the two women, both literally and figuratively. 'Um, they didn't get brought to the shoot or something?' I suggested.

'Don't be stupid,' Skye snapped. 'They were in *last* season. We're not using them in this issue.'

Oh, they were in during the neo-goth vampire chic season? *I must have been too distracted by the actual vampires to notice.* Not that either of these two haughty women seemed to recall one darned thing about the vampires, or about what happened to them with the Blood Countess the night after the fashion parade we'd attended. Their memories of the incident seemed to have been erased. Just like my date Jay's memory. I'd quickly guessed that much. Any attempt to remind them that I'd kind of *saved their lives* was totally useless.

So I was just Pandora English, lowly subordinate assistant. Still, I dared to ask another question. 'So if we aren't using them for this issue, then why . . .?' I began. The two women turned to look at me and I swallowed the rest of my question. 'Why does it matter?' I finally squeaked, finishing the sentence so softly the words barely formed at all.

'You aren't to leave for lunch today. Scour the office for those samples,' Skye ordered.

'But . . .' I protested.

By the time I closed my mouth again the two women were inside Skye's office, and the door was slammed shut.

At close of business, I sat on the edge of the wide reception desk, looking and feeling deflated. My stomach rumbled. My head hurt. It had been a long, particularly unpleasant day, made significantly more unbearable by the lack of a break. I was glad to be heading home. Morticia re-laced her Doc Martens, gathered her things and we left together without a word.

'Well, that was a day,' I said at the base of the stairs.

We stepped out into the cool winter air and I felt relief wash over me.

'Yes, I could see. What was Skye chewing you out about? Something about a tattoo?' Morticia said. 'I didn't know you had one.'

I managed a laugh, and dug my hands into my coat pockets. My breath made a little white cloud that drifted away on the cold street air. 'I don't have any tattoos. She said something had gone missing from her office, some kind of Chanel tattoo, and she wanted me to find it.'

I hadn't found it. As I had been reminded again and again through the day.

Morticia's animated face lit up with recognition. 'The Chanel temporary tattoos? She got the new ones in? Cool!'

I shook my head and stopped in my tracks for a moment. 'Okay, I'm confused. You do mean Chanel, right? The Chanel with the pearls and the suits and things? *Coco Chanel*, Chanel?'

Celia had given me something of a lecture about the iconic French designer Coco Chanel and her impact on the fashion world – her pioneering look of menswear-styled women's tailoring, pant suits and layers of chic pearls at a time when many women were still expected to wear restrictive corsets and elaborate, cumbersome costumes. Celia even lent me some of her vintage Chanel from time to time; in particular, a lovely Coco Chanel designed jacket that had probably helped me get the job at *Pandora*. I could not afford something like that myself, not even secondhand. Needless to say, I found it hard to reconcile this image of Coco Chanel with tattoos.

'Yeah,' Morticia said. 'They are amazing. Haven't you seen them? They totally rock, even though they're temporary. Just beautiful.'

Once again I was reminded that I really wasn't much of a fashionista.

'I've got a new tattoo,' Morticia said. 'A real one.'

'Oh, can I see?'

We had stopped on the sidewalk, and now she pulled her dyed red hair to one side, ignoring the flood of pedestrians passing us. 'It's on the back of my neck. It's only a week old.'

I pulled her collar down a touch and saw a big cartoon skull. The skin around it was still slightly red. 'Ha. I like it,' I told her. 'It suits you.'

Morticia and I parted ways at the subway, as we always did. And I wondered, not for the first time, if I'd ever be able to introduce a friend to Celia. Or to Spektor.

I had the feeling Spektor wanted to keep its secrets.

# CHAPTER
# FOUR

*It is possible to feel totally alone in a sea of people.*

This thought occurred to me as I made my way up the steps at 103rd Street station, exiting the coarse musk of the subterranean subway to take a deep breath of crisp winter evening air. Rugged up locals rushed past on the sidewalks of Spanish Harlem, and a male stranger bumped hard into my shoulder without seeming to notice me or what he'd done. Taxicabs and cars filled the streets, honking and moving in starts. I even saw a black car like Vlad's, but could not see inside the windows. After growing up with the slow pace of staid Gretchenville, the charismatic chaos of Manhattan still jolted me at times. New Yorkers were always in a hurry to get somewhere, see someone, do something. Did they ever stop to smell the roses? I wondered. It was the state flower, after all.

I took the subway nearly every morning and evening of the working week, and it still amazed me how little human contact there was on those journeys, despite the throng of people. Commuters did not make eye contact, and even the buskers and beggars who occasionally boarded to sing or recite poetry, or simply ask for money, often had trouble attracting so much as a glance. Of course, sometimes Vlad picked me up to take me home – usually unannounced – but I resisted making that a habit. Maybe it was my small-town upbringing, but the idea of being ferried everywhere by Celia's statuesque chauffeur seemed wrong to me, despite her curious claim that she needed to 'keep him busy'. New York might be a big, strange place but, after being cooped up so long in my small hometown, I needed every part of my independence.

There was no subway stop in Spektor so I rode the subway uptown and walked the last stretch through Central Park. If my great-aunt thought this routine of mine was a show of stubbornness, she didn't bother to mention it.

I wrapped Celia's cashmere coat tight around me, and began the solo walk home. On my first date in Manhattan a rather handsome New Yorker named Jay Rockwell – *roses guy* – had driven me home and said, 'I hope you don't go walking through Central Park on your own at night.' It had seemed condescending at the time, as if he thought I was fresh off the boat and didn't know a thing about personal safety. Yet here I was walking alone through the park most evenings after work.

Thing is, after the events of the past couple of months, human villains no longer seemed so scary.

Thankfully I was not accosted by any balaclava-clad baddies in the park, and the stroll rewarded me with the final minutes of a sunset of gold and red hues before the sky turned to total darkness. As I entered the omnipresent fog of the tunnel to Spektor I pulled the small bag of rice from my satchel.

I could never be too careful.

Half an hour later, I opened the heavy door of Celia's building, balancing my satchel and my shopping from Harold's Grocer, including a box containing the spider vivarium he'd got in for me. Oh yes . . . and I had a small box of live crickets to feed the spider before it starved to death. A box of *live* crickets. I hadn't considered that. This wasn't going to be pleasant.

I stepped inside the lobby, juggling my parcels with difficulty, and let the door close behind me with a puff. When I turned to cross to the lift I saw that I was not alone.

'Well, who do we have here?'

*Oh no.*

It was my nemesis, Athanasia, and her trio of supermodel cohorts – my 'housemates'. Athanasia was a disturbingly beautiful creature, from her mane of auburn hair down to her stylishly stilettoed feet, and she had a striking ability to mesmerise people on first meeting. (I'd seen her practically hypnotise a whole room of cynical fashion types. An incredible feat.) Her physical attributes certainly helped; she possessed a lithe, willowy physique and a tiny waist. Her eyes were dark, feline and wideset, and she had a full pout to make even Angelina Jolie jealous. Her three friends were also exceptionally attractive, as I suppose one would expect of professional fashion models, though not one of them could outshine the dark beauty of their ringleader. One of the women was blonde, one a brunette and the other a redhead; and all were tall, pale and equally stunning in their own way. They were a kind of lethal version of the Spice Girls, except each one was Scary. I'd seen these four work the catwalk. They'd had a moment of popularity when vampire chic was in. The New York fashion scene really hadn't known what they'd bargained for there because hidden beneath the models' pretty lips were genuine ivory fangs the size of a wild cat's.

They were *Sanguine.*

Not vampires. Sanguine. I'd been told that 'vampire' was a loaded term with a lot of negative baggage, and I should never, *ever* use the 'v' word in the face of the undead unless I wanted to get myself necked. (*Nosferatu* is no better. It means 'plague carrier'. Bram Stoker has a lot to answer for, Celia says.) *Sanguine* is the correct term, from the Latin *sanguineus*, 'of blood'. These were all things I'd learned fairly recently.

In addition to the requisite blood-thirst of their kind, these four models had a penchant for expensive, figure-hugging designer clothes and, it seemed, leather. Tonight Athanasia was wearing tight leather pants. We'd got off to a rather bad start when I'd arrived in New York and she was caught up with an entrepreneur named Elizabeth Báthory. Athanasia had worn those same leather pants the night I'd found her on the ceiling of the lobby, head twisted round, baying for my blood.

I'd staked her.

She'd survived.

Things had been tense since.

'It's the small-town hick,' Athanasia said, answering her question with a rather derogatory answer.

I moved across the tiles of the lobby, brushing past the four hideously beautiful women, and aiming for a quick escape to the lift. I knew perfectly well that these four creatures hated my guts with the eternal passion of the undead and would suck me dry in a mortal heartbeat. Only one thing prevented them – they lived under Celia's roof, and they had to play nice. The middle levels of the sprawling mansion were a kind of halfway house for Sanguine, hence the blocked-out windows. Or at least that was how it had been described to me. It was an arrangement Celia had here in Spektor – goodness knew why – and it had been going for some time. Sanguine could come and go, and reside on the middle floors if they pleased, but they couldn't come up to the penthouse. Celia, as mistress of the house, could revoke their invitations at any time. Celia had assured me she'd spoken to her friend Deus, who was a very powerful local Sanguine, and he'd ordered that I not be harmed by these demon-women. I was Celia's ward and they weren't to lay a hand on me. That rule had been clearly explained.

But it was something of an uneasy truce.

As I passed the glowing glares of these four deadly models I tried to remember that I was safe. *They wouldn't want to harm you. They wouldn't want to be homeless. You'll be fine . . .*

'Nice dress. So modern,' Redhead hissed as I strode past her, keeping my head down. She clearly had no appreciation for vintage.

Blonde followed close behind me, and sniffed my hair. 'Oh, smell the *virgin!*' she cried. 'Yummy.'

*That's none of your darned business,* I wanted to shout, but I held my tongue. It did not pay to provoke Fledglings. They had notoriously little restraint. Celia could kick them out on to the street, sure, but if they'd already ripped my throat out it would do me little good. No, I just had to get out of the lobby and into the elevator and I would be fine. I scurried up to the lift, feeling extra clumsy with the burden of all my parcels, and found I could not quite press the call button with my elbow. With my heart beating a touch too quick, I placed the vivarium on the floor and pressed the button with a free, shaking hand. Thankfully the lift was on the lobby floor. The doors opened, I hastily regathered my things and I stepped into the lift with my jaw tight and my breath quick.

'Oh, listen. Her heart is beating *fast*. Yummy little *morchilla* . . .' Brunette said.

*Morchilla*. Blood sausage.

I felt my temper flare. 'Vampire chic is out this season,' I blurted. 'How sad for y'all.' I pressed the button for the penthouse floor.

A hand shot out to stop the lift door from closing, and I regretted my quip immediately. The manicured hand was clenched tight on the ironwork of the sliding door; long blood red nails, the wrist decorated with what looked like drawn-on bracelets.

'I *will* get you back, you know,' Athanasia hissed. 'I'll have your throat!' she shouted, as if I hadn't got her point, and now she was showing fang – a lot of fang. This was rapidly getting out of control.

'For now you'll have to do with rice,' I cried out, and threw a big handful of plain white rice grains outside the lift. They hit the lobby tiles, bounced and scattered. Athanasia let go of the door and it slid shut.

'Oh!' Brunette said and bent over to begin counting.

Soon all four of them were on their knees. 'One, two, three, four, five, six . . .' I watched the pathetic display through the ironwork as the lift ascended.

The undead are obsessive compulsive.

In former times it was common practice to scatter grains around graveyards, and in ditches alongside cemeteries, to slow the progress of the undead when they rose from their graves to feed on the living. Some misguided superstitions specified that vampires counted at the rate of one grain per year, but sadly, that wasn't true. They counted fast, but still, they counted. Evidently they had to. Eastern Europeans sometimes favoured carrot seeds for this purpose, but my great-aunt swore by rice. Rice grains are small to carry, and cheap to acquire. She told me there were still wise folk in New York State who scattered grains outside their homes, just to be sure. At Halloween they put all those unwanted pumpkin seeds to use on the steps of their homes to help identify undead intruders dressed up as trick or treaters.

You could never be too careful.

I arrived at Celia's midnight blue penthouse doors out of breath and a little shaken by the encounter with Athanasia and her gang. That was by no means the first run-in I'd had with those four, but it did seem our uneasy truce had become increasingly fraught.

I knocked and entered. 'Celia, I'm home.'

Relieved to be safe, I slipped off my shoes and unburdened myself of the vivarium, satchel and bags. I saw Celia's stocking-clad feet up on the leather hassock. Freyja was with her, and at the sound of my greeting she hopped down from the chair and strode over with her white tail in the air.

'Hi Freyja, how are you?' I said and leaned over to pat her silky back.

'*Meow*,' was her pleased reply.

'And how are you, young Pandora?' my great-aunt said, turning to me.

'Oh, good thanks. Except . . .' I hesitated.

'Goodness me, you've been having trouble with Athanasia and her friends again?' She marked her page and closed the book she was reading.

'It's no big deal,' I said quietly and stood at the doorway for a moment. My heart was still beating hard from the confrontation – just as the Sanguine women had known. It was downright creepy to imagine that they could sense the rate of my heart, even from metres away. What a horrible skill. And due to some long established pact I didn't understand, Celia allowed those horrible creatures to live in her mansion. There was at least one more Sanguine down there I knew of, too. *Samantha.* The woman in the photograph in my desk at work. She'd worked at *Pandora* magazine before Athanasia turned her, and by some mad twist of fate I'd taken her position there. But Samantha was different from the others. I felt sorry for her because I knew she'd been a victim. It wasn't her fault that she'd been made into a monster. Perhaps that was one of the reasons I couldn't bear to toss away the wrinkled photograph of her with her mother; it was a reminder that she'd once been human.

It was also a reminder of the danger of the Sanguine. Samantha and I had been friendly from time to time, though

I hadn't seen her much lately. And even *she* had once tried to eat me. It was a terrible habit those Sanguine had. You couldn't trust them not to try it. And yet my great-aunt allowed them here, and she even had a friend who was Sanguine, and a very powerful one at that. How could she stand it? How could she stand those creatures? Celia stood. This evening she was wearing a stunning dress in black and deep ruby red, with black silk stockings and her omnipresent widow's veil. She slipped her feet into her fluffy slippers and walked gracefully over to me, the heels making a faint click on the hardwood floors. 'Come now,' she said and gave me a brief hug. Her embrace was cool but heartfelt. 'I'll have to let Deus know if they're harming you in any way,' she said.

*Deus. Not Deus.*

'I'm unharmed,' I assured her. 'It's nothing.'

'Did you have to use the rice again?'

I nodded. My cheeks became warm.

'Oh dear,' Celia said, and put her hands on her hips. She tilted her head to one side. 'I should probably have a word with him.'

'Don't!' I said. 'It's not necessary, really.'

Deus was Celia's powerful Sanguine friend. I'd not met him, but I was already positively terrified of him. Celia made him sound very civilised, sure, and I knew they were close. Heck, from what little she would tell me, he seemed to be the primary reason for her unnaturally youthful good health. I could see how she'd be grateful for that. But my run-ins with the fanged had been less than pleasant, so the thought of a very powerful Sanguine was extra terrifying. He was no Fledgling. I couldn't just rice him.

'I see,' Celia said, and sighed. She thought for a moment. 'Well, let's have a look at this.' She indicated the box containing the vivarium. I too was happy to change the subject.

We opened the box together to find a surprisingly beautiful, lightweight container inside. It was certainly not your standard pet shop vivarium. This one was modelled on, of all things, a castle. It had been designed with little turrets and an arched doorway that acted as a locking front. The top lifted off and shut with a little padlock. It was constructed of a clear material like glass, giving it the effect of an ice castle. Freyja sniffed at it and seemed not to know what to think.

'This is beautiful! Where do you think he found it?'

'Harold is very clever. He can get anything, you know,' Celia replied.

I'd heard him claim that, but really, a princely spider vivarium?

'What do you suppose it's made out of? Is it glass? Or some kind of plastic? Do you suppose it is made for spiders, or for something else?' I rambled excitedly.

Celia shrugged. 'It's a fine house for your friend.'

*Gosh.* 'It's almost a shame I won't have it for long.' I dusted the packing material off it, and placed the castle on Celia's shelf. It fitted perfectly, though snugly, between the shelves, the turrets just making the squeeze.

'It looks like it belongs there,' Celia said.

Funny, but it did.

She returned to her seat and watched me as I cleared the packing material away.

My gaze was drawn to the jar on the shelf. The tarantula was quietly watching us. It was strange how intensely I felt its eyes, like it actually knew what it was seeing. It somehow appeared self-aware. *Peculiar*, I thought again. *Peculiar.*

'Have you told anyone about your little pet?'

'It's not a pet,' I protested. 'In fact, it's a shame this is such a lovely vivarium because I think I may have already found the pet shop the spider escaped from. I'm going there tomorrow. I'm sure they'll be missing this little guy.'

Celia smiled enigmatically. 'That will be interesting, I think. Be sure and let me know how you go.'

I set about transferring the tarantula into the vivarium. It worked with surprising ease – the animal just slid down the glass of the jar and walked right in like it owned the place. I refilled the tiny water dish, slid it inside and locked the little door at the front. *Ah, the food*, I remembered. I took out the small box of live crickets Harold had given me. Celia watched with one cocked, perfectly sculpted eyebrow as I clumsily took one of the insects by two legs. I was afraid I'd hurt it, so I let go. *Oh, this is awkward.* I tried again, and it squirmed and wriggled but I managed to quickly throw it inside and shut the castle door again. I was pretty sure I never wanted to do that again.

I covered my eyes, and watched through laced fingers.

Seconds ticked by. Minutes.

It turned out to be a rather anticlimactic meeting of creatures. The spider just sat in its castle, watching me.

*Don't look at me, look at the cricket!* I wanted to point and tell it to eat. Surely it must be starving by now?

I was confounded. 'Maybe I got the wrong thing. I figured the cricket would be okay,' I said.

'Yes, it looks like the cricket will be fine,' Celia said.

I frowned.

# CHAPTER
# FIVE

I arrived to work at *Pandora* magazine on Wednesday morning with some trepidation. I had no idea what kind of mood Skye might be in and I really didn't want a repeat of Tuesday's unpleasantness. As a pre-emptive strike, I arrived with a bagel and cheese in case Skye felt like starving me again, but I desperately hoped to get away on my lunch break. I had plans.

Morticia had her Doc Martens up on her desk and a lopsided smile on her face when I walked in. 'Good morning,' she said.

'Hi. Is she . . .?'

'Here? No. Not yet.' I relaxed a touch. I slipped Celia's coat off and sat on the edge of the reception desk. I gently placed the satchel on the floor. Only a couple of staff were in so far. They paid us no attention, as usual. 'How was your night?' Morticia asked.

I thought of Athanasia and the way she'd bared her fangs at the mouth of the lift, ready to lunge.

'The usual,' I said. 'And yours?'

'The usual,' she replied, but with a barely detectable touch of melancholy. She paused, and then her eyes lit up. 'So, want to hear some goss?' she asked excitedly.

'Sure.'

She took her feet off the desk and leaned in to me. 'You know the whole thing with Sandy Chow?'

The name was familiar. 'The designer, right?' I was still learning who's who.

'Yeah, the designer. Well, apparently she's *missing*. Like for real missing. It's all over the news. Did you see?'

Celia and I didn't watch the evening news. In fact, as far as I was aware, she didn't have a television. Would television reception even work? I wondered. There was no phone or Internet access, and my cheap mobile didn't even get one single bar of reception. Morticia flicked a few strands of shaggy hair to one side of her face. 'And get this – Sandy's workshop was *destroyed*. All the samples, the patterns, everything gone. The police are treating it as a possible kidnapping. Even murder.'

'Really?'

'And it gets even crazier. Richard Helmsworth – I'm sure you've heard of him – well, his workshop was apparently all packed up and he's vanished. Some think he might have . . . you know, been responsible.'

'Why do they think that?' I asked.

'They had this big public rivalry. I'm sure you've read about it.'

I hadn't.

'And now she's missing, and he's missing too,' Morticia concluded with a look of thrilled shock.

'I remember the stylist on the shoot saying something about how she couldn't get the Sandy Chow samples. I wondered what that was all about,' I said.

'Yeah. It's weird, huh?' Morticia's eyes were wide. She seemed excited by the whiff of drama. 'Watch this space,' she concluded.

I nodded. 'I'll do that. I'd better get to my desk,' I said.

I picked up my satchel with extra care and made my way to the back of the office.

Skye DeVille arrived at work two hours later. Some part of me had dared to hope she might show up after lunch, so I knew I could get away. She was becoming increasingly tardy of late. But at eleven thirty she breezed past me wearing a short, quilted jacket and a neat scarf tied elegantly around her neck. She wore riding boots with designer jeans and it looked like she might have just stepped off an equestrian fashion spread.

'Good morning, Skye,' I said.

She didn't look particularly well, I thought. She was probably battling a cold.

'No phone messages this morning,' I told her and she shut her door without a word.

For the next thirty minutes I watched the clock anxiously. I had plans for my lunch break and the sooner noon came around the better. I was worried she might —

*'Where is the jewellery!'*

Skye's office door burst open and I turned in my chair and braced myself for her wrath. Standing in the doorway with her fists clenched, and her fuchsia pink lips pressed into a thin, mean line, she stared right at me with hollowed eyes. Frankly she seemed a little crazed. I sincerely hoped this wasn't some initiation phase at the magazine – work for two months and then the abuse really steps up?

'Where is the jewellery?'

'Umm,' was all I could muster. 'I . . .?'

'The *jewellery* from the shoot. The *Chanel* jewellery. It has to be returned today,' she said, enunciating each word slowly, and with venom.

I'd never seen her quite like this and I was so shocked that I couldn't grasp what she was talking about or how I should respond. Jewellery from the shoot? Would the stylist have these things from the shoot, perhaps? 'The stylist . . . maybe she —' I began clumsily.

'It was in my office yesterday!' Skye roared in response.

I pulled myself together. 'Do you mean the temporary tattoos you were looking for? We haven't managed to locate those,' I told her. 'I'm sorry —'

'Brilliant,' she responded, seeming at last to calm a touch. Her voice became low and even. 'And now the jewellery is missing as well.' She narrowed her eyes at me. 'Open the drawers of your desk.'

I abruptly stood up. 'But Skye . . .'

*'Open them!'*

The blood drained from my face. This was a new level of humiliation. In two months of working at *Pandora* she had treated me rudely – usually by ignoring me – but now she was accusing me of theft? Horrified into a stunned silence,

I bent over and pulled open the drawers of my desk one by one. I saw pens and paperclips and notepads, and that sad, crinkled photo of Samantha and her mother that I couldn't quite bring myself to throw away. Of course there was no jewellery in there. I didn't even know what jewellery she meant. I tried to think back to the shoot and what the model was wearing. Something brightly coloured? First Skye was missing some temporary tattoos and now some jewellery? What was going on?

'And your bag,' Skye demanded after I'd shown her the contents of each drawer.

'My bag?'

By now we'd attracted quite a little crowd. Pepper had walked over with her brow furrowed. She watched the display with agitation. Crowded behind her was the rest of the staff of *Pandora*, none of whom had bothered to get to know me. *Some impression this will make*, I thought. *Pandora the suspected thief?*

Morticia, I noticed, hadn't left the reception area, but was craning her neck to see what was happening. She held one hand over her mouth and her eyes were large. She looked concerned for me. That was something we had in common.

Skye and I locked eyes again. 'Open it,' she demanded again.

*I really don't want to do this . . .*

I carefully pulled my leather satchel up on to the desk, my face positively radiating with humiliation. I opened it for her. 'See,' I said. 'Nothing.'

She stepped forward and rummaged around in my bag, and then to my complete horror she picked up the satchel and turned it upside down. She shook it roughly and all the contents spilled out.

*No!*

I somehow caught the jar with the tarantula in it before it hit the desk. In a flash it was in my hand, hidden behind my back. I'd never moved so fast in my life. I couldn't even recall catching it.

I backed up a few paces, and then realised that, from her position, Morticia could see what I was holding behind my back. I glanced over my shoulder to see her eyes fixed on the jar. They were the size of dinner plates. The hand returned to her mouth. She said nothing.

*What a day to bring a tarantula to work.*

Amazingly, Skye didn't seem to notice what I was holding, or care. She was too intent on seeking out the jewellery. Of course the jewellery wasn't in my bag. I may be a strange girl. I may even be living a double life, but I am no thief.

Pepper finally stepped in. 'Pandora, I have an errand for you to run,' she said.

I nodded stiffly.

'I want you to get a quote from Victor Mal for the knitwear feature. Just a few good lines will do. Something about his collection and knitwear in general. Okay?'

I nodded again. 'Okay.'

'Nothing else,' she said pointedly. She put an address in my hand. She guided Skye back into her office while I gathered my things into the satchel.

'Everyone back to your desks,' Pepper ordered, and the rest of the staff scattered as she closed the door of Skye's office. A tense quiet descended.

I grabbed my coat and bag, and walked to the reception desk. I took a deep breath.

'Wow,' Morticia whispered.

'I know,' I replied in a low voice, and put my coat on.

'Are you okay?'

I nodded. 'Pepper has given me some errand to get me out of the office.'

'Good,' she said. 'And . . .' Her gaze fell to the jar in my hand, and I slipped it into my satchel. It wasn't the time for show and tell. I had to get the tarantula out of the office. The poor thing would be quite distressed after being tossed around like that. I'd been foolish to try to save it in the first place. I probably should have let someone else take care of it at the studio. Imagine if Skye had found it, in front of everyone?

'I know,' I replied. 'I know.'

I left.

The fresh air outside was a godsend. The cold hit my hot cheeks with a sting at first, and then slowly the cool winter breeze and the anonymous, impersonal flow of traffic helped me to feel human again. I was no longer the centre of attention or the subject of indignity. In this crowd I was nobody, and that felt like a good thing.

I questioned my future at *Pandora*. Could I quit? Should I? Finding a job in New York was hard, I'd discovered. Heck, these days it was hard to get a job anywhere – or that's what everyone said. I hardly had impressive qualifications. I'd been lucky getting work there on Celia's advice – *really* lucky – and I couldn't count on having that kind of luck again. I'd worked in Bettina and Ben's Book Barn through much of high school, before they went out of business when everyone started buying books online. (The shop had been a boon for my voracious reading habit.) And then I'd been Skye's assistant for a short time. That was it. I had never landed that job at the local paper or got any of my articles published. And my 'special' talents (as Celia so encouragingly referred to them) didn't amount to much in the business world. Who wanted to hire a strange girl with a penchant for unconventional feelings about supernatural occurrences, and an ability to speak with ghosts?

I held Pepper's note in my hand. Victor Mal. I needed to get some quotes from him for the feature. *Nothing else*, she'd said, as if I needed a reminder that the last time I'd put my reporter skills to work I'd uncovered a huge story about the cosmetics industry, and Pepper had taken all the credit for it. As if I needed reminding of that.

I felt around in my satchel and pulled out the jar with the spider in it. It was looking at me again. It seemed surprisingly docile – I was worried that was because it was starving to death. As good as Celia had been to let me keep it at her house, it needed to be with people who could feed it and look after it better than I could. It needed to go back to where it belonged. And I was confident I knew where that was.

'Hi there,' I said, looking over the desk of SoHo Exotic Pets. The pet store was surprisingly unkempt, lined with glass vivariums and fish tanks. It harboured the strange smell of reptiles.

A woman was on her knees behind the desk, but she stood when she heard my voice. 'Welcome to Exotic Pets. How may I help you?' she said. She was wearing very thick glasses, and an even thicker cable-knit sweater. She looked like she didn't leave the shop very often.

'I was wondering if you might have lost someone?' I said with a cheer I didn't really feel. I fished around in my satchel and pulled out the jar. I placed it on the desk. The tarantula inside shifted a little and then turned around to sit facing me. Again, I felt its stare.

'Do you need some food for your pet?' the shopkeeper said. 'We have crickets, and all kinds of gut load available . . .'

*Gut load?* 'Oh, no, it's not my pet. I found it nearby and assumed it had escaped from your shop,' I explained. 'A lost tarantula in New York.'

'Hmmm,' she said. 'Hang on a moment.' She leaned away from the desk. 'Jason!' she shouted. 'We missing any tarantulas back there?' There were only two customers in the shop. They both turned around to stare.

I winced.

After a few minutes, Jason appeared. The two were related, if the glasses and sweaters were anything to go by. 'You want us to buy this off you? You a breeder?' he said and scratched his short, grey beard.

'A breeder? No. No. I thought you might have lost it. I found this guy practically next door, at the studio.' I motioned to the photographer's studio just down the street. 'I felt for sure it had escaped from here.'

'Not from here,' he said.

'Well, you're the only exotic pet shop around.'

'We aren't missing any animals,' he said.

*Darn it. How did I get myself into this?*

I couldn't insist that it was theirs if they said it wasn't. But what could I do? I picked the jar up and looked at the spider. It was still staring at me. 'I can't keep it,' I finally said, feeling deflated. 'Do you know of anyone nearby who would be missing one? It seems so docile, it must be a pet.'

'No one has come in looking for a spider.'

I put the jar back down on the desk. 'It's a tarantula, right? It's not native to New York, is it?'

The woman bent forward and looked. 'It is a tarantula. I'm not sure what breed. Not a Chilean Rose Hair or Mexican Red Knee,' she said, and adjusted her glasses.

'Not the Red Leg. Or the Honduran Curly,' Jason added, peering down to look as well. 'The markings are a little unusual. Is it Old World, do you think?'

'Well, it's not the Malaysian Earth Tiger, or the Thai Black. Look at that colouring . . .'

I watched them study the spider for a while, as it, seemingly, studied me. I couldn't get past that feeling of being watched by those eight tiny eyes.

And then it happened.

I felt a familiar coldness in my belly.

*Death.*

*Danger.*

I stiffened. The tiny hairs on the back of my neck stood on end. In a flash I turned around, my blood already coursing with panic. *Something is wrong.* Danger was approaching, unknown danger. The feeling was so strong I felt I needed to flee the shop immediately.

I backed away from the counter. 'I have somewhere I need to be,' I called out as the two shopkeepers continued to argue over what kind of tarantula it wasn't. 'Will you take it?' I said.

They looked at each other. 'We can't just buy this off you —' Jason began.

'I don't want any money,' I said, gathering my satchel and already heading for the door. They both looked at me strangely. 'Please just take care of it. It hasn't eaten.' I pushed the door open and made it out on to the street, feeling as if I were in the grip of an attack of claustrophobia. The cool winter air felt refreshing on my face after the stuffiness in the shop, but unfortunately my sense of foreboding didn't improve. I loosened the collar of Celia's coat for more air and hurried up the street towards the subway station.

When I reached the top of the steps I felt compelled to turn. There were countless pedestrians moving past me on the sidewalk, but one person stood out.

Her.

An unusually tall woman about ten feet behind me, moving in my direction. I felt sure she'd seen me come from the pet shop. She paused now that I had stopped moving. She was swathed in black and she sported a short, dark bob and large black sunglasses. My eyes were drawn straight to her, and beneath those dark glasses of hers I felt my gaze was met.

There was something there. *Something.*

I didn't pause to find out what. I turned and hurried down the subway steps.

# CHAPTER
# SIX

The green oasis of Washington Square Park opened before me.

I'd been tense on the subway trip to W4th, shaken by my strange foreboding and the tall woman with the dark hair. I'd jumped at every loud noise and every stranger's voice. After the humiliation I'd endured at the office, my overactive imagination had got away from me. I needed to relax. Now, as I walked towards the park on my way to the address Pepper had given me, I revelled in fresh air and snatches of winter sun, happy to be outdoors. Thanks to Pepper's errand, I could take a moment to escape the oppressive concrete of this urban island for the temporary company of trees.

Washington Square Park was a sanctuary, though a bitterly cold one. Wind whipped past the barren trees across expanses of grass, kicking up fallen leaves and littered newspaper. On this weekday afternoon the park was peopled with joggers, dog walkers and students from the surrounding university campuses lingering after lunch. Despite the cold, I found myself smiling as I entered the square by the north-west entrance, my long hair whipped by the breeze. The sense of foreboding I'd felt at the pet shop had disappeared and

I reminded myself that, despite my panicked behaviour, the spider was finally in good hands.

No one had killed it. My mother would be proud.

With my mother on my mind I passed under the dark, barren, silently reaching branches of an ancient elm tree towering a hundred feet over me, far above the other trees, and the cold thing reawakened in the pit of my stomach.

*Death.*

People died every day, and nearly every square foot of the Earth had seen that normal cycle of life. But wrongful deaths – murders, executions, unspeakable suffering – left a lasting imprint on a place, and often the spirits of the dead could not fully escape the place of those final, terrible moments. Some spirits circled endlessly, trapped in their own private torment. Some reached out to me. On this occasion I heard an unearthly choking, and I closed my eyes and tried not to see the faded shapes of perhaps twenty men, many of them young, all of them skinny and sad in their worn rags, gasping with ropes around their necks, just as they had two centuries before, sentenced to hang for crimes only some of them committed.

*The Hangman's Elm.*

A couple of students sat beneath the Hangman's Elm, chatting and snacking on sandwiches in the winter sunshine. Unbeknownst to the woman, the dangling feet of a murderer hung not inches from her mouth. I looked away and hurried through the park at a brisk pace, making for the other side. By the time I'd reached Washington Place and Greene Street I'd rid myself of the image of the Hangman's Elm and her victims. But strangely, my stomach was no less cold. I stopped by the Brown Building and caught my breath. I had not run terribly fast, but my throat felt tight, my lungs constricted.

I coughed.

I coughed again.

Could I smell . . . *smoke?*

I looked up and stifled a scream. A young woman was falling through the air above me, caught in a death leap. I cowered beneath her falling form before realising that she was suspended there. She too was a spirit faded in the daylight; the essence of a lost life caught between worlds. Her mouth was open in a silent scream and her clothing flared out behind her in wings of flame. And she was not alone. Above her were others like her, trailing into the sky. All young women. On fire.

These spirits, or imprints, appeared not to see me. They weren't ghosts like Lieutenant Luke. I could not talk to them. I could not interact, but I could see them, *feel* them.

I shivered.

What a place for Victor Mal to have his showroom, I thought. Though I supposed not everyone remembered those long ago events, or felt the tragedy of the largest industrial accident in New York's history as if it were still happening. As it was, I had to work hard to block the psychic aftermath of the terrible Triangle Shirtwaist fire of 1911 and the imprint left by the deaths of the 146 women, most younger than me, who burned within the locked doors of the textile factory, or plunged a hundred feet to their deaths down the elevator shaft or from window ledges trying to escape the flames. Over a century later, they were still leaping to their demise, forever trying to escape.

A New Yorker strolled past in a smart business suit, toting a briefcase, clearly immune to all the death. He didn't look up.

*Pandora. You are strange.*

I found the address Pepper had given me, mere metres from the falling bodies of the century old fire's victims. Feeling drained, I walked through a lobby and into a lift, where I found a sign for Victor Mal. When I stepped out on his floor I found myself in a brightly lit reception area the size of a small baseball field. This was Victor Mal's studio all right. Each letter of the words VICTOR MAL DESIGN was taller than I was and flanking this impressive signage were floor-to-ceiling reproductions of his advertisements over the decades.

*Is that Cindy Crawford? Claudia Schiffer? Gisele Bündchen?*

I stopped midway through the reception area to gawk.

'May I help you?' The words were polite. The tone was not.

I turned to see the receptionist looking at me. She was blonde, petite and unseasonably tanned. I guessed she was wearing one of Victor Mal's creations. She appeared to be midway through packing some things.

'Um, I am Pandora English of *Pandora* magazine, here to interview Mr Mal.'

She raised her head from what she was doing, and then she raised an eyebrow.

'Ah, yes. I wondered when you'd come,' she replied, as if I was late, which I didn't imagine I could be. 'No photographer?'

'Photographer? No. Just me. I have a few questions. It shouldn't take long.'

Two men who seemed somewhat more groomed, plucked and waxed than I was strode past me without a second glance. They were wearing the fashionable satchels that were once called 'man bags'. The office was emptying out for lunch.

'I'll take you to the work room,' the receptionist said. I followed her down a short hallway towards a large, white door. She was indeed wearing one of her employer's creations – a figure-hugging knee-length knit dress with a vibrant criss-cross pattern and asymmetrical draping around the hemline that swayed when she walked. She stopped at the door and knocked.

'Victor, there is a journalist here to see you.'

I became a touch taller. I wasn't sure anyone had actually called me a journalist before. It sounded nice.

*Pandora English. Journalist.*

It beat being called a freak.

There was a muffled reply, and the receptionist swung the door open and left me at the mouth of an oversized room filled with spools of yarn and fabric swatches. There were a few half-finished designs on mannequins in the room too and I made my way around them as I entered.

Victor Mal was a surprisingly diminutive man – no more than five feet tall – but I could see right away that he was the type to compensate for his size in other ways. He turned to me, unsmiling, and leaned against a giant wooden workbench that took up one whole side of the long room. As I made my way closer, he crossed his arms and lifted his chin by way of welcome. He was wearing a bright knit top with a startling V-neck, the type usually worn by women. He was so deeply tanned he made his fake-tanned receptionist look pale.

'I'm Pandora English from *Pandora* magazine. Thank you for taking the time to see me,' I said, averting my eyes from the cleft of his man-cleavage.

'I don't have much time for you, darling, but I can always use the publicity. *Pandora* magazine, is it? You have fifteen minutes. Shoot.'

I gathered he meant I should shoot him with my questions, so I proceeded. 'Tell me what it is about knitwear that you love so much,' I asked. As soon as the words left my lips I knew my question was a mistake. It was hardly an interesting way to begin. His eyes glazed over, and he turned to his work table.

'Darling, it's all *about* knitwear. This is New York, the knitwear capital.'

Was it? *Knitwear capital*, I wrote on my pad.

I noticed he had a way of saying 'darling' that made it clear you were not very darling. I positioned myself against the table to catch his eye, worried I might have already lost him. I'd have to work on my interviewing technique.

'I can see you are very hands-on with your garments,' I said. 'Your work is beautiful.'

'I don't just design, I *create*,' he informed me with what I took to be a haughty look. I dutifully took a note on my writing pad. *Doesn't design. Creates.* Just then the receptionist marched back in with a parcel, hem swaying.

'For you. Just arrived.' She was a woman of few words. Considering she was addressing her employer, her tone seemed a bit hostile. She scowled as she passed the package to him. There was clearly some unresolved issue between them. Or was hostility in fashion? I didn't know.

Victor studied the parcel and turned it over in his hands, effectively ignoring her. Whatever it was, it was beautifully wrapped in ribbons and bows of jet black and emerald green. 'I'm leaving for lunch,' the receptionist informed him, and Victor nodded absently in response, evidently mesmerised by the box. The fashionably hostile receptionist closed the door behind her and we were alone again. Victor and I both stared at the box for a spell, before I realised how odd that was. It did seem rather magnetic, I thought. Strange.

I quickly decided to jump in with another clumsy question. 'How did you first become involved in design . . . uh, creation?' I asked. I hadn't done a lot of live interviewing in the past, and it sure showed. At my question he placed the captivating box on the work table and crossed his arms again. 'When you were a kid, did you want to be a designer?' I asked as a follow-up.

'I have always wanted to create something beautiful,' he replied flatly, as if I'd clicked the 'frequently asked questions' button and was getting a recording.

*This is excruciating. Now for the real questions*, I thought.

'Victor, I was wondering if you had heard about the recent disappearances of Sandy Chow and Richard Helmsworth? The three of you are considered to be among New York's top knitwear designers. I was wondering if you had any theory on what had happened to Sandy and Richard?'

This question took him off guard. He straightened.

'You really can't compare my creations to Sandy Chow's, or that of Richard Helmsworth.'

'Pardon?'

'They were hacks.'

Interesting. I took a note: *Hacks.*

'Really,' he continued. 'Everyone knows I am the best knitwear designer in the world. In fact, I'm probably the best there has ever been.'

'You are the best knitwear designer ever?' I repeated back. He rated himself better than Missoni? And Sonia Rykiel? Even I thought that seemed a rather overblown claim.

'Well, darling, *yes*. It's no boast. This is my area. I mean, I'll leave the suits to Hugo Boss, but in knitwear, I am king.'

My eyebrows went up. It seemed an incredible boast to make, but worse, he seemed genuinely not to care about what had happened to the other two designers. Could he really care so little? Or maybe he was hiding something?

He seemed to sense my surprise.

'Maybe they're faking their deaths for publicity, or something,' he concluded with a wave of his hand.

'Together? I heard they didn't get along.'

'Well, how should I know?' he responded. 'Anyway, I must go. When is this coming out?'

'The next issue of *Pandora*,' I told him.

He nodded and then folded his arms. *Interview over.* He clearly didn't like being asked about the disappearances. There didn't seem to be anything more I could get out of him, so I took the hint. I thanked him and led myself out.

Well, I had a few quotes for Pepper's feature, I supposed.

A few quotes and nothing more.

It was just past six in the evening when I knocked and entered the penthouse. Grateful for the rest ahead, I slipped off my shoes and hung Celia's beautiful winter coat on the mirrored hatstand by the door. I caught a flash of my reflection in the small, oval mirror and did a double take. Was it my imagination, or had something indefinable changed in my appearance? Was it the look in my eyes? Increasingly, I had the impression that I was shedding the skin of my former life. Gretchenville was visibly falling off me.

'I had the most bizarre day . . .' I began, turning and walking into the lounge room. I thought of Skye's bizarre and humiliating outburst, the strange feeling I'd had at the pet shop, and the woman I'd seen at the subway station. And to top things off, meeting the famous Victor Mal had been distinctly uninspiring. His boasts seemed like a new level of conceit. Or did everyone in this town talk like that? At times, the rest of Manhattan seemed stranger even than Spektor. Which was, admittedly, something of a statement.

' . . . Celia?'

I noticed then that for once my great-aunt was not in her chair. Before long I heard the delicate click of her heels, and she came around the hallway corner with a compact in one hand and her deep red signature lipstick in another. My great-aunt wore emerald drop earrings, a wasp-waisted black satin knee-length dress with a matching emerald brooch, and, of course, her omnipresent widow's veil. She looked particularly stunning, I thought.

'Are you going out?' I asked. She looked ready to attend a fine dinner or concert. Then again, I'd never seen her 'dressed down'. I wondered if she even owned a T-shirt.

'Perhaps later,' she said. 'But we have company right now.'

'We do?'

'Yes.' She finished applying her lipstick. 'Pandora, we have something to discuss.'

My heart skipped. When Celia said we needed to discuss something it tended to be of grave importance. (So to speak.)

'If it's about the spider, I know. I shouldn't have brought it here in the first place. I took it to a pet shop today. It's gone now. We won't be seeing it again. It's in good hands.' I turned to look at the empty vivarium on the shelf. 'And we won't be needing the castle, so I can take it back to Harold.'

'Don't worry about all that for now, Pandora.' She stepped towards me and placed a cool hand on my arm. 'Deus is here to see you.'

My jaw dropped. All thoughts of the tarantula left me, all thoughts of Skye and Victor Mal, and everything else that had crowded my day.

*Deus* . . .

*The Sanguine* Deus was here tonight . . . to see me?

'I'm not sure I'm ready for this,' I blurted.

'You are,' Celia said calmly.

My entire body came up in goose flesh. 'Well . . . Do I need to . . .' I stopped. 'Should I arm myself with —'

'Rice doesn't work on older Sanguine,' Celia said. 'They usually outgrow the obsessive compulsive condition of their Fledgling years. I've already told you this. Don't embarrass yourself by stuffing your pockets.'

*Gotcha.* 'And you know how I put on that crucifix that time, thinking you were —'

'Yes, I remember,' Celia said, beginning to sound unimpressed.

I'd thought at one point that she was a vampire. After all, she looks pretty good for someone pushing ninety. Plus she wasn't big on garlic or taking strolls in the sunshine.

'Well, I remember you said something about how that crucifix wouldn't work on any Sanguine, or something to that effect. Did you mean it wouldn't have any effect because it was a plastic Madonna eighties cross or because crosses don't work at all?'

Celia squinted and folded her arms. 'The Material Girl crucifix is particularly useless, I'd be willing to guess,' she responded, with some measure of sarcasm.

'But is that because —'

'It has much to do with the power of belief.'

'It does? So if you believe deeply enough you can make a cross work?' I had thoughts of anti-vampire seminars: 'How to Make Belief Your Weapon!'

'No, darling, if the *Sanguine* believes it deeply enough. Which I assure you is unlikely. That would have to be a lot of belief.' I supposed she was right. 'And think about it . . . If crucifixes – or indeed any two sticks placed at right angles – caused such a reaction, you have to ask yourself how any revenant rising from a grave could last even a second in the hallowed ground of a cemetery dotted with crucifix tombstones? Bram Stoker . . . Ridiculous.'

I had wondered about that.

'Now what are all these questions about?' Celia demanded. 'You know all this.'

*I don't want him to eat me.*

'I can see you are panicking, but you really needn't,' she assured me. 'Deus is an ally. I have told you this before. A lot of rumours about the Sanguine are purely propaganda – they are supposedly "demons"; a crucifix makes them burst into flames, et cetera, et cetera . . . all great reasons not to miss your Sunday sermon. I've seen Sanguine drink holy water for kicks. Put all that stuff out of your head.' She put her hands on her hips. 'You're not planning to greet our friend Deus with some sharpened stake or some such, are you? Because, really, you would make a less than ideal first impression.'

I blanched. 'No. No, of course not. I wouldn't do anything like that.' *Unless he tries to hurt me.* 'I just don't want to do the wrong thing . . . like wear something that could make him burst into flames.'

'I assure you, Deus is not that flammable. Now run along and freshen up. He'll see you shortly,' she said, and walked into the kitchen, leaving me in a delicate cloud of her fine perfume.

There was no further discussion to be had on the topic, that much was clear. In truth it wasn't really Stoker's tale I needed to get out of my head; it was my own run-ins with less than mannerly Sanguine. Nonetheless, it seemed that after hearing about him for two months, I was now going to meet the Sanguine responsible for Celia's unique condition.

I wondered if I was ready.

# CHAPTER SEVEN

Sometimes it seemed that Celia believed everything could be solved with fresh lipstick and a cup of tea.

I emerged from my room to find her waiting with a beautiful silver tray with a pot of tea and two cups neatly arranged on it. Two, I noticed, not three. But of course Deus wouldn't drink – tea.

'Would you take this tray?' she said, and I did as she asked.

I'd changed into one of my favourite dresses. It was an amber colour that matched my eyes. Celia had once designed it for the movie star Lauren Bacall. It fitted perfectly. I thought it might be a little too dressed up, but something told me it would be rude to meet Deus in anything less than the best.

'You look wonderful, darling Pandora. And I see you haven't covered yourself in crucifixes. Good choice,' Celia assured me. 'Now don't be anxious. He really is quite lovely, and *very* powerful. He could be a great ally for you.'

*Very powerful.* Well, that was precisely why I was nervous about meeting him. That and the fact that he was immortal and probably had fangs like a tiger. Mostly, I'd found that fanged types wanted to eat me. And some of them felt it necessary to continually mention my virginity, which seemed rather impolite.

(I didn't even want to think about how they knew such things.)

'Just one last question. How do I talk to him?' I asked.

'Talk to him like he is a man, Pandora. The Sanguine can be very powerful and they have a certain otherness, but it would be wrong to think they retain nothing of their human origins.'

*Otherness.* The otherness being that they fed off humans?

I thought of Athanasia with her teeth bared, and failed to see traces of her humanity. 'Is there any special etiquette?' I persisted. 'Do I bow? Curtsy? Is it rude to shake hands or show the sole of my foot? Should I be alarmed if he sniffs me?'

'Just don't call him a vampire,' Celia quipped in reply, and made a final adjustment to her black widow's veil.

Celia compared the 'v' word to that 'n' word Mark Twain recently had stripped from his novels, and rap stars sometimes still used in their songs. It was okay for a Sanguine to use it, perhaps, but it was unwise for a non-Sanguine to utter the term. I was sure I wouldn't slip up.

'This way,' she instructed and, to my considerable surprise, my glamorous great-aunt led me towards her quarters. When I had first arrived she had been very specific that I was never to venture this way. So strict had her instructions been that in the event of a fire I would have been hard-pressed to do more than bang on her door.

'You know, many of mankind's most talented leaders, thinkers and artists have chosen the way of the Sanguine,' Celia informed me in a calm, soothing voice, clearly trying to put me at ease. 'Queen Victoria, Nietzsche, Michael Hutchence —' she went on.

'Queen Victoria? Nietzsche, the philosopher?' I replied, disbelieving. It was perhaps inevitable that some well-known figures would have become undead, but Queen Victoria? Could it be?

(Somehow INXS's Michael Hutchence didn't seem a stretch.)

'Oh yes, the Widow of Windsor came to the Sanguine just before the end of her sixty-three-year reign. I suspect she wasn't happy to just sign off after all that. She has something of a cult following now among those in the know. And I'm not sure why you'd find Nietzsche such a surprise. He was always fascinated with "vampirism". What was his famous quote? "Of all that is written, I love only what a man has written with his own blood."'

Well, that did seem a bit dark.

'Didn't he die of . . .' I thought for a moment.

'Syphilis, they said it was,' Celia told me.

Ouch.

She stopped at the end of the hall, just outside her door. 'Most choose to fake their deaths. Well, in truth, they aren't *faking* their deaths to become undead, but they must fake the manner of their deaths,' she corrected herself. 'Still syphilis seems an odd choice. I think he was going for "death by madness". Nietzsche is a complicated character.'

Celia was speaking of Nietzsche in the present tense. How peculiar.

'Who else?' I asked, deliberately stalling.

'Let's see . . . There are so many. Well, there's Napoleon, Ludwig I of Bavaria, Marie Antoinette, Picasso, Frida Kahlo, Oscar Wilde, Jim Morrison, Aaliyah, Courtney Love —'

'Wait, Kurt Cobain's widow? The singer? But she is still alive,' I protested.

'Is she?' Celia replied, and her words hung in the air for a while. 'Well, perhaps that one is only a rumour,' she finally conceded.

'What about Bela Lugosi?' I remembered him from the 1931 *Dracula* film that made him a horror legend.

'I don't think so,' Celia said.

That seemed a bit cruel, what with him being buried wearing his vampire cape and everything. 'And you don't want to be Sanguine?' I pressed.

'No. Or I'd probably already be one.'

'But you aren't ageing.' I was dying to know how she did it.

'Well, thank you for saying so, darling,' she said. 'Okay, enough trivia. It's time.'

*Oh boy.*

She slid a key smoothly into the lock and opened the door. For the first time, I was able to see beyond the door that had held such curiosity for me for months. The smell hit me first. The scent of frankincense was in the air. Frankincense and something else? The aroma was pleasant, if slightly cloying.

The door opened into a sunken chamber. It appeared to be a small but plush sitting room with Persian rugs, heavy velvet drapes and a stunning, carved sideboard on which several candles glowed in little silver holders. I saw two closed doors, one next to the sideboard and one at the far wall. There was no window. Two exquisitely carved wooden chairs with plush burgundy velvet seats were set out around a low circular table in the centre of the room. A velvet chaise lounge was pushed against one wall.

'Watch your step.'

There was a drop of three stone steps into the room. We walked down these, and Celia motioned to the carved, circular table. I placed the silver tea tray on it. I heard knocking and straightened abruptly. It wasn't coming from any of the three doors. It was coming from behind me. I turned, and took in a shocked breath. I had considered my powers of observation to be good. Not so. How else could I have missed the enormous coffin behind me?

*Oh god, Deus is inside. He's in the casket!*

The full-sized coffin sitting in the shadowy corner was of deep, polished mahogany.

'Come in,' Celia said cheerily, in a slightly raised voice. She turned to me. 'He always knocks. Isn't that just darling?'

There was a slight creak, and one set of fingers appeared beneath the lip of the coffin's lid. Someone . . . or *something* was pushing it open. I thought of horror movies with rotting zombies rising from their graves. I covered my mouth with my hand, looked away and shut my eyes. There was a shuffling sound, and further creaking, and finally I faced the creature I feared.

'Deus, meet Pandora English. Pandora, meet Deus,' Celia said.

The creature before me wasn't rotting. In fact, he looked rather well, if a little pale. (Understandable, considering the whole sunlight allergy thing.) Still, he had a darker complexion than I'd imagined and if I'd expected a tall Euro-vamp in a dinner suit and red-lined cape, I'd have been disappointed. He wore a very attractive skinny suit, as the fashion mags called it. He looked like he might be going to the same dinner party as Celia. Deus was a bit taller than me, perhaps five foot nine or ten, and he had dark, dramatic eyebrows and the longest eyelashes I had ever seen on a man. But of course he wasn't a man, was he? He was a Sanguine. And he was at least a few hundred years old, from what I knew. How does one even have a conversation with someone with that much experience and power? How does someone have a conversation with a creature who has been hanging out in a casket?

'It is a true pleasure to finally meet you, Pandora,' Deus said, smiling.

I couldn't pick the accent, but it wasn't Romanian.

'Um, yes . . . ah . . .' I stuttered, trying to find my tongue.

'I'll leave you two. You have much to discuss,' Celia said.

*No!*

Celia seemed to catch my panic. We traded a glance and the look in her eye told me to relax. But how on earth was I to relax?

Deus gave her a courteous nod before escorting her to the door. I watched for a kiss or lovers' gesture at the top of the little steps, and didn't see either. Still, I noticed Celia was positively glowing. Was she blushing? She stepped back into the penthouse and closed the door behind her. Deus turned and I averted my eyes.

'Sorry for the entrance. It must seem rather theatrical to you,' he said as he came back to join me.

'Oh no. Not really. I mean, you are . . . It's . . . No, that's fine.' I stuttered awkwardly, looking at my shoes. *A coffin. Did he really just rise from a coffin? Celia keeps a casket for him?*

'May I sit?' I heard him say.

'Oh yes, uh, please,' I replied. I took one chair and he took the other.

I crossed my legs and fidgeted, trying to avoid his face. The desire to look at him was frighteningly intense, and I fought against it. From what I'd seen he wasn't handsome exactly, but he was extremely attractive in a magnetic sense. I knew he was smiling. I had to say something. The stretch of silence had become excruciating.

'So, yes . . . nice to meet you Deus . . . Isn't Deus Latin for God?' I asked, evidently unable to stop myself rambling as soon as I opened my mouth. I flicked my eyes up to his face, saw its smooth texture, saw that large, pleasant grin, and I looked down again.

No, not handsome, but . . .

'Well, yes it is. We know some Latin, do we?' he replied calmly.

I blushed. 'Not really . . . just . . . I know a few words from my mother's books. That's all.'

There was a long silence. 'Shall we have some tea?' he finally suggested.

'Oh, I didn't know you . . . Well yes, of course . . .' Before I could finish embarrassing myself with my sudden inability to string a sentence together, he had poured us both a cup.

'Cream and sugar?'

'Thank you.'

He handed me my cup and placed some sugar in his. He didn't touch the cream. 'Lactose intolerant,' he explained.

*Oh.*

I took a sip of tea.

'You have a problem with my kind?' Deus suggested.

I nearly choked. 'No, no! I have nothing against your kind. Nothing at all.'

'I meant that I understand you are experiencing a problem with someone in particular.'

Now I understood what he meant. 'Oh yes, there are a few vampir . . . uh, Sanguine models in the building and they really don't like me.'

*I can't believe I nearly said vampire! Idiot . . . . idiot . . .*

I looked at his face now, finally. And immediately I thought, *Oh no.* He *is* handsome. A handsome vampire. It seemed a horrible idea. Horrible because of the hold a Sanguine like Athanasia had over others, particularly men. She hypnotised them so easily. They went silly around her. They gawked. Was the same going to happen to me now with Deus? Was I going to gawk helplessly at him?

'You've been having some troubles with Athanasia, I understand,' Deus gently prodded.

I nodded enthusiastically, tearing myself away from my strange thoughts. 'Yes. She wants to kill me.' I paused. 'Actually she wants to kill me and eat me.' I took another sip of tea. Great-Aunt Celia sure knew how to make some wicked Earl Grey.

'I see,' Deus responded calmly, the grin still on his face. *An eternal smile*, I thought.

'And you staked her,' he said.

I bit my lip. 'Wait, that's not fair. She attacked me. It was purely self-defence. She attacked me in the lobby downstairs. And another time after a fashion show, and yesterday she would have attacked me if I hadn't produced some rice.'

'Hmmm, she hasn't outgrown her counting.' He thought about that. 'You didn't provoke her, then?'

I thought of my comment about vampire chic being out of style. I guess someone like Athanasia might find such a comment provocative, but it hardly warranted a murder attempt.

'Not really,' I said.

He nodded. 'I see. I'll have a word with her and her friends.'

'I don't want to make things worse,' I said. 'I don't need any more trouble. I just want her to leave me alone.'

Deus nodded. 'I've heard there are things afoot at the moment, but Athanasia will leave you alone now.'

'Things are afoot? What kind of things?'

Deus bowed his head. 'Celia warned me that you like to ask questions.' His grin didn't falter. Nor did he elaborate on just what kinds of things were afoot. 'So, how is *Pandora* magazine working out for you?' he asked.

I was taken aback. I hadn't imagined Deus would have given my work any thought.

'Um, my job is fine,' I said cautiously. 'It's not easy to get work in New York.' I squinted at him. 'Why do you ask? You didn't have anything to do with me getting that job, did you?'

'Me? No. I didn't get you that job. Though of course I did know it was available, after what Athanasia had done.'

'You mean after she *killed* my predecessor.' And turned her into a Sanguine.

'Yes,' he replied.

And Deus had told my great-aunt about it, who'd told me to go to the magazine. And there it was. I'd got my first job in New York because of Athanasia. A vampire. And that same vampire was trying to kill me. I was quiet for a while as I absorbed that bit of info.

'I've not seen Samantha around lately. Is she okay?' I asked.

'I believe so,' he said. 'But it wasn't her I wished to discuss. I was wondering about your colleagues, Skye and Pepper.'

'What about them?'

'I'm sure you've realised they don't remember anything of the incident that took place the other month.'

Yes, the incident. The incident when I saved them. 'I'd noticed,' I said and watched his face. 'You . . . did that?'

'It fell to me to erase them, yes. I haven't had the chance to discuss it with you. I was wondering how that was working out.'

Deus had erased them. Of course. I knew something had done it. I supposed you couldn't have two women roaming around Manhattan blabbering about what they'd seen. They'd probably be in straightjackets by now if he hadn't intervened.

'Well, you did a good job,' I conceded. 'They don't remember anything.' I put my head in my hands and sighed. 'I understand. I do. Or I'm trying to understand. You have to erase their minds.'

'The world isn't ready for what we are, Pandora.'

I had no comeback for that.

'Couldn't you have just taken away their memories and maybe left a bit of gratitude in there for the fact I saved their lives? Couldn't they at least like me a little, even if they don't know why? Ah, never mind.' Then I thought of Jay. *Roses guy.* 'Did you erase my boyfriend as well?' I had to ask.

'No. It was already done.'

I sighed. 'Oh. He doesn't even know who I am now. And he's the only real boy I've met in New York.'

*Sharing boy problems with a long-dead Sanguine? My love life was getting ridiculous.*

'Never mind,' I finally said under my breath.

Deus straightened his tie. 'It's been a pleasure, Pandora, but if you'll excuse me I do have a tight schedule this evening.' He rose from his chair and extended his hand.

I shook it, and felt a strange pull as our skin touched. His hand felt smooth, cool and somehow sensual. I blinked a few times and wondered . . . could he really be dead? With such a strong presence?

'Please thank your lovely great-aunt for the tea,' Deus said, and then paused. I looked at his face, and found that I didn't want to look away. Those eyelashes were so long. His skin seemed *silky.* How could it feel like that? He inclined his head towards me, still gently gripping my hand. 'You have a question?' he stated more than asked.

I swallowed. 'Yes. I do,' I said. I disengaged and let my hand fall to my side. 'Um, is it true that you are . . . dead? That your heart does not beat?'

Deus let out a curious sigh, something like a quiet laugh, and asked, 'Do you really want to know?'

I found myself nodding. I did.

He took my right hand in his and guided it towards the left-hand side of his chest.

I gasped. His flesh was cold, *but his heart beats.* I could feel it clearly and steadily beneath my palm. The rhythm was slow and hypnotic.

'But . . . I'd been told —'

'I'm sure you've been told a lot of things,' he said, echoing Celia's words.

I was stunned into silence. He had his hands clasped behind him now, and I kept my hand there on his chest, feeling the beat.

'Now, it has been my pleasure to finally meet you, Pandora, but if you'll excuse me, I have some other matters to attend to this evening,' he said. 'Please thank your beautiful great-aunt for her hospitality. I'm sure we will see each other again soon.'

'Yes. Uh, thank you,' I said and took a step back. I curled my hand into a ball and let it drop at my side.

*His heart beats. I felt it. It beats.*

Still smiling, Deus walked back to the casket on the floor, opened the lid and slid into the darkness inside. Each movement was smooth as water. Slowly the lid closed, and then he was gone.

I squinted and cocked my head to one side.

It took perhaps a minute to come out of the strange, mesmerised feeling Deus had left me with. Once I did, I went right up to the casket, put my ear to the lid and listened. At first I heard nothing, and then there was a slight echo of footsteps.

*Aha!*

I pulled open the lid.

The coffin was bottomless. I leapt up, grabbed one of Celia's glowing candles and lowered my arm inside. There were stone steps leading down into darkness.

*A private entrance. Of course.*

And to think that for a moment there I'd believed Deus actually hung out in a coffin in Celia's room. Ludicrous.

'Pandora?'

Celia was calling for me. I took one last look through the coffin's empty base and then hurriedly closed the lid. The doorknob on the door leading to the hallway turned, and my great-aunt appeared. She found me standing in her sitting room with her candle in my hand, looking guilty.

'Watch it now or you could burn yourself,' she said casually, then glanced down at the coffin and the corners of her mouth turned up for a moment. 'I hope you'll forgive the entrance.'

'The entrance?'

She leaned against the doorframe and crossed her arms. 'The hidden entrance. It was here before I bought the place.'

'Oh.' *It was? But who would . . .?*

'It's not really my style, I'm sure you'll agree. I've been thinking of just putting a trapdoor in its place, but I never get round to organising it. Besides, I imagine the coffin would rather prevent nosey people from finding the passage-way. Come,' she beckoned. I placed the candle back on the sideboard and stepped into the hall. She re-locked the door behind us and followed me into the main penthouse. 'There are reasons why Deus cannot come in through the main door,' she told me as we reached the main lounge room, casting her eyes on the doorway that I came and went from every day.

*Oh. Sanguine cannot enter the penthouse.*

'And it would be most bothersome for him to run into some of those Fledglings on the main street. All the grovelling and so on. Some of them really don't know when to quit.'

'I'm sorry, I left the tea.' I suddenly felt the need to sit down.

'Don't worry about it, darling. I'll take care of it. You have a lie down.'

Instead I sat on the hassock near her reading chair. I felt strangely depleted from being in Deus's presence. It was like I'd spent a prolonged period of time pressed up against a lion's cage. Now that the adrenaline had passed, I felt so drained I needed to rest, perhaps even sleep. I'd been near Sanguine before – not by choice – but Deus was different. Even compared with the four-hundred-year-old Elizabeth Báthory, his presence was somehow more intense. I hadn't realised how shaken I was until he had gone.

'Don't you find his manner . . . strange?' I couldn't help but ask.

Celia perched on the arm of her chair. 'How do you mean?'

I thought of that permanent grin and felt my stomach do a little flip. It was pleasant, and yet . . .

I wondered how best to put it. 'He's always *happy* looking.'

'He is a Kathakano, Pandora. They always grin.'

'He's a what?'

'Kathakano,' my great-aunt said. 'The traditional Sanguine of ancient Crete.'

Ancient Crete?

*Oh boy.*

'Oh yes, *ancient*.' The corners of her lips curved up ever so slightly.

Had I really just spent time with someone who had walked the earth since the days of ancient Greece? What was it like to live so long . . . and still be grinning?

'The effect he has on you will get easier to control.'

'What do you mean?'

'His presence can be quite overwhelming at first,' she explained. 'It's a natural predatory effect the Sanguine have on humans. As a rule, the more ancient they are, the more skilful they are at using Sanguine trickery, so the more powerful the effect. I suppose you spent half the meeting looking at him, or trying desperately *not* to look at him, or thinking about his face and wondering what exactly it was that made it so alluring. Wondering what it would be like to be closer to him? Wondering what it would be like if he just reached out and touched you? Or *you* touched him?'

I blushed.

'It's okay. It's a perfectly normal reaction to the presence of a Sanguine, particularly a powerful one. It would not have been personal. He wouldn't have been trying to seduce you.' She raised an eyebrow, and threw me a salacious look. 'Because if he *had* been trying to seduce you, well, we'd know about it.'

I blushed even worse.

'But it will get easier. Especially for *you*, Pandora. You are gifted.'

'Is that part of being the Seventh?' Celia had often told me that I was the Seventh – the seventh Lucasta daughter. This role meant I had responsibilities as well as powerful, innate gifts. She still hadn't explained exactly what those gifts were. The seventh son of a seventh son was nothing compared to a seventh Lucasta daughter, she'd informed me. I was hoping she would now enlighten me as to why.

Celia just smiled. 'The next time you meet him, you'll be more in control of your reaction.'

*Next time.* Did I want there to be a next time? Part of me really did. The part of me I was going to ignore, however, because I felt like I'd been tricked. It was Sanguine trickery. I mean, I touched his heart. I felt his heart beating!

'You touched his chest, didn't you? That was brave,' Celia remarked.

'Oh, I . . . yes. I-I thought their hearts didn't beat,' I stuttered.

'How do you think the blood pumps through their bodies?' she said, as if it was the most obvious thing in the world. 'They are Sanguine. The blood is the life.'

*The blood is the life.* Was my great-aunt now quoting Count Dracula himself?

'I thought you hated Bram Stoker.'

Celia chuckled slightly at my reaction. 'Well, it is a good line.'

I had never in my life felt so incredibly naked. My great-aunt had known everything I was feeling – everything I was feeling about her . . . *boyfriend?* Was that what he was? What was it that he had going with Great-Aunt Celia, exactly? He was keeping her young somehow, but he hadn't turned her. I'd spoken about it with her before, but she was cagey about the specifics and I still didn't understand. Her approach to keeping me in the loop seemed to be on a need to know basis. Was it love? I knew what my paperback novels said – the eternal love of the vampire and all that – but even with a beating heart, could a predator, a Sanguine, really *love?*

'What is it that you two have?' I blurted and, as soon as the question popped out, I knew I'd been too rash, too rude. My great-aunt did not respond to rudeness.

Her eyes flashed wide and then narrowed. 'That's a bit personal, darling,' she said, and smiled, but her pale, beautiful face was closed to me. I knew that look. It meant *end of discussion.* 'A lady has to retain some mystery,' she added and straightened her dress. 'Now, darling, you look exhausted —'

'Great-Aunt Celia, I'm sorry if it's rude to ask all these questions . . . but . . . How do you know you're safe with him?'

At that, she smiled wickedly. 'You needn't worry about me. I'm not so powerless.'

I pondered that. What powers did she have, exactly? How could she feel safe with someone as clearly powerful as Deus? Someone centuries old?

'Much as I am touched by your concern, I assure you I am safe with him. There is much I can know about a person,' she insisted, and the sparkle in her eye returned. Though Celia had never directly said so, I was increasingly sure that she could read my mind. Perhaps she could read other people's minds. Could she read his?

She reached a hand out to me, and I took it. 'Come. You need your rest. There are things afoot in Spektor, I can feel it.'

'Deus said that too. What things?' I asked.

'We'll soon find out, won't we? For now you must rest. I left a drink by your bed. Something to help you sleep tonight.' She helped me to my feet. My limbs felt filled with lead. 'Sleep well, Pandora. I'm glad you and Deus have finally met.'

I nodded. I took a step forward and stopped. 'But he's not a person,' I said.

'Pardon?'

'You said there is much you can know about a person. But he's not a person.'

'No? Well, he *is* more than that, yes. But then, so are you, Pandora.'

# CHAPTER
# EIGHT

On Thursday Skye DeVille did not come in at all. This was by no means normal, but selfishly, I was relieved. Perhaps she'd delegated her work to Pepper for a couple of days while she recovered from her flu. (Or her attack of insanity.) Maybe she'd got her cold medications mixed up. In any event, the office was more peaceful for her absence.

At the end of the day, as I was packing up, Morticia came over to gossip. She was clearly buzzing with excitement about something. She obviously couldn't wait until we left so she'd taken the unusual step of coming to my desk first.

'Did you read the news today?' she asked.

I picked up my coat and slid it over my arm. 'No,' I said, and neglected to mention that I'd spent the previous evening chatting with an ancient Greek vampire who had stepped out of a casket. Such things tended to make fashion industry news seem a bit dull.

'It's all over the websites,' she went on.

'What's happened?' I asked, prepared for news of some celebrity coupling, reproduction or split, or the latest goss on some fashion collection. Morticia followed that sort of thing so I didn't have to, I figured.

She leaned against my cubicle, all striped leggings and long limbs. 'Apparently last night another designer went missing,' she told me.

'Another designer?' That *was* interesting.

She nodded and her eyebrows were fixed high on her forehead. *'Victor Mal.'*

I gasped. 'No! I only talked to him yesterday.' We hadn't exactly bonded, but it was a real shock to imagine that something could have happened to him, and so quickly. I shook my head. 'He didn't seem like he was planning to go anywhere. In fact, he had seemed pretty intent on remaining "The King of Knitwear" in New York. There's no way he would have taken off by choice.'

Morticia threw her arms in the air. 'I know. It's crazy.'

'It must be foul play,' I said. 'Do they still suspect Helmsworth?' I'd never met the man, but he would have to be pretty insane to organise something like this, and not think the finger would be pointed at him. Kidnapping people? All knitwear designers? Did he have a bone to pick with all of them?

Morticia shrugged. 'I don't know.'

I had a very bad feeling about the whole thing, and this latest news was unsettling, to say the least. I tried to imagine the events that might have taken place since I'd seen Victor. Had he packed up his things and left? But why? Had he been abducted? I turned off my computer and grabbed my satchel, and Morticia and I walked towards the door. Pepper was hunched over at her desk. She was probably doing the job of two.

'Goodnight,' Morticia said to the remaining staff in the office. There were a few mumbled responses. *Don't fraternise with the freaks*, I could almost hear them think.

'Hey, did Skye phone in sick or something?' I asked quietly as Morticia and I reached the staircase.

'Pepper told her to take some time off, I guess,' she said, uncertain. 'She wasn't looking really well.'

'No,' I agreed. 'She really wasn't.'

With our coats bundled around us we walked to the subway entrance at Spring Street, and parted ways. I had something I wanted to do before I made my way home to Spektor. I was pretty sure SoHo Exotic Pets would be open late on a Thursday.

I was right.

A bell chimed when I walked in. The shop was empty of customers, but crowded with vivariums, aquariums and fusty animal smells. In other words, nothing much had changed. I wondered how they stayed afloat.

The bespectacled shop assistant rounded an aisle of shelves to greet me. 'Exotic Pets, how may I help you?' She adjusted her frames.

'It's me again,' I said, just as she appeared to recognise me.

'We hoped you might come back.'

'You did?'

'How is your spider? Did you find out what breed it was?' she asked.

I squinted at her. 'The spider I came in with wasn't mine . . . like I said. And I wouldn't know how it is because I left it with you.'

'Left it with us?' She looked surprised but then smiled. 'You're kidding, of course. It was quite a lovely looking tarantula. Unusual, but —'

'Wait,' I said, stopping her. 'Are you telling me you don't have that tarantula here? Did someone claim it?'

'Of course we don't have your tarantula.'

*It was never my tarantula,* I wanted to say, but dropped it. 'But I left the spider with you, remember?'

'Jason!' she called out in a shrill voice, and took a cagey step back from me.

The male shopkeeper soon appeared from the back wearing the same sweater I'd seen him in last time. It didn't look like it had been washed in the interim. There was a big dirt patch on one shoulder, which he dusted off casually as he approached. 'Oh hello again. Did you find out what kind of tarantula you have? The Thai Black, right? Maybe a new hybrid?' he asked.

My brows pulled together. I looked at their faces. They honestly believed I'd taken the spider with me. I could hear it in their tone, see it in their eyes. I didn't understand. How could they think that, when I'd left it right on the desk with them and run out in such a dramatic fashion?

'Jason, this lady seems to think she left her pet with us,' the female shopkeeper said quietly. She sounded a little nervous that I might be crazy. She'd backed away from me another step.

'What? Hey,' he began, 'I don't know what your game is, but —'

*They honestly think I kept it.*

'I was only kidding,' I squeaked. 'Sorry . . . I, um, wanted to thank you for your help the other day. I was hoping you knew what sort it was. Never mind.' I laughed nervously. 'And I have these crickets.' I removed them from my satchel. I had no need of them anymore, and I couldn't exactly set them free on the streets of Spektor. I could hear them scratching around in the little box. 'Please take them. Anyway . . . um, bye.' I turned on my heel and walked out. If they hadn't thought I was strange after my last departure from their shop, they certainly did now.

I walked to the Spring Street subway station, deeply puzzled. They sincerely believed that I had left with that tarantula. Why? I'd been in such a fluster to leave, perhaps someone else had been there to snatch it? Was that possible? Who would do that? It seemed unlikely, to say the least. And yet I could not believe those two were lying. It just didn't add up.

I hopped down the subway station stairs and put my ticket in the turnstile. The first train arrived only seconds after I'd stepped on to the platform, and I pushed my way inside the car. As usual, there were a lot of after-work commuters.

My belly twinged strangely and I looked up.

*There.*

The train pulled away just as I caught sight of a woman staring at me. She stood on the platform with her dark hair blowing sideways in the breeze brought by the train's movement. She was exceptionally tall. Her face was delicate, classical. Her eyes were dark and intense, and she was looking right at me.

*The tall lady.*

A shocked 'Oh' escaped my mouth.

She'd followed me from the pet shop the day I'd dropped the tarantula off. Or the day I *thought* I'd dropped the tarantula off. And here she was again, staring at me.

I had that awful, cold feeling in my belly.

And then the vision of her disappeared, replaced by a fast-moving slab of concrete as we hurtled through the tunnel and sped away from Spring Street. I stayed riveted to the glass window, still picturing the tall woman who made my stomach freeze like ice. I steadied myself on the rail and, at the next stop, took an available seat. I looked around me from time to time, in slight panic. I had a feeling that the tall woman was following me, and might appear at any moment on one of the platforms just beyond the glass. Crazy, I know. Eventually I managed to settle in to my latest book.

I was two stops away from my destination at 103rd Street when I felt the familiar coldness in my belly return.

*Thanatos. Death.*

I looked up with a start, and searched the crowd for signs of the tall lady. *She's following me!* Was she here on the subway car? I couldn't spot her. I struggled to concentrate on the feeling, as Celia had been teaching me to do, and I noticed the sensation was different, although barely perceptible. Under the sense of alarm and danger and death, there was another familiar feeling. Just as I was beginning to think it must be a ghost reaching out to me from the subway tunnel or trapped amongst the travelling cars, I realised that I knew exactly who it was.

*Athanasia.*

Oh fiddle. The nastiest supermodel I'd ever met was on the same train as me? (Okay, so she was also the only supermodel I'd ever met.) If she wasn't following me it was an awful coincidence that she was on the 6 line at the same time. She'd probably heard that Deus knew about her latest exploits, thanks to me, and she probably had a thing or two to say about that.

*Please let it not be her . . . Please . . .*

Sure enough, as the subway car rattled and shifted along the tracks, the door at the end of the car opened and in she walked, followed closely by Blonde, Brunette and Redhead. The inseparable four laughed and chatted amongst themselves with a kind of fake nonchalance that begged you to look while they pretended not to care. Each wore designer clothes that were completely inappropriate for the winter climate, with pale, toned arms and legs exposed to the elements. It made the contrast with the rugged-up mortal passengers around them even greater. Blonde was in a fashionably ripped shirt and fetching leather miniskirt with spike-heeled boots. Redhead wore a skin-tight stretchy tube dress that showed off her enviable figure, and Brunette was wearing fish-nets and a lycra suggestion of a skirt under a silk top that dropped suggestively off one shoulder. Athanasia was wearing tight jeans and a sleeveless leather vest that nipped in at her waist. She had strings of jewellery around her pale neck. The four of them looked like they might be in a band. Or at least in the band's rock video.

New Yorkers tend not to look at each other on the subway. It's an unwritten rule in Manhattan that you don't ever catch the eye of a stranger on public transport. Only crazy people did that. Yet, quite unwisely, several men had decided to break that rule. They looked up from their phones, or their newspapers, or their daydreaming, and ogled the fearsome four. These vampires probably didn't need to try very hard to pick up a snack after dark.

Blonde swung from one of the subway poles like it was another kind of pole, then let out a cruel laugh and sneered at an old woman who'd clearly found her display unladylike.

I shook my head, but said nothing. I really didn't need to be dealing with Athanasia's nonsense right now. She was certainly aware of my presence on the car and had probably even sought me out. I travelled this train route nearly every day after work, but today I was later than usual. Perhaps when I hadn't shown up as scheduled in Spektor, she'd decided to come and pester me? I wondered exactly what she planned to do. I had my pockets filled with rice, as was my custom, and I doubted they had outgrown their fetish for counting. I'd be fine on the subway car. (Wouldn't I? They didn't want a bloodbath on public transport, I hoped.) It was when I got off that I would have a real problem on my hands.

Too quickly the car slowed and the tiled platform of 103rd Street came into view. It wouldn't pay to stay on board till we were in the Bronx. I'd have to lose these four somewhere in the station or in Spanish Harlem, otherwise the walk through Central Park could be dangerous. Feeling wary, I got up from my seat and made my way to the doors. In a flash the quartet were on me.

'Hello little *morchilla*,' Redhead whispered. Her breath on my face was less than pleasant. 'Nice hair.'

'Yeah, nice do,' Brunette pitched in. 'Very *country*.'

'Can we save this for another time?' I said under my breath.

It was Athanasia who answered me. 'Looks like you need an escort. You can never be too careful in Central Park at night.'

I said nothing more.

The doors opened and I stepped on to the tiled platform and headed for my exit. The four fashionable creatures were on my heels, followed by a couple of mortals. At the base of the stairs I hurried ahead of them, not quite in a run, but pretending I had somewhere to be in a hurry, which come to think of it, I did. I flew up the steps two by two, my legs burning from the exertion. *Thank goodness for sensible shoes*, I thought. *And for silly Fledgling obsessive compulsive urges*. I spilled some rice grains just before I rushed out of the station, and then hit the open air of the crowded street. About a block away I turned down a buzzing main street and caught my breath. The street was filled with open shops and takeaway places, and I ducked into the nearest one I could find. It was a tiny pizza joint and didn't look very flash, or fresh.

I rested my satchel at my feet and urged my heart to slow.

The strong aroma of pizzas baking surrounded me. A light flickered overhead. After I'd loitered for a minute or two, a large, moustachioed man behind the counter gave me an impatient look. He wore a streaked white bib and he had a strong mixed Mediterranean accent. 'Lady, you here to sightsee or what?'

With a quick apology, I put in an order.

I waited against the wall by the corner of the grease-slicked counter, as far away from the window as possible. My heart was still pounding too fast.

Unfortunately it acted like a beacon, and after a few minutes the four Sanguine appeared outside the glass door, chatting and carrying on as if they hadn't just been counting rice grains on a grungy subway staircase. They were just four unnaturally good-looking underdressed young women having a little street party in Spanish Harlem. The party, I was afraid, involved me. There was no way around it.

Eventually the food I had no interest in eating arrived in a greasy box and I paid the hirsute man behind the counter without enthusiasm. I stepped outside with the box under my arm.

'Ewww, that place stinks,' Brunette said as I strode past.

'Pizza makes you fat, little *morchilla*,' Redhead taunted.

'I have bigger problems than you bunch right now,' I muttered and continued walking towards Central Park.

Athanasia sidled up close. 'Then stop meddling in my business, bitch,' she spat.

Always with the classy language. Always.

I stopped and looked at her. My eyes went to her neck. 'Wait, is that . . . Are you wearing the jewellery from Monday's photo shoot? Oh, you are kidding me.'

The jewellery around Athanasia's neck was brightly coloured strands of enamel. Precisely what the model had been wearing at the knitwear shoot. Precisely what Skye had accused me of stealing. I saw the little linked C shape of the branding.

'It's Chanel.' Athanasia placed her fingers on the strands, caressing her designer haul.

'It doesn't belong to you,' I said with a disapproving glare. I turned and continued to walk, my jaw set. 'I don't have time for this.'

'It does belong to me if I say it does,' Athanasia said, her unreasonably long legs easily keeping up with my stride.

We had finally reached the entrance to Central Park, but there was still an expanse of green grass and shadows to traverse before I made it to Spektor and to the safety of Celia's Sanguine-free penthouse. I couldn't wait to get into the lift. *The lift . . .?* In a flash I remembered Athanasia reaching out to stop the lift door from closing the other day. She'd had a tattoo on her wrist. It had looked like drawn-on jewels. It wasn't there now, I noticed. It had been a temporary tattoo.

'I see your tattoo wore off,' I said bitterly. *'Thief.'*

The undead supermodel just laughed at me. 'Oh, you are so naive. It's really quite touching.' She matched my pace as we passed benches in Central Park.

'Why are you stealing from my boss's office?' I demanded. I thought of how Skye had accused me, how I'd had my bag upturned in front of everyone in the office. 'On second thought, never mind. I don't care.'

Athanasia laughed again. 'It's no fun when someone screws up your career, is it?'

I resisted rolling my eyes. 'Athanasia, it's not my fault that you got mixed up with the Blood Countess. That was always going to go wrong. Just leave me alone.' I walked ahead as fast as my legs could take me without breaking into a run.

Athanasia growled at me. Actually growled. She pushed my shoulder with a violent jab and I stumbled forward.

*Oh dear. Here we go . . .*

In seconds she pounced, knocking me sideways, and we tumbled on to the grass. My satchel went flying, and the takeaway box flipped upside down and opened up beside us. She straddled me, the stolen necklaces tangling in my hair. Her undead friends gathered around chanting, 'Feed, feed, feed!'

'Hungry?' I managed. 'Have some garlic bread.'

In one swift motion I planted the hot slab of garlic bread on her face. It stuck like a cream pie on a clown.

'Ahhhgh!' Athanasia screamed and reeled back, swaying on her knees.

I slipped out from under her and scurried back across the grass towards my satchel. I watched in amazement as the long, flat greasy bread clung to the left-hand side of her face. It just stuck there, peeling downwards in slow motion. Athanasia seemed frozen in disbelief. She knelt with her hands in the air, as if ready for some dark prayer. Finally she gripped the corners of the bread with the tips of her fingers and, with a pained howl, flung the bread on to the grass.

'You . . . You bitch!' she cried shakily. Still she didn't move. She gasped again and again, horrified into speechlessness. Her mouth hung agape, and her manicured fingers flitted helplessly around her damaged face. Her skin didn't smoke exactly, but it did seem to be, well . . . *melting.* Boils began to appear. 'Look . . . look at what you did!' she screamed. 'Look!'

Her eyes filled with something dark, something that began to roll down her cheeks as she screamed and moaned. *Tears. Tears of blood.*

*Oh boy.*

It was time I bolted.

Fast.

# CHAPTER
# NINE

I sped down Addams Avenue at a half-jog, still expecting to be grabbed by one of Athanasia's cohorts at any moment. By the time I reached Celia's penthouse I felt I'd run a marathon. I knocked and then threw myself inside, panting.

'Darling, is everything okay?' Great-Aunt Celia called out from her chair. Freyja was asleep on the hassock next to her stocking-clad feet. I didn't pause to say hi.

'Um, excuse me for a moment,' I replied, and disappeared quickly into my room. I closed the door behind me and leaned back against it. My satchel slid to the hardwood floor at my feet. I'd never felt such profound relief to be safely in my room. Even with all that had happened since I'd moved to Spektor, I'd never really considered returning to my stifling hometown of Gretchenville. And now I wondered − really wondered − if I was up for this strange new life. I was going to have to arm myself with more than garlic bread if I was going to stick around. A wooden stake wouldn't do either, I'd learned. I'd once staked Athanasia (as I kept being reminded) and Celia had calmly explained that stakes were only utilised to hold vampires still while you performed the rest of the ritual − head removal, stuffing mouth with garlic, et cetera. *Yuck.* I was no vampire slayer. I couldn't exactly wander the New York subway system with an axe at the ready.

Something large – perhaps a bird – flew past my bedroom window, and I shut the curtains. I made a beeline for my ensuite and washed my hands once, twice, three times, until I couldn't smell the garlic anymore, and the sight of Athanasia's melting face was, for the moment, out of my mind. I pushed my hair off my face and looked at myself in the mirror. My eyes were large and a little terrified. This was becoming a regular look for me.

*I can't keep doing this.*

I leaned on the sink with my shoulders hunched. Some help talking to Deus had been. I'd just known it would only make matters worse. And what about Athanasia stealing those things from Skye's office? Was she trying to get me fired? That figured. I'd been the reason she'd lost *her* job. But it was hardly fair to compare such things when my job was legitimate and hers had involved procuring virgin blood. And virgins.

'Horrible,' I muttered aloud.

*I hate Sanguine. I hate them!*

'Why won't they all leave me alone!' I cried in a fit of frustration and leaned my forehead against the cool mirror. Something caught my eye in the reflection, pulling me out of my spasm of self-pity. The wall behind me was turning white. No, it wasn't the wall . . . it was the air behind me. I felt a cool mist gather at my back.

'Miss Pandora?' Lieutenant Luke said, even before he'd fully materialised. His handsome face appeared, but he looked disturbingly faint in the mirror reflection. He was a poor, see-through version of himself. I turned around quickly in a panic, but, outside of the mirror, I was relieved to see he looked less amorphous. I hugged him and clung to his chest. He felt solid enough to embrace, and for a while I did exactly that. His chest felt firm under my cheek, his uniform crisp and spotless under my skin. He brought a hand up to gently stroke the back of my hair.

'Miss Pandora, are you okay?' he asked.

I slid my arms down around his waist, hands resting against the leather belt that cinched his frockcoat tight.

'Miss Pandora, you aren't going to leave, are you?'

I shut my eyes tightly, and warm tears gathered in my lashes. 'Just hold me,' I whispered.

We stood there for a while. I didn't open my eyes. I didn't move. He didn't speak.

There was a knock on the door of my room.

I sighed. Celia would be wondering if I was okay. It was unlike me to lock myself in my room. I disengaged from Luke's comforting hold, and stepped out of the bathroom.

'Celia?'

'Yes, darling, it's me,' she said through the door.

For some reason I was overcome with a guilty urge to hide Lieutenant Luke, as if I were a teenager caught with a boy in my room. But Luke was no boy, and I was the only one who could see him. It was times like these when I felt fresh sadness at Luke's otherness. He was real to me, yet I knew we lived in very different worlds. I could never do things with him that I could do with a normal, living guy. We could never walk down the street holding hands. We could never go to a movie. I could never introduce him to my friends. (Not that I really had many.) I could never introduce him to Celia. And there were . . . other things, too – other things any normal woman craved. With Luke, those dreams were impossible.

It would have been nice to have known him as a man.

Luke materialised at the doorway to the ensuite and we exchanged glances. I arranged myself on the edge of my bed. 'Please come in,' I said. I grabbed one of the vintage *Vogue* magazines Celia had stacked on my bedside table for inspiration, and placed it in my lap as if I'd been reading.

The door opened. 'Darling, I can see you are distressed,' she said. 'May I sit?'

I nodded. 'Of course.'

My stylish great-aunt had a special glow about her, I noticed. Beneath her omnipresent veil, her pale skin was luminous. She had reapplied her scarlet lipstick and was wearing a pair of fine leather gloves that added an extra layer of glamour to her outfit. Once again, it looked like she was ready for an important night out with the likes of Cary Grant or Humphrey Bogart at some divine house party or cool jazz bar.

'You look lovely,' I said. I was reluctant to tell her about my problems with Athanasia, in case she spoke to Deus again and things became even worse.

'You have a visitor,' she told me calmly.

*I* have a visitor?

'Deus is here.'

I got a little chill. Luke frowned and looked at Celia, who naturally did not return his gaze.

'I think you know why,' she finished.

The garlic bread incident. *Word travels fast.*

'It's important that you sort this out now,' she said gently.

I took a sharp intake of breath. I was still too shaken. I wasn't ready for visitors. I certainly wasn't ready for the likes of Deus, and his strange, hypnotic face.

Luke furrowed his brow. He moved close and set a protective hand on my shoulder. My great-aunt could not see him, nor could she hear him say, 'Are you sure that's necessary?'

'Um, are you sure that's necessary?' I asked Celia, hyper-aware of the strangeness of the moment. She knew I had a ghostly friend, but she didn't know he was right next to me. Should I tell her, out of courtesy? I wondered.

'I'm afraid it is necessary,' Celia responded. 'It's better to resolve this.'

I knew there was no point in trying to argue. 'I'll need a few minutes to get ready,' I said.

'Take a little while if you need to, dear. Oh, and tell your friend – he *is* here, isn't he? – tell him it would be best if you went in alone.'

My face went hot so fast it must have turned purple.

Instinctively, I looked up at Luke. Celia followed my gaze but looked through him to the wardrobe. She'd told me that seeing spirits was not one of her gifts, yet somehow she knew he was there. Perhaps it had been our voices before she knocked. More likely, she'd read my mind.

Ten minutes later I emerged reasonably composed. I'd cleaned my teeth, run a brush through my long, naturally light brown hair, and taken a few deep breaths. Luke was still in my room, and when I walked out the door I glanced back and noticed that he had started pacing. It was kind of sweet, I thought.

'You are quite fond of your friend, aren't you?' Celia said in a low voice as I joined her.

'I am,' I replied, with a heavy feeling of sadness. I knew Lieutenant Luke was real, or as real as spirits could be, and yet he wasn't a real man.

'And he has been helpful to you, hasn't he?' Celia gently prodded.

'Yes,' I answered.

'He's handsome. I know that much,' she said, and I blushed again. 'Tell me, how is he dressed? Is he in uniform?'

I nodded. 'He died in the Civil War. He was a second lieutenant in the Lincoln Cavalry. I sometimes think he understands something of what is going on, something of the same things you've been telling me.'

'That's very good,' she said and fell into a mode of quiet contemplation for a moment. I wished I could read her mind as she seemed able to read mine. She placed her gloved hands on each of my wrists. The slim-fitting leather was soft. 'We will discuss this later. Deus will see you now.'

I followed her into the kitchen and she handed me the silver tray, already neatly prepared with all the fixings for tea. I was relieved to see there were three cups this time. She moved down the hall towards her private quarters, and I followed at her heels. She opened the door with her key. The small room was candlelit again, and chairs were set out. Deus was already there, and he rose to greet us. He was again dressed in a suit, and his hair was perfectly coiffured. To my complete and utter horror, however, he was not alone.

*Athanasia.*

*No!*

'Go on,' Great-Aunt Celia whispered, and encouraged me forward. Like an automaton I walked down the little stone steps carrying the tray. Celia shut the door behind me, and for a moment I thought I might have a severe attack of claustrophobia – something I'd been feeling a bit lately. The feeling probably had something to do with being locked in a confined space with two vampires; one who was ancient and held some mesmerising power over me, and the other who had very recently tried to rip my throat out. How could my great-aunt do this to me?

Deus gave me a cordial, cool-skinned handshake, and grinned his eternal Kathakano grin. 'Pandora, thank you so much for seeing me again. You remember Athanasia.'

I nodded numbly. Yes, I certainly remembered her.

'Let me take that,' he said, relieving me of the tray. 'That's very kind of you,' he said, as if it wasn't Celia who had thought of providing the tea. 'Please take a seat, if you will.'

I noticed that the low, circular table between the seats was carved with a pentagram. I took a step and stopped.

Athanasia's appearance was quite shocking. Even under the dim illumination of flattering candlelight I could see that one half of her face was terribly scarred and pitted where the garlic bread had made contact. She had her arms tightly crossed, and her legs too. Her jaw was set. Her black eyes were fierce and red-rimmed. I found myself staring at her ruined skin. I almost felt sorry for her. *Almost.*

'Please take a seat, Pandora,' Deus instructed for a second time.

There was an empty chair close to the door. I bent my knees and sat in it very slowly, instinctively avoiding sudden movements, as if Athanasia were a wild panther or a wolf that might lunge at any moment. I ended up perched on the edge of the cushion. After a moment I automatically patted my pocket for rice, but of course I hadn't brought any with me. That was an oversight. But how could I have known that my nemesis would be in the room? How did she even get in here? I guessed this chamber wasn't part of the original penthouse, hence the steps and the stone walls and floor. Was it a kind of antechamber leading between the penthouse and some other area? Had Athanasia come in through the coffin with Deus? Was my great-aunt safe with all these Sanguine crawling around this end of the mansion?

'Now, as you can see, Pandora, Athanasia has sustained an injury to her face,' Deus began with unnaturally polite charm.

I looked at her again while she fumed silently. Her scars resembled melted plastic. Or pizza. I wondered how long they might take to heal. Or did Sanguine not heal as quickly as vampires did in the movies? She'd survived my staking rather well, I thought. I was also quite sure it would take her a lot less time to heal from my garlic bread application than it would for me to heal from her lethal fangs.

'Yes,' I finally replied to Deus, though the word barely came out. 'I can see that.'

'She tells me you are responsible for this injury.'

I gaped. '*Responsible?* She tried to kill me tonight when I got off the subway! She came after me with her friends.'

'Is this true?' Deus asked Athanasia in a level voice.

'We were talking,' she said in a low voice.

'Talking? *Sure.*' I shook my head.

'Why were you at the subway station?' Deus asked her.

'Coincidence. We got on the same train.'

Oh please.

'I seriously doubt it was coincidence and she certainly wasn't keen for a simple chat,' I said. 'She tried to kill me.'

It was like being in the school principal's office. Only the principal was undead, and smiling strangely. He had also probably just risen from the casket in the floor. I hated to think what kind of detention he could give us.

Athanasia kept her arms crossed and her eyes averted. I knew Deus was very powerful, and if Athanasia was going to listen to anyone it would be him, but the idea that she was going to confess the truth to him seemed surreal. As if Athanasia had one honest bone in her undead body!

'You meant to feed on her?' he prodded her.

'That wasn't all,' I said, interrupting. 'Not like that would be okay either . . . Athanasia tried to kill me. Simple.'

'Oh please. This is pathetic,' Athanasia said.

I crossed my arms. 'She's been stealing from my place of work, too. The Chanel jewellery she's wearing right now, and some fake tattoos I saw on her the other day. She stole them. She wants me to lose my job.'

At that Athanasia jumped up from her chair and pointed an accusing finger at me.

I swallowed a scream and almost jumped out of my own chair in fright. She was positively terrifying in close proximity. I wanted to leap up and flee the room.

'She staked me,' Athanasia yelled. 'She killed my employer, and she staked me!'

It was true.

'In self-defence,' I managed to say. 'How many times do I have to explain this? *Self-defence.*'

I could see she was getting fired up. Her fangs began to show – big, white fangs. But I wasn't scared now. I wasn't going to back down. I kept my arms crossed and held her hard gaze.

'We have discussed this, Athanasia,' Deus said calmly, and her accusing finger closed into her fist. She seemed to deflate under his influence, and eventually she sat down and folded her arms again. Her fangs slipped back beneath her lips.

There was a stretch of deeply tense silence before Athanasia spoke up again, this time with less vehement certainty. 'Come on. She can't be the Seventh,' she said. 'Look at her.' But the words only seemed to deflate her further, or perhaps it was the steady gaze she received from Deus. Finally she slumped in the chair, chastened into silence.

What did my being the Seventh have to do with this?

'Athanasia will not harm you,' Deus said, as if the conversation were over.

'Good,' I replied. 'I also need her to stop stealing things from my work.'

He turned to Athanasia, but she said nothing. Her full lips were pulled tight into a grimace.

'And you won't disfigure her again?' he said.

'I will defend myself if I'm attacked,' I replied in a firm tone. 'But she needs to take off that stolen jewellery she's wearing right now and give it back.' I held out my hand.

At this Athanasia sat up in her chair and raised her eyes to me. A cold, calculating smile pulled her plump lips tight. 'This isn't stolen. It's a gift,' she replied, touching her manicured hand to the enamel pieces around her throat.

*A gift?*

'Whom are you feeding off?' Deus asked her.

'That's none of her business.'

*I remembered something.* 'You're feeding on my boss, aren't you? You're feeding on Skye!'

The scarves Skye kept wearing around her neck every day. Her tardiness coming to work. Her pallor.

Athanasia was smiling at me. 'It's not like I attack her. She comes to me.'

My goodness, Skye was the mortal Luke had seen in the building that night. Athanasia must have hypnotised her and turned Skye into her personal meal service!

'I can't believe it.' I pulled a face in disgust.

Deus's strange, mesmerising smile didn't falter. He didn't seem surprised.

'You knew about this?' I blurted, and then held my tongue. *Of course he knows.*

'Non-lethal feeding is encouraged,' he said.

I blinked. *Right. Better than the alternative. I get it.*

I felt my strength rise up. 'I don't wish to encourage lethal feeding, far from it, but is there any way you could get her to leave my boss alone? And maybe even leave me alone, while we're at it?' I narrowed my eyes at Athanasia. 'And she'd better not think that is the worst I'm capable of,' I said, gesturing to her disfigured face. *'I am the Seventh.'* I'd never said those words aloud, and honestly I didn't quite know what they meant, but Celia had said it was an important title, and it seemed to have some impact on both of them. They were listening.

Athanasia's dark eyes grew wide, and she quickly looked down.

'Athanasia will stop feeding off your boss,' Deus said.

'Good.'

The deflated look on Athanasia's face was priceless. She must have really thought she'd hit the jackpot when she'd sunk her teeth into Skye – a meal service and a direct line to free fashion samples. And Skye couldn't remember any of it. Terrible. Athanasia might still be a Fledgling, but she appeared to be good at hypnotism.

I held my hand out. 'The jewellery.'

Begrudging every moment, Athanasia undid the strands of Chanel jewellery around her neck and handed them to Deus, who placed them gently in my hand.

'And you promise not to disfigure her again?' he said.

Her face really did look rather bad. The misshapen and pitted skin glowed with a painful red hue in the candlelight. 'Only if she promises not to try to kill me. And if she leaves me and my boss alone.'

'Will you do this, Athanasia?'

She nodded.

'Then it's decided.'

'And one more thing,' I said, surprised by my growing confidence. I'd had another idea. Athanasia seemed to be at the heart of any trouble. 'I want to know if she or her friends have anything to do with the missing knitwear designers.'

Athanasia looked up. Her eyebrows were raised.

'What?'

'Sandy Chow? Victor Mal?' I pressed.

'Who?'

I could see she knew nothing.

'Never mind.'

'Okay. Now go in peace,' Deus said to both of us.

*In peace?* Could a Sanguine go in peace? Deus seemed to be able to. It was hard to believe they were the same species. Athanasia stood and bowed to Deus. I wasn't sure if I should do the same − I hadn't before. I stood up from the chair and watched their exchange with interest.

'Go to ground for a while, Athanasia,' he told her, and her face dropped. Well, half of it was already dropping, I supposed.

She nodded and backed away from him with surprising reverence. She retreated right up to the casket, opened it and left us.

I have to say, the sight of her scurrying away gave me no small degree of immature pleasure.

*Suck on that*, I thought.

In truth, I was a little surprised at myself. I'd never thought I was someone who would enjoy that kind of mean satisfaction. It was a bit shameful, really.

'She won't be bothering you again,' Deus said after a moment.

'For a while, perhaps,' I replied.

He nodded sagely. 'Could I have you for a moment longer, Pandora?'

Have me? 'Um, sure.'

'There is another matter I wish to discuss with you.' He indicated that I should sit again and I took my seat, puzzled. I was beginning to feel much more confident in his presence, just as Celia had promised, but I didn't exactly want to hang around to see what he could do.

'Your great-aunt tells me you have a friend here. She tells me he is unable to leave the walls of the mansion.'

*Lieutenant Luke.*

I sat up a touch straighter. 'Yes. Yes, that's true,' I said. 'Do you know anything about him? His name is Second Lieutenant Luke Thomas.'

'I believe I may know something of interest.' Deus leaned forward, and I found myself looking into his eyes and watching those long eyelashes blink. I had much better control over my reaction to him, but I was still far from immune to his surprising aura of power and energy. 'I'm sure you realise this particular building is well known in Spektor. The architect and original owner, Dr Barrett, was quite an unusual man and performed experiments.'

'Yes,' I said. I'd heard a lot of morbid reports. Barrett was a founding member of the Global Society for Psychical Research, a group formed in the late 1800s to investigate reports of telepathy, psychic ability, ghost sightings and so on.

'Pandora, some of the experiments were about necro-mancy,' Deus said.

I lifted my eyebrows. 'Raising the dead?' I said.

From what I understood, necromancy was the practice of raising the dead for the purposes of fortune-telling or divination. Corpse prophecy. Without physical bodies, spirits were thought to be no longer limited by the earthly plane, and therefore in possession of great secrets – the future, hidden truths about the past, the real cause of their deaths or the deaths of others. My relationship with Luke seemed to gel with that idea. He seemed to know so much, but was forbidden from telling me many of the secrets of the dead. Necromancy, along with witchcraft and other occult practices, was severely frowned upon by the church. The Victorian establishment would certainly have disapproved of Barrett's experiments.

Deus continued. 'Barrett was in the habit of acquiring cadavers for these attempts.' Still that grin did not leave Deus's face, despite the morbid topic.

I grimaced. 'He used actual bodies?' Obviously getting a medium around and summoning energy from an old wedding ring wasn't enough for Barrett. 'But he couldn't have possibly had Luke's . . . um, *remains*. He died in the Civil War,' I protested. 'He was a second lieutenant. A war hero.' Well, I didn't know if he was technically a war hero, but that's certainly how I thought of him.

Deus shrugged. 'I'm not sure where the lieutenant was buried, or whether his remains were put to rest properly, but there was a flourishing underground trade in bodies during Victorian times.'

How grisly. I thought of the store next to *Pandora* magazine, and the skull Morticia wanted. How much of a person was left in their bones? What happened when someone was not 'put to rest properly'?

'Soldiers were thought to be strong spirits,' he said. 'Strong enough to travel to the underworld and back.'

When I emerged from the candlelit antechamber with the silver tray, my great-aunt was waiting. She re-locked the door behind me and led me into the kitchen. My head was reeling with everything I'd learned. I wondered if I would be able to sleep a wink.

I placed the tray on the counter. I'd barely touched the tea, but I felt jumpy. 'Can Athanasia get in here now?' I asked. 'Into the penthouse? Because she was invited into that room?'

'No,' Celia assured me. 'She can't come in. The Sanguine are not invited here.'

'Is that why you lock the door? So they can't get in?'

She smiled. 'They can't cross that threshold. It is forbidden.'

It was one of those supernatural rules. Sometimes they got me quite confused. Celia had mentioned this one before, of course. According to her, needing to be invited into a home was one of the few rumours about the Sanguine that actually was true. That, and the whole fang thing, I'd noticed. Yes, that rumour seemed strongly founded.

'It's time I gave you the key. You've been here long enough to understand the dangers.' To my surprise, she had a key ready and pressed it into my hand.

I blinked. Did that mean I could now enter the ante-chamber and explore the hidden staircase?

'Thank you. I appreciate it,' I said. It seemed as if I'd passed some kind of test. I slipped the key into my pocket.

'It may fit a few doors in the house.'

I raised an eyebrow. A skeleton key? Was she suggesting I could finally explore?

Great-Aunt Celia took her fine leather gloves off, brought the cups to the sink and prepared to do the washing up. 'No, no. Let me do that,' I said, taking over. It felt good to do something distracting and useful with my hands. My body was charged with nervous energy and my head was busy trying to process everything. I poured the tea out and ran water into the sink.

'Deus mentioned the necromancy experiments to you?' my great-aunt said.

I nodded mutely and reached for the detergent. The idea was a bit hard for me to take. For starters, my feelings about Luke were a little confused already, even without imagining his disinterred corpse lying around in the mansion, or lying around *anywhere* for that matter. I couldn't think of him that way. He wasn't just any old dead guy to me.

Great-Aunt Celia said nothing, she just watched thought-fully while I cleaned the cups and put them back on the cupboard shelf. When I was finished she led me to her reading chair in the lounge room. I sat on the leather hassock with Freyja purring around my ankles. Celia balanced herself elegantly on the wide arm of her chair, posing like a designer who instinctively understood the most flattering position for the garment she wore. She looked like a fashion illustration from 1949. Some habits never disappeared, I supposed.

'I know you've had a big night,' she began, 'but I do want to discuss something important with you. It's better that we discuss this now.'

I nodded. My brain felt pretty full already.

'Now listen to me carefully. When you first arrived here, I told you not to explore the other floors of the building under any circumstances.'

'I remember. It was because of the Sanguine,' I said. I had gone against her wishes and explored one of the other floors on one occasion, and I'd nearly been necked for it.

'The dangers of the Sanguine. That was part of it, yes,' she replied.

*That was only part of it?*

'Pandora, there are some passageways you may not be aware of.'

I thought of the casket on the antechamber's floor, and the staircase beyond it. 'I wanted to ask you where the hidden passageway in the coffin led,' I said. 'Does it meet up with the mezzanine, or . . .?'

'That passageway is one of many. Dr Barrett had some mysterious motives when he built this place. It's possible that he wanted to keep some of his experiments secret from the rest of the world, and from his wife, in particular. She was of a sensitive disposition, by all accounts, and his work was sometimes dark. He dabbled in things Victorian society did not appreciate. Forbidden things. Necromancy was only part of it.'

I swallowed. Celia had told me before that Barrett came

from a wealthy and prominent family, but even that had not been enough to protect him when his experiments clashed with the standards and ideals of his colleagues. He had been banished from the Society for Psychical Research. If he was in the habit of acquiring stolen corpses, I could understand why.

'He used bodies,' I said with displeasure. 'That's what Deus told me.'

'Yes,' she confirmed. 'So he retreated to this house to conduct his experiments in secret. Now, there are some hidden doors and passageways in this house, Pandora. You have been here long enough to earn the right to explore the house and, frankly, I know you will anyway.'

I felt the heat on my cheeks.

'Eventually you will find some of these hidden areas. But there are some things you should know before you do. If you are to explore this building, you must do so carefully. There are dangers.'

I imagined stumbling into rooms infested with hordes of vampires. 'If I explore, I should do it during the day.'

She shook her head. 'Not necessarily.'

I was surprised. 'The Sanguine aren't the danger then? What is?'

'Dangers even I can't know.'

I was taken aback. It seemed to me there was very little my great-aunt did not know. What dangers would she not know about here, in the building she owned? That thought was mildly terrifying.

'You would do best to bring your guide,' she said.

'There's a guide? Like a map?'

'Not a map. Your friend, the soldier. I believe he is your guide.'

I couldn't have been more surprised. *Luke? A guide?* Well, of course. He would know the house inside out, wouldn't he?

'Don't assume he knows everything that is here,' she warned me, and I was sure she'd read my mind. 'And don't assume he has the power to tell you all that he does know. There are things even he needs to discover in this place. Perhaps you will help him to find what he searches for.'

I opened my mouth to ask *what things*, but she placed a firm hand on my knee and continued. She had more to tell me tonight.

'I have something for you,' she said, and took something small from the silk pocket of her dress. She held the object in her palm, and closed her eyes for a moment. When she opened them again she was uncharacteristically serious. She opened her milky white hand to reveal a piece of jewellery – a ring. The gemstone was jet black, held with ornate, pale gold claws. It was delicate looking, and clearly very old.

'This ring is very special. I believe it belongs to you,' my great-aunt said.

'Belongs to me?' In my former life I might have protested that I hadn't seen the ring before, and therefore it could not be mine, but I'd grown used to Celia's manner of speaking. She believed that certain things were predestined. This ring, she believed, was meant to be mine. Whether or not she'd tell me why was another matter. 'It's gorgeous. What is it made of? Is that polished jet?' I asked.

She shook her head. 'No. I love my Whitby jet, but no. Look at that shine. Really *look* within the crystal.'

I did as she said. Deep within the black there seemed to be some small blazing pinpoint of energy.

'It is the eyes of the dead Pharaohs, the eyes of the Moai on Easter Island, as dark as the soul but with a star of life inside.' She shifted the ring in her pale palm, and the black blazed and shone. 'A symbol of rebirth and protection, historically used in talismans and amulets to conjure up spirit energy to safely interact with Earth-bound souls.'

'Black obsidian,' I said, marvelling at it.

She nodded. 'Very good. This ring belonged to your great-great-grandmother, Madame Aurora. It has been waiting for you, Pandora. It will protect you and assist you.' She handed it to me.

'This belonged to Madame Aurora?' Celia had shown me clippings from her infamous days with Barnum and Bailey. She was a gifted psychic in her day, and she was a Lucasta, as I was. Apparently she could even make objects move at her will, which must have really stunned anyone who witnessed it. I imagined tarot cards floating past astonished faces, and clients parting with their cash. I was part of a curious family tree of women with unusual abilities. For reasons I didn't fully understand, my mother had never told me about Madame Aurora. She'd tried to shield me from her family history.

'I'm honoured. It's beautiful . . .' I held it gently by the band and examined it with awe. The pale gold setting was forged a long time ago, that much was clear. The tiny carvings looked almost like melted wax. The setting had a wonderfully aged patina, but the crystal itself was bright. I couldn't take my eyes off the inky depth of the blackness, or the light it reflected at its core. It seemed imbued with a mysterious energy. 'I don't know what to say. It is truly beautiful.'

Celia nodded. 'Go on.'

I slipped the ring gently on to my ring finger. It fitted perfectly.

'There. See how it fits you like it was always there on your hand? Wear it day and night, Pandora.'

I nodded, still staring at it. Was it my imagination, or was the crystal slightly warm?

'Now Pandora, listen to me carefully.' Celia was as serious as I'd ever seen her. Her eyes were intensely direct. *'Never travel below Barrett's basement laboratory, not under any circumstances.'*

'There is a basement?'

'It is said that there is.'

'That's where the fire was, right? The fire that killed Edmund Barrett?'

She nodded.

'But you haven't seen the laboratory yourself?'

'This house has not opened all its secrets to me. But I do know this, Pandora – *never ever travel lower than the laboratory*. If you discover a passage that leads underground, *do not take it*. Do you hear me? Not even with your guide.'

'Yes, of course. But how will I know if I've found the laboratory?'

'You will know.'

'But if you haven't seen it yourself, how can you be sure I will know if I find it?' I asked.

'You will know.'

We were both silent for a time.

'Luke is my guide?' I finally said.

She nodded.

'The Seventh always has a spirit guide. And a personal talisman.'

I looked to the ring.

My talisman?

# CHAPTER TEN

I woke up early on Friday morning to watch the first washed-out rays of sun filter across the ceiling of my room. My hair was spread out across the pillow, and my arms were tucked beneath my cheek, the warm sheets sitting high on my collarbone.

*The obsidian ring.*

I lifted my right hand, flexed my fingers out and stared at the fascinating new addition perched on my ring finger. When Celia had first given me the ring, it seemed slightly warm, but now it felt pleasantly cool on my skin. Nothing had changed about the puzzling depth of that inky crystal, nor the strangely beautiful pinpoint of light at its centre.

This was my personal talisman?

I wondered where Madame Aurora had acquired it. Through the Lucasta line? Or from some exotic dealer? I didn't know much about my great-great-grandmother, and I was increasingly curious about her powers. Was she truly the psychic and medium Celia said she was? I tried to imagine what her life might have been like, travelling with Barnum and Bailey.

I thought of the key my great-aunt had entrusted me with, and almost before I knew it, I was dressed and slipping out the door of the penthouse. I took the rattling old lift down to the dusty lobby, stepped out and stopped in the centre of the tiled space beneath the broken chandelier. Arms crossed, with one finger at my chin, I studied the space around me.

*Hidden passageways?*

The oval, high-ceilinged lobby was cool, as always, and I buttoned Celia's beautiful winter coat up to my neck. I closed my eyes for a moment, collecting myself, and when I opened them again I noticed things I hadn't seen previously. The tile-work of the floor, for instance, was cracked from one side to the other, with several smaller splits spreading out from the main line, not unlike the divided lifeline of my palm. (What would Madame Aurora have made of that?) Though not immediately visible the split in the tiles was significant, and I wondered what kind of movement would have caused such damage. There was also a split up the wall that snaked out into several branches. I cast my eyes over the dusty wall sconces and the spiked fleurs-de-lis of the elaborate lift cage. They were magnificent, if broken in places. Nowhere, though, did I see a door or an entrance I hadn't previously been aware of. I approached the walls and began looking for gaps or cracks. I confess I even pushed on a protruding tile or two on the floor. I walked up the snaking staircase to the sealed wooden door of the mezzanine, pushed and pulled at it, and then walked down again. It wasn't exactly a hidden door, but I'd never seen it opened. Perhaps Luke could tell me what was beyond it?

I looked for concealed entrances, levers, buttons. What kind of hidden passageways had Barrett built? I had to think in terms of Victorian technology, I reminded myself. Any special levers might even be broken.

*Tonight. Tonight I will explore. And I'll bring my spirit guide.*

I emerged from the subway steps in SoHo to find that the skies had opened up. My black umbrella proved almost too unwieldy to manage as the rain moved sideways across the street in violent gusts, pummelling cars and pedestrians alike. It was in these moments that New York was its most impersonal and cold. Commuters were faceless and hurried. The spikes of passing wet umbrellas battled silently as if jousting. My brolly turned inside out, and I jabbed the ground with it until it flipped round again.

I got through plenty of paperwork and filing during the day as there was no sign of Skye DeVille. It was a relief not to have to brace myself every time her office door opened. I prepared three hot beverages all day – a mere pittance compared with Skye's inhuman caffeine demands. I also must confess I spent a guilt-inducing amount of time taking advantage of the office's Internet connection to research necromancy. I'd read about it in my mother's many books back home, but I had never thought I would find myself considering it as deeply as I was now. Necromancy certainly had a long and motley history across cultures. I wondered what Barrett had hoped to achieve with his experiments. Had he been motivated by prophecy, money, or simply curiosity?

'What are you doing?'

It was nearing the end of the day, and thankfully I'd heard Pepper coming before she'd got near enough to see the window open on my computer screen. I closed the giant image of the Witch of Endor I'd been looking at, and returned to my inbox.

'Nothing. I mean, working,' I responded quickly.

She stood over me, unsmiling and fashionably severe. 'I need a quote or two from another couple of designers.'

'For the feature?' I asked, though it was obvious enough.

She nodded. 'I want to wrap this up on Monday.'

'We're still going ahead with the knitwear spread? Even with all the, uh, news?' I said. It seemed incredible that the piece wouldn't need to be reworked. Or even put on hold.

'Fashion doesn't stand still just because of some disappearances. Here are the addresses. Or you can just call.' Pepper handed me a scrap of paper. Both were in the Garment District. Again, the fashion industry's sense of concern was really moving. Pepper was almost as sympathetic to the plight of those designers as Victor Mal had been. Until he became one of them.

'No problem,' I told her, putting the paper into my bag. 'I'll go in person. I might be able to get more that way.' As always, I was eager for an excuse to leave the office.

'I don't need you getting into this whole scandal, okay? We want to steer clear of it. Keep it about the fashion. The rest of this stuff could be old news by print time.'

Could it really? Could three missing top designers be old news? Even if they turned up by the time the magazine came out? 'You don't think it would be a bit of a glaring omission to not even acknowledge . . .'

Pepper glowered at me.

*Okay. My views are not wanted here. I get it.*

I nodded obediently. 'I'll keep it about the fashion.'

Once she was satisfied that I wouldn't ruffle any feathers – as I clearly had the last time I'd used my actual brain to do a bit of reporting for her – Pepper let me be. I packed up my satchel and coat, turned my computer off and breezed over to Morticia.

'You're leaving early,' she commented.

'Yeah, Pepper gave me an errand. I've got to go up to the Garment District to speak to a couple of designers. See you Monday.'

She nodded. 'Any hot dates this weekend?'

'Nah,' I said, but thought of my Civil War crush.

'Me neither,' she replied, and pouted. 'It's depressing. Hey, would you like to see a movie? That new Johnny Depp one is out.'

'Oh. That's a good idea.' It was one I wanted to see, and I had been hoping to get to know Morticia better, but I was unsure I could spare an evening so soon, considering all I was learning about Lieutenant Luke. Was he really my spirit guide? What did that mean?

'I'll be a bit busy this weekend but maybe next?' I suggested and scribbled my cell phone number on a piece of paper. 'I finally have a phone, but the reception is pretty awful where I live, so if you don't get through, leave a message.' Of course, Morticia couldn't know that there was no reception where I lived because it was a suburb that didn't exist – to phone companies, anyway.

'Cool,' she said. 'I'll put you in my phone.'

Finally I was forging a normal friendship in this new town. I smiled. 'By the way, I don't know if I ever mentioned this, Morticia, but I really like your name,' I added.

Morticia was a weird name and I guess it had made me feel closer to her from the first day we met. My name had always made me stand out, and not always comfortably.

'Your parents must be cool to give you a name like that,' I continued. 'They must be big fans of *The Addams Family*.'

I noticed Morticia frown. 'My parents? Oh, no. My parents named me "Bea". Can you imagine? I changed my name the day I turned eighteen.'

She sure didn't look like a Bea. I'd never considered changing my name. It might have been weird, but then so was I. 'What made you change it to Morticia?'

'The obvious, I guess. My parents weren't happy about it, you could say that much. Yeah . . . we don't, um, get along,' she said, and I saw a flash of sadness in her eyes. 'I moved out last year and we don't see each other much.'

'I'm so sorry, Morticia.' I felt terrible for bringing up the whole subject.

'Yeah, well . . . I guess I'm not what they expected. Or wanted . . .' She took the scrap of paper with my number on it, and played with it listlessly. 'It's cool,' she finally said. 'You have a good weekend.' She offered her lopsided smile, but it didn't quite disguise the hint of sadness in her features.

'Let's catch that movie soon,' I said.

'Cool. Oh, and look out,' Morticia added, as I headed out the door.

I stopped in my tracks and turned.

'It's a full moon tonight. The crazies will be out.'

The closer of the two addresses I'd been given was for the brand Smith & Co. I recognised the name. Their headquarters were announced by a stylishly understated sign on a doorway on W36th Street, next to an alley. I looked up and saw banner advertising in the first floor window above, confirming that I'd arrived at the correct location. The door on street level was unlocked, and I walked up a clean but nondescript stairwell to reach the glass door of the office and push my way inside.

'Good afternoon. How may I help you?'

The waiting area was small and modern. An attractive, slim young man wearing a close-fitting top and fashionably retro black-framed spectacles sat behind a wooden desk. As with Victor Mal's studio, there were ads decorating the walls of the waiting area. The Smith & Co ads were much more understated, however, and seemed to include only the latest campaign.

'I'm here for a quick interview with Mr Smith,' I told the man at the desk.

'*Pandora* magazine?'

'Yes, that's right. I hope this is a good time.'

'It's nice to meet you.' He stood and shook my hand. 'I'll take your coat and umbrella. If you'll please take a seat, I'll just see if Laurie is ready.'

'Sure thing. Thanks.'

The receptionist relieved me of my coat – which he hung on a designer coat rack that looked like a small, flattened tree forged of stainless steel – and he popped my umbrella in a red plastic umbrella stand while I took a seat on a low-slung minimalist leather lounge that probably cost more than everything I owned.

I waited.

I lifted my hand and examined Madame Aurora's obsidian ring once more. I'd been doing that a lot through the day. I loved objects with history. No doubt it was a trait I'd picked up from my late mother, the archaeologist. Perhaps that was why I was more interested in vintage fashion than the latest offerings. I liked the idea that things were lived in, that they had stories to tell. This ring would have seen a lot, I guessed. I didn't really know if I believed in talismans, but if so much was possible in the spirit world, so much that the world did not acknowledge or believe in, the existence of a real talisman was not such a stretch.

'He's in the atelier, if you'd like to go in,' the receptionist said when he returned to the waiting area. 'He's working on a new collection.'

'Wonderful,' I replied, and sprung up.

I was led into a long, narrow, high-ceilinged space – obviously another warehouse conversion – to find Mr Smith smiling and walking towards me. He was tall and he sported artfully dishevelled hair, like a kind of fashionable Einstein figure. He wore a chocolate-brown suede blazer over a thin knit top that seemed like a masculine version of the Smith & Co clothing I'd seen on the shoot. I guessed he was mid-fifties. Several half-dressed couture mannequins filled his workshop. Lining one wall were hip-height tables layered with textiles.

A large bulletin board was tacked with images, sketches and cloth samples.

A diminutive Chinese–American woman slipped past me to the door. 'Goodnight, Mr Laurie,' she said on her way out.

'Goodnight,' he said, and then whispered to me, 'that woman can do *anything*.'

I perked up. 'That's impressive,' I replied. 'I'm Pandora English, from *Pandora* magazine. Thanks for taking the time to talk to me this afternoon. I won't keep you long.'

'I'll likely be up all night anyway, I think. New collection.'

'Yes, your receptionist mentioned that. How is it coming along?'

He swept his gaze over the room. 'It's coming...' He pulled up a chair for me, and cleared it of layers of half-constructed garments. 'So, your real name is Pandora?'

'Yup. That's me. The lady who let all the evil into the world.'

'I thought that was Eve,' he said.

'She's the *other* lady who let all the evil into the world. I was the one with the box, apparently. Actually, I think originally it was a jar.' Celia had told me that my name meant 'gifted' or 'all-endowed', but it was the ancient Greek myth of the woman with the jar (or box) of evil that was most remembered. Why was it always women's curiosity for opening jars or eating apples that was blamed for everything wrong in the world?

'Was the magazine named after you?' Laurie Smith asked.

I wasn't sure if he was joking. I was hardly a nineteen-year-old people named things after. 'Not at all, I'm afraid. Mere coincidence.'

He cocked his head and smiled. 'I don't know if I believe in coincidences.'

There was a light knock on the open door of the workshop, and we both turned. The attractive bespectacled receptionist held a beautiful parcel, immaculately wrapped in bows of black and green. I'd seen something like it before, I thought. Recently.

'Sorry to disturb you both, but a package just arrived for you, Laurie. It might be the one you were waiting for?'

'Thanks, James,' Laurie said. 'You can leave it on your desk. See you tomorrow.'

'It was nice to meet you, Pandora,' James said, and left us.

Laurie sat up on the work table and let his long legs dangle. I noticed him pick up a large pair of work scissors and move them to one side. 'I'm, um, no good at interviews,' he said to me finally, and I smiled.

'I'm not that good at conducting them,' I replied.

'No, no. I'm sure you're fine. Besides, you are young. There's time.'

I smiled, and pulled the pad and pen from my satchel. 'Interview starts now, if that's okay with you?' I adjusted myself on the little chair and got started. I asked Laurie Smith a few basic questions about the knitwear industry and his latest work. I kept it short and fashion-focused, as instructed, and he didn't make me feel like an idiot the way Victor Mal had. He didn't bring up the missing designers, and I resisted broaching the subject. It was possible that he was so focused on his collection deadline that he hadn't heard the news. Or perhaps Pepper was right, and it just wasn't appropriate for our interview.

'You know, I have to say, you seem refreshingly humble,' I said once I'd filled a couple of pages with my notes. 'I had to interview someone else for this piece and he said he was the best designer in the world. With knitwear, anyway.'

And now he was missing. It was a bit hard to believe.

'I used to be like that,' Laurie confessed. 'I was the worst of them. I thought that if you didn't boast the loudest no one would respect you in this business.' He paused and pointed at my notepad. 'I hope you're not going to put that in?'

'No, I won't. I promise. Is there anything else you'd like me to add about your collection?' I finally asked.

'We worked hard on this one. I just hope people try it.'

'Very good.' I closed my notepad and slipped it away. 'Thanks again for your time this afternoon . . . ah, evening.' It was almost five, I realised. Perhaps I could get to the next place before five thirty? It wasn't far. 'It's been really lovely to meet you,' I told Laurie. 'Here's my card in case you have any questions, or if you have anything else to add.' I didn't have my own card, but I did have one for the magazine. I wrote my name and email on it and handed it to him. 'Good luck with the new collection.'

Laurie saw me out himself, which I thought was very courteous. Before this afternoon I had been starting to wonder if rudeness was fashionable, but the experience at Smith & Co had made me think differently. I noticed the receptionist had gone home and the office seemed empty. Laurie would be pulling a late night by himself. That was dedication. I took my coat off the strange, flat tree and wished Laurie Smith goodnight, and good luck with his all-nighter.

By the time I stepped out on to W36th Street it was growing dark, and a wind was blowing hard. The air was thick with electricity. It felt like a storm was coming. By my calculations the next address was only a few blocks away. It was possible they might still be in. I was less than halfway there when the first drops of rain landed on me, and I realised what I'd overlooked. *Your umbrella! Idiot.* I'd only been gone perhaps fifteen minutes, but when I returned to Smith & Co I was nevertheless relieved to find the door was still unlocked. I stepped inside the waiting area and called out, 'Hello? Sorry, I just forgot my umbrella.'

Then I froze.

Something was wrong. Something was profoundly wrong. That familiar foreboding chilled my stomach. It became more intense with each passing second.

'Um, is everyone okay?' I ventured, but there was no reply. 'Mr Smith?' I heard a strange moaning sound, and stiffened. From the direction of the workroom there was the hard bang of something falling over. 'Mr Smith? Are you okay?' I pushed open the door to the atelier and stepped inside.

What I saw then was hard to comprehend.

In the middle of the workshop a shape was moving violently from side to side, erratically, like a small tornado, knocking into work tables and toppling mannequins over. The shape was like a six-foot-high silky cocoon. The whole thing turned and thrashed before me as I stood frozen at the door. What was it? I had no idea. I thought perhaps I could almost make out the shape of . . . a man? And then I heard another moan and I realised that it was coming from *inside* the cocoon, and in that moment I knew that someone was in there.

I sprang into action. 'Hang on!' I shouted and sprinted forward. 'Hang on. I'll . . . I'll . . .' I looked around in a panic. 'I'm going to cut you out!'

On instinct I grabbed the scissors I'd seen earlier on the work table and I pushed the cocoon against the wall to hold it still. My palms became sticky and for a second I had to struggle to free them. I wiped my hands on my clothes in disgust. The cocoon was some sort of large, sticky web. A web that seemed to have a life of its own?

'Don't move,' I instructed and the person inside moaned unintelligibly in reply. The violent movements were reduced to a kind of wild shivering. I thought it was Laurie Smith in there – somehow – and it was clear that he was suffocating. I needed to get his head out, and fast. At the hollow below the chin I inserted one point of the scissors inside as carefully as I could, and then began cutting the cocoon open. Using all my strength, I pulled it back with both hands. My hands kept sticking to the material, and though it was silky and thin, it was remarkably strong. I tore hard at it, and after some effort Laurie's face emerged, purple from lack of oxygen. He gasped for air and let out some garbled cries, his bloodshot eyes bulging out of their sockets. The poor man seemed half out of his mind with confusion and terror. Wasting no time, I tore the cut larger, and then had to resort to the scissors again to work down the body. It all happened so fast that I was half kneeling on the floor, cutting a hole at his waist, when I realised that the sack itself was squirming . . .

Spiders were pouring out.

*Oh!*

I screamed and jumped back, dropping the scissors. Spiders of all shapes and sizes spilled out of the holes I'd cut in the cocoon. Orb-weavers. Tarantulas. Jumping spiders. Wolf spiders. Crab spiders. I stifled a scream. Laurie moaned again, bringing my attention back to him. He slid down the wall into a huddled position. He could not yet free himself. There was no choice but to continue cutting him out.

*I hope none of these little fellas are deadly.*

I quickly went in again, gritting my teeth. Spiders crawled out of the holes in the sack, spreading across the webbing and over my hands and up my arms in a slow, steady stream. Those that did not crawl on me dropped to the floor and swarmed around my feet. There was a seemingly endless supply. My spider-covered hands shook as I worked away at the cocoon. I worried I might be hallucinating, experiencing some horrific arachnophobic nightmare. Or worse, that I wasn't hallucinating at all.

Soon I'd cut the body of the cocoon open and helped Laurie out. I flicked spiders off his clothes while he danced awkwardly about the workshop like Mick Jagger on bad acid. I thought the poor man might have a heart attack. Heck, I thought *I* might. I flung Celia's coat off and did some awkward dancing of my own to remove the spiders still clinging to me.

'What on earth happened? What was that? Are you okay?' I asked in an excited ramble, shaking a fat orb-weaver off my shoe. Laurie didn't seem able to answer, and I didn't blame him. I hauled him to one end of the workshop, away from the discarded pile of sticky webbing and the seething mass of arachnids that surrounded it. I brought the chair over and sat him in it.

*Okay, breathe, Pandora. Breathe.*

'Have you been bitten? Should I call 911?' I asked.

Laurie finally spoke. 'What . . . was that?'

'I have no idea,' I said. 'I was hoping you could tell me.' But he didn't seem capable of telling anyone anything just yet. 'Maybe we should get you to a hospital,' I suggested and moved towards a phone on the wall.

He shook his head emphatically, and reached out a hand. 'No. No, no, my partner is waiting for me. I'll just go home.'

'I thought you said you were pulling an all-nighter? Do you want me to call your partner for you? Let them know . . .'

He shook his head vigorously. 'No. I'm fine.'

'That's crazy. How long were you in that sack?'

'What sack?'

'The sack I just cut you out of . . . with all the spiders . . .' It sounded crazy to say it, and Laurie's confused reaction made it seem even crazier.

He touched his fingertips to his forehead. 'I don't know what happened,' he said, seeming deeply confused. 'I opened that package, and then . . . I don't know.'

*The package.*

I looked around me. There was little sign of the extraordinary struggle that had just taken place. A few mannequins were knocked over, and the scissors and some scraps of textile had slid on to the floor. I noticed the green and black parcel on the ground, opened and upturned. Black tissue was torn open. Amazingly, the pile of sticky webbing was shrivelling and jerking across the floor where we'd left it. The spiders that had swarmed out of it were crawling away into the shadows, and the cocoon itself was . . . *disappearing*? The whole mass was shrinking up like burning paper.

I was totally baffled. My mouth hung open. (It seemed to be doing a lot of that lately.)

'I think I'll go home,' Laurie said behind me. 'I'm fine.'

I shook my head. 'You can't possibly be fine. I really think —'

'My partner is waiting for me. I'll call him. He'll come pick me up. He's not far away,' he said.

I was tempted to wait until his partner arrived, but I began to get the not-so-subtle feeling that Laurie just wanted me out of there, so I took the hint. I finally backed down. I dusted off Celia's coat and took my things – including my umbrella – and, after a few last words, left the workshop. If there was one thing I had learned after a lifetime of seeing impossible things, it was that when you saw something clearly supernatural it was best not to insist on talking about it with people who didn't want to discuss it, didn't understand it, or flat out denied it. That was a one-way ticket to unwanted psychiatric attention. Incredibly, there was no sign of the spiders or the shredded webbing when I closed the door behind me. It had literally shrivelled into nothing.

Shakily, I made my way down the stairs and out on to the dark streets of the Garment District. My adrenaline was still pumping hard.

*What on earth do I do now? How can I not tell anyone?*

It had stopped raining, I noticed.

'You've been asking after me,' a voice said, and I stopped.

The voice was unfamiliar, with an accent I couldn't place.

I turned, prepared for almost anything after what I'd just seen. A woman was leaning in the mouth of the narrow alley next to the Smith & Co studio entrance. I recognised her. She was tall, swathed head to toe in black, and she had a perfectly chic jet-black bob cut sharp at her high cheekbones, the geometrical fringe framing large, penetrating eyes and a mouth that was small and dark. She had a face like Louise Brooks in the 1920s.

This was the woman from the subway station. The woman who had followed me.

'Pardon?' I replied.

I hadn't been asking around about her, but I was beginning to think that perhaps I should have been. There was an intensity to her presence that was unnatural. It disturbed me, just as it had the two times I'd noticed her before. As she approached, something cold twisted in my belly, and I found myself on high alert again. The tall woman moved to the edge of the alley, the streetlights casting harsh shadows on her face. Though her features were classically beautiful, they were set with unhappiness. I saw faint lines etched into the delicate skin straight as an arrow from her left temple across her cheek to her feminine jaw. But these faint lines did not rivet me. It was something else. As she neared, I saw that her mouth was cruel, despite its even, attractive shape. The wide, dark eyes glinted with bitterness, and her features combined like a beautiful, but warped painting. Louise Brooks on broken celluloid.

I wanted to turn and walk away, even run, but I held fast. This was the third time I'd encountered her. There was a reason.

'You are Pandora English,' she said.

'Yes,' I replied, surprised, and not at all liking the sound of my name on her lips. I gripped my umbrella and satchel. What did I have with me? My phone, subway ticket, map, book, a few cosmetics, hairspray, rice, notepad, pen. The coldness in my belly was so strong it actually hurt, like I'd swallowed dry ice. I was in danger. That much was clear. I struggled with my instinct to run.

'You've been asking around about me,' she said again.

'I'm a journalist,' I said by way of response. I wasn't sure why she thought I was asking about her.

'I've been asking around about you, too,' she went on. 'Though I can hardly believe you'd come in such a pathetic form.'

*Pathetic?* I furrowed my brow. That kind of rudeness was a bit unnecessary, wasn't it?

I was just thinking up a suitable comeback when movement drew my attention to her shoulder. I watched with a sinking sensation as thick, insect-like legs appeared, followed by the bulbous body of an arachnid. It was a tarantula, and it crawled slowly across the fabric of the woman's top and came to sit on the edge of her collar, watching me just as the other one had done.

Wait. Was that the same spider?

'Why did you take it home? My little spy?' the tall woman asked me.

*The tarantula. It was hers.*

'I don't know what you're talking about,' I replied.

'Oh, I think you do. Did you think you could watch me? Did you think you could tap into the hive mind and spy on me? As I could spy on you?'

I may have gawked a little at this. I struggled for a suitable response. *The hive mind?*

The strange woman looked me up and down. She must have caught my expression of bewilderment, because she cocked her head, her perfect bob falling in a sharp line across one cheek. 'I think they are wrong about you.' She folded her arms. 'You? The Seventh? I don't believe it.' She chuckled then. It was a joyless sound that sent icy shivers through me.

*The Seventh.* There was that title again. Celia had been trying to explain its importance to me, in her way. Her ways were a bit mysterious though and seemed to involve telling me things when she felt I needed to know. There was something important about the fact that it had been one hundred and fifty years since the last Seventh. And the Seventh held a very important role. I had powers. But what exactly? Celia said it would all reveal itself in time, but right now I felt like I needed to know a whole lot more.

I did my best to stand tall. 'What business is it of yours if I am the Seventh?'

I kept my eyes on her, and she took another step forward. I realised then that her movements were wrong. For a moment I could fool my eyes into believing that what I saw was normal. But there was something disproportionate about the way she moved. Her legs were too long. The black clothing she was

184 · TARA MOSS

wearing appeared flowing and elegant, but it was disguising something. It wasn't the cut of the garment that created the oddness of movement. It was as if her joints were actually in the wrong places. I gripped my umbrella, thinking I might soon need it to defend myself. With my other hand I fished around in my satchel.

The woman's eyes narrowed. 'I won't let you get in the way,' she said with a low-voiced anger. 'Laurie Smith was mine. He deserves my wrath.'

As if in slow motion, the sweeping knits that covered her oddly statuesque form fell back, and revealed the most hideous, confusing anatomy I'd ever seen. Legs – not human legs, but sleek black *spider legs* – darted out towards me. Even in the harsh shadows of the alley I could see that she didn't have a torso – not a human one, anyway. She appeared to have a round, distended black belly and several legs . . . six legs, to be exact. *Six spidery legs*. And now those legs reached out to me.

*Oh!*

A scream escaped me, and I leapt backwards just in time to stay out of the reach of those horrible extremities. I popped open the umbrella with a quick click and began wielding it like a shield, while with my other hand I found the cool cylinder of hairspray in my bag. I pointed it at her face and depressed the button as if it were mace, causing a cloud of faux lavender to stream into the air. It was a sad excuse for a weapon, to say the least.

One of the sharp ends of the spider legs pierced through the umbrella and narrowly missed my leg. I threw the empty hairspray can at the woman, heard it bounce, and then chucked the open umbrella.

*Time to run!*

I hit W36th Street fast and passed two older men in business suits and wool coats. They must have heard my scream, and they asked if I was okay.

'Just run!' I yelled without bothering to turn around. 'Run!'

I ran full tilt down the rain-slicked sidewalk and ploughed into a middle-aged woman carrying her shopping. She let out a shocked gasp and her bags hit the ground, potatoes spilling on the sidewalk. *Sorry!* I thought, but didn't stop to help her. I just held my satchel close to my body and kept running as fast as I could.

I didn't pause to look back.

By the time I placed my subway ticket in the turnstile of the first subway station I found, the rain had returned and I was soaked to the bone. I had frozen, shaking hands. I'd not even stopped to look at my map, and I wasn't sure how far I'd sprinted. I was so flustered that I boarded the first train I saw, before realising it was headed in the wrong direction.

I just managed to compose myself enough to transfer to the green line before I was off Manhattan Island and headed for Brooklyn.

*You're fine. Everything is fine now. Breathe . . .*

The 6 train was still packed from the post-work rush when I boarded. Frankly I was relieved to be surrounded by strangers

– normal, *human* strangers. I stood in the crush of people and wrestled with everything I'd just seen.

It seemed I had interrupted the tall woman with the spider on her shoulder. Interrupted her doing what exactly? Why did he deserve her wrath? Who was she? *What* was she? One thing was for certain. She'd known I was the Seventh and she didn't like that very much. I had to get home and warn Celia. *'Something is afoot.'* Something was afoot, indeed. And that something had eight limbs.

*A spider woman*, I kept thinking. *There is a spider woman in New York.*

# CHAPTER
# ELEVEN

'Great-Aunt Celia, I'm home.'

I closed the door, dropped my satchel, hung up my coat, slipped my shoes off, and caught a brief glimpse of my harrowing reflection in the Edwardian mirror. My hair was plastered flat against my head, and my eyeliner had smudged into dark circles. I looked away.

'Darling, you've had some excitement,' my great-aunt said, and closed the book she was reading. She peered around the corner of her reading chair and took in my appearance.

Diplomatic as ever, she didn't comment.

I walked over to her in a kind of daze. She was reclining in a blood red ensemble made up of a gloriously well-fitted jacket with exaggerated shoulders and tight sleeves, and a full, knee-length skirt. A large black button closed the jacket at the waist. She wore fine black fish-nets, and, of course, her veil. I wondered – and not for the first time – whether anything ever fazed her.

'Celia, I saw something extraordinary tonight,' I began. 'Something I wouldn't have believed possible only a short time ago.'

'Good,' she said.

*Good?*

'Come. Sit.' Freyja jumped down from the leather hassock and I took a seat. The albino cat circled my ankles, then sniffed and stared at me. I patted her. She seemed disturbed by some faint scent I'd brought home. 'Young Pandora, it is good that you are coming to better realise the extent of what is possible,' my great-aunt told me. 'Arm yourself with an open mind, and you will not be blind like other mortals. It will serve you well.'

I nodded, thinking of Laurie Smith and how he didn't seem to remember anything that had happened to him after he'd opened the mysterious green and black package. It was as if his mind had simply rejected it. In the last two months I had noticed people rejected Spektor in a similar way. Taxi drivers would tell me there was no such place. Jay Rockwell – *roses guy* – hadn't ever heard of it and later remembered nothing of it. (Or me, as it happened.) Spektor didn't exist because it *couldn't*. The suburb was invisible to the closed mind.

'Celia, I met a woman tonight. I know this will sound crazy, but she was human from her head to her chest, but the rest of her was like some kind of . . . *spider.* She had spider legs.'

In response Celia arched one eyebrow.

I recounted what I'd seen – the suspicious green and black parcel at Victor Mal's studio and then at Smith & Co, the webbed cocoon suffocating Laurie Smith, the spiders, and the tall spider woman in the alley who I had seen twice before, and who gave me that awful, cold feeling in my belly.

My wise and beautiful great-aunt closed her eyes and nodded, absorbing my tale.

'Do you know who she is?' I asked eagerly.

Celia tilted her head and considered my words. 'I think it's time for a cup of tea, darling.'

I sat up. 'Um, okay . . .'

Great-Aunt Celia rose elegantly from her chair, slipped her toes into her heeled slippers and sauntered into the kitchen. I dutifully followed behind. Freyja watched us both, disinterested, and then hopped back up on the hassock to steal my spot.

Celia's kitchen was compact but well appointed. She boiled the water while I prepared some cups. She was quiet for a good ten minutes while she worked her magic (I don't know how she always got her tea tasting so good) and finally she poured us both a cup and walked slowly back to her large, leather reading chair holding her cup and saucer. I followed with mine. She took her seat and Freyja jumped off the hassock again, with a slightly dissatisfied meow. My great-aunt clearly believed in the power of a good cup of tea, which made me wonder what she was preparing me for. I had to be patient when she was like this. There was no sense in pushing. She took a sip. I did the same. I felt the energising effect of the tea almost immediately. I waited. I took another sip. So did she. I felt I might burst with questions. She took another leisurely sip.

'Well, Pandora,' she finally began, just as I thought I might explode with impatience. 'It sounds to me like the spider goddess has come to New York to settle some scores. The only real question is, which spider goddess is she?' she mused.

'There's more than one spider goddess?'

'Well, yes, but don't trying telling any of them that. The gods and goddesses have a terrible egoism. Always have. They are always "the original", "the greatest", or "the most powerful". I guess that's why they call it a god complex.' She leaned back, placed her empty cup on the arm of her chair and casually straightened the fall of her beautiful red skirt.

Only Great-Aunt Celia could talk of gods and goddesses so flippantly.

'Let's see . . . there are the weavers of the universe, the Hopi Spider Woman, the Navajo Spider Grandmother.' Celia counted them off in the air with one slim hand. She stopped. 'Did she seem grandmotherly to you?' she asked me.

'Grandmotherly?' I thought of the woman's cruel mouth, and that icy laugh. 'Not at all. But then, you don't seem great-aunt-ish,' I remarked.

That was certainly true.

'Of course I don't, darling. Anyway, it doesn't sound like the Navajo Spider Grandmother or the creators. They are generally rather beneficent. Your spider woman was testy, wasn't she?'

I nodded. 'You could put it that way. I had the feeling she wanted to eat me.'

*Why does everyone want to eat me?*

I finished my cup of tea, and felt a torrent of adrenaline fill me. I went to place the empty cup and saucer on the floor, caught the disapproving look on my great-aunt's face, and reconsidered. I delivered both of our cups and saucers to the kitchen sink. I was back in a flash, hoping Celia would feel compelled to continue our discussion without any further breaks.

'Thank you, darling. Well, I hope this woman you encountered isn't the Japanese spider goddess. Did she look Japanese at all?'

'Not really, no.' I pulled my feet up under me on the hassock and tried to remember everything I'd seen. 'She had black hair cut in a bob, but . . . no she didn't look or sound Japanese.'

'Good.'

I had to ask. 'Why? Who is the Japanese spider goddess?'

'There were many female *Tsuchigumo* in Japan at one time – "ground spiders", or "earth spiders". But the Japanese spider goddess was really something. She was quite fierce. She lived in the Japanese Alps and preyed on travellers. As legend has it, the hero Raiko saw a skull fly into a cave one night while he was travelling with his servant. Or was it that the skull was flying out? It never seems clear. Anyway, he went to investigate and became ensnared in a sticky web. The weaver of the web appeared to be a comely woman – aren't they always beautiful women in these stories?' Celia remarked. 'He struck her with his sword and the woman fled, and when the servant helped Raiko out of the web they found a giant spider on the floor of the cave, impaled through the stomach with Raiko's sword. They split her belly open and the skulls of her many human victims tumbled out, as did her spider children, whom they killed one by one.'

That sounded rather grim. 'But if she was killed, then it can't be her?' I reasoned.

'Ah, there is much we can learn from legends, Pandora, but never take those heroic endings literally. Men like to boast. Heroes always feel they have to claim a goddess or two. It rarely happened in reality.'

'Oh.' I wasn't heartened by that idea. It doubtless meant that if a goddess wanted to destroy me, I'd have a hard time protecting myself, let alone vanquishing her. I had no interest in being a hero, of course, but that hardly seemed to matter. 'She said something about not believing I was the Seventh? What could she have meant by that?' I asked.

Celia pondered that. 'She knew who you were. She might have expected a fight.'

I thought about my efforts with the umbrella and the can of hairspray. Hardly awe-inspiring stuff.

'Being the Seventh is a gift, Pandora. But it won't be easy. They'll be drawn to you, and you to them. It is the way of things.' She contemplated something for a moment. 'Raiko's sword was called *Kumokirimaru*, or "spider killer". I wonder if it exists,' she said, possibly thinking it might come in handy.

'Wait, you need to explain this to me. What do you mean, "the way of things"? And who is *they*?'

Celia placed a cool hand on my knee. 'Well, all this is not so easy to explain in common terms, Pandora. You have to cast aside what you learned back in Gretchenville. You have to open yourself to the fact that you are the Seventh. You are special, and you can be sure that those who are powerful will be drawn to you because of it. It is the natural order of things. Every one hundred and fifty years, there is this tension, or agitation, this explosion of activity from . . . well, from *different* forces.'

'Different forces? You mean like this spider woman? Like the Blood Countess?'

'Yes. And others besides.'

*Others. Great.* 'So these people, or whatever they are, they will come here looking for me?'

'Well, not exactly. Many of them will come here and hope to avoid you, in fact. But yes, they will come, and you will be drawn together.'

'I'm a little confused.'

'That, darling, is quite natural,' she said.

Some time passed as we sat there in silence. Freyja continued to sniff at me occasionally. Her pink opal eyes regarded me with curiosity.

'Supernatural hive-mind spiders,' I told the cat in a whisper. 'And a spider web cocoon. That's what the smell is.' Freyja cocked her head to one side, considered my explanation and lay down at my feet, evidently as perplexed as I was by it all.

'I know you sometimes think it would have been easier if you hadn't come here, Pandora,' Celia said. 'But believe me when I tell you that these forces would find you no matter where you were.'

I swallowed.

'You were the Seventh long before you came to Spektor. But the time – your time – is now.'

'Why every one hundred and fifty years? What does that mean?'

'Your friend will understand. He knows.'

'Luke?'

She nodded.

'Great-Aunt Celia, how do you know all these things?' I'd read so many of my mother's books on mythology and ancient cultures – read them over and over in my youth until the stories of gods and monsters were as familiar to me as fairytales were to other girls. And yet I didn't know half of what my great-aunt seemed to. I'd certainly never heard of anything called 'the Seventh'.

'It's rather become my business to know,' she responded, typically evasive.

'But how do you separate myth from reality? How do you know which of these goddesses or creatures really exist?' I pressed.

'I don't,' she said simply. 'But if they do exist there's a good chance they'll show up in Spektor.'

I watched her face carefully. She didn't betray any sign of jest.

'You are serious, aren't you?' I said.

'Indeed I am, Pandora.'

Spektor was an unusual place. That much was clear from the first time I'd set foot in the suburb. Perhaps we had the Victorian-era architect and psychical scientist Edmund Barrett to thank for that?

'Pandora, what most people call folklore is generally just a report passed down over so many generations that the facts seem fantastical. A bit like a game of Telephone. The details change, but there is truth at the centre. More often than not, folklore begins with the truth.'

In the past two months I had discovered, with great surprise and some alarm, that some folklore the modern world thought was ridiculous was indeed true: mediums existed, psychics, ghosts, the undead. And if vampires existed – though they'd hate you to call them that – then what else was real? How many monster stories were founded on a real species or supernatural being? How many ancient legends were based in truth? I thought of the spider woman, whose power and poison could be felt like an aura around her. And that body . . . those spider legs. She was sinister, there was no doubting that. She was no beneficent spider goddess.

'So if she isn't Grandmother Spider or one of these Japanese spider women, then who is she?' I asked.

'There is one more suspect who comes to mind. I'm surprised you haven't mentioned her yet.'

I drew a blank. 'I don't know who you mean.'

Celia frowned at me. 'Really now, Pandora. The name *Arachne*? You mean to say that doesn't ring a bell? With all your love of ancient mythology?'

The legend of Arachne did ring a bell. And I'd seen the name somewhere recently, too, hadn't I? I searched for the context, but for the moment it eluded me. 'But that story is definitely a myth,' I protested, thinking of the ancient Greco-Roman tale. 'Obviously there was no Arachne, or Athena for that matter.'

'That's an interesting perspective,' Celia said and folded her arms. I knew that look. It told me I had much to learn.

*Arachne* . . .

'Wait. Now I remember where I saw that name! It's the other address Pepper gave me,' I said, and leapt from my seat. I fished the piece of paper out of Celia's coat and brought it over. Sure enough, the word was scrawled across the page in Pepper's tiny writing. Arachne was the name of the last remaining designer that was to be interviewed for the knitwear feature. There was an address in the Garment District, and a phone number.

Celia raised an eyebrow. 'That's quite a coincidence, isn't it?'

The ancient story of Arachne was that she was once a great mortal weaver, praised for her work. Eventually she became so proud that she boasted she was greater than the Greek goddess of crafts, Pallas Athena. The goddess heard of these boasts and was angered by the young woman's conceit. She set a weaving competition, during which Arachne wove a beautiful tapestry, but cheekily chose to depict the sins and transgressions of the gods. Enraged by her defiance, and perhaps even jealous of the beauty of her work – and in some tellings, also jealous of the beauty of the young woman herself – the goddess destroyed Arachne's tapestry, broke her loom and cut her face before turning her into a spider. Athena clearly had some fierce temper. I could remember a few words by the Latin poet Ovid from his famous work *Metamorphoses*, in which he wrote of Arachne's curse: 'You shall live to swing, to live now and forever, even to the last hanging creature of your kind.'

Arachne was cursed to become a spider – the spider woman, *the spider goddess*. She was cursed for her conceit.

*Everyone knows I am the best knitwear designer in the world. In fact, I'm probably the best there has ever been,* Victor had said, only hours before he went missing. He had been boastful. Had the others? Was Arachne the one sending the mysterious parcels?

Destroying the designers' workshops? For revenge? Because of their boasts?

I hesitated. 'But it's just a tale. It's a parable. *Metamorphoses* was written in, like, 8 AD or something. There's no way . . .'

And then I thought of the beautiful but warped face of the woman who had confronted me. Those faint lines I'd seen. They were *scars*.

'Just because it's in a book doesn't mean it isn't real,' my great-aunt answered with a level gaze.

# CHAPTER
# TWELVE

It was midnight, and I had little chance of drifting to sleep. I'd long since bathed, dried my hair and changed into my nightie. I sat on the end of my bed gazing at the deep pitch of the obsidian ring for an incalculable stretch of time before deciding to give up the notion of going to sleep. My mind was crowded with thoughts of supernatural spiders, ancient myths, necromancers and mad psychical researchers, and my veins were still charged with my great-aunt's tea. Thankfully, I didn't have to be up for work on Saturday, so sleeplessness seemed not to matter.

*Should I head to the Garment District in the morning? Just check out the address?* I wondered. Surely it could wait until Monday. What would I find, anyway? Even after what I'd thought I'd seen, and everything Celia had told me, the idea that Arachne herself was loose in New York seemed too incredible to be true.

*No.* It just wasn't possible.

But nor was sleep. I hopped into my favourite pair of jeans, a T-shirt and warm sweater, and I stepped out into the lounge room. The curtains were open over the tall windows, and moonlight fell across the room. In the distance, the Empire

State Building was silhouetted by a bluish full moon against the dark sky. Celia was no longer reading at her chair. If she were any average great-aunt, she would be fast asleep, but I fancied she was out somewhere in her sumptuous red ensemble, painting the town black. As if to confirm my suspicion, her fox stole was gone from the Edwardian hatstand. I was alone.

I stepped out of the front door of the penthouse and stood by the rail. The mansion was quiet below me. I gazed at the lobby tiles of the ground floor and wondered if there was some secret passageway down there. Perhaps a passageway that led to Luke's resting place.

*Luke. My spirit guide.*

'Lieutenant Luke?' I called out tentatively.

In moments I felt a coolness descend, and my ring gave a surprising but brief burst of heat. I was looking at it when he materialised at my side, first as a white misty shape, and then as the handsome soldier I knew.

'Miss Pandora.'

'Luke. Hello.' His luminous blue eyes met with mine and I grinned helplessly for a moment. He seemed to be getting more handsome. Or maybe there was something unreasonably attractive about having him appear when I called? Probably it was both.

'Is your hand okay?' he asked.

'My hand?'

'You were looking at it.'

'Oh, yes.' I turned my hand over and frowned. 'It's this ring Celia gave me . . . It became almost hot for a moment. Or I thought it did.'

He looked at it and two creases appeared between his brows. 'That ring has power,' he said.

I was taken aback. 'In what way?'

'You are anchored,' he told me. 'It helps to keep you on this plane, while you communicate with the dead.'

The dead. Like Luke.

I leaned against the rail and watched him. 'How do you know?'

'I can feel it,' he said.

'Oh!' I stood to attention. 'Should I take it off? Is it hurting you?' I felt a touch panicked.

'No, Miss Pandora,' he assured me. 'It anchors you and gives you strength, but it does not alter me. It protects you.' As with so much of what he explained to me about the spirit world and his connection to the mortal world, I did not fully understand, but I felt comforted. Celia had said Madame Aurora's ring was a talisman. I wondered about its powers. What had Madame Aurora experienced with it? Or accomplished with it?

'Luke, can I talk to you about something? Do you have time?'

'I have no time, and nothing but time, Miss Pandora,' he told me. He removed his cap, and held it close to his breast. 'What I do have, I give to you.'

I felt my knees weaken a touch. My cheeks grew warm and I looked to my feet, willing my face to return to a normal colour. Blushing in front of a ghost? How ridiculous. Even worse, to be blushing *over* a ghost. I felt my father's disapproval even from the grave.

This time, Lieutenant Luke's words were no riddle. Ghosts like Luke were already departed, if not really gone. They had no time left, in the mortal sense, but also no schedule. No possessions. No earthly body. No daytime presence. Only spirit. Luke brushed my chin with one cool, misty finger, lifting my face up to him. 'I wish I could do more for you,' he told me. 'I wish I could be more.'

I felt the compulsion to kiss him. 'I . . .' I began, not even sure of what I wanted to reveal. The silence was too awkward. I needed to say something. 'Will you come downstairs with me?' I finally asked and swallowed.

'Of course, Miss Pandora.'

We took the lift down to the lobby. Luke probably could have drifted down through the mansion and met me there, but he stood attentively in the confines of the little rattling lift as it descended, holding his cap neatly in front of him with both hands. I thought about how we'd never be able to walk along the street together. Or go to the movies. Even leave the house . . . And yet I felt so safe with Luke. I looked down at the ring on my finger again. Why had it grown hot? What did it mean?

We emerged from the lift and walked across the tiles of the lobby.

I had an idea.

When Luke saw that I was heading for the entrance, he slowed. I walked straight up to the large wooden front door and pulled it open. The night air blew in, along with the faint smell of Spektor's curious fog.

'Come,' I beckoned.

Lieutenant Luke stopped just under the dusty chandelier. 'I cannot pass out of this mansion,' he said. 'I am trapped here.'

I thought about these strange supernatural rules I was learning about – how a Sanguine needed to be invited into a home, and how they could be affected by a crucifix if they really believed in the power of it. (Though Celia said it would take a *lot* of belief to burst into flames . . .) I thought about the ring. Who knew how much power and magic it held? 'I think you can make it,' I told him. 'You just have to believe.' I said it with conviction, and I found that a good part of me believed what I said. Had Luke ever been invited to *leave*?

'I cannot. I am sorry, Miss Pandora.' He stood fast.

I stepped through the door into the cold night, and held out my hand to him.

His whole body seemed to stiffen within his tailored uniform. For a while we stood a few metres apart, each firm at our posts. I hoped to feel something in the ring, another flash of heat perhaps, something that might indicate that this strange talisman Celia had given me would help him to pass through the doorway. Nothing happened, and then, just as it seemed we were at an impasse, Luke fixed his cap on his head, and began to walk slowly towards me.

'You can do it, Luke,' I encouraged him.

*Please* . . .

I kept my hand out, and he neared me, taking slow steps, his leather boots unnaturally silent on the tiles. Closer. Closer still. Soon we were nearly touching. And just as he stepped over the threshold, inches from my outstretched fingers, he disappeared.

208 · TARA MOSS

'No!' I gasped.

I raced back inside the lobby. The door slammed shut behind me, pushing dust into the air. 'Luke? Luke?' He was gone.

'I told you I couldn't leave.'

I looked around for where his voice had come from and after a moment Lieutenant Luke's form materialised as a white shape near the base of the winding mezzanine staircase. In time he became whole again, and I let out a deep breath I didn't even know I was holding.

I ran a hand over my face. 'I'm so sorry. I was just hoping . . .'

'I'm the one who must apologise, Miss Pandora,' he replied. 'I am meant to remain here. I do not know why.'

The sincerity of his voice only added to the shame I felt for having pushed the issue. I'd thought it was at least worth a try, but now I felt selfish. I sat at the base of the staircase, defeated. Luke came to sit next to me.

'There is a woman out there . . . a spider goddess,' I found myself explaining. 'She's been following me all week and tonight she attacked me. I guess maybe . . .' I hesitated. 'I guess I'm afraid. I guess I hoped you could help me somehow – because you are my spirit guide.'

It felt strange to say it aloud and, even stranger, Luke made no protest or comment. It was as if he already knew or suspected his role.

'I don't know what all this means,' I said, and leaned forward on my knees. If he was my spirit guide, how did that work? Why couldn't he leave the building with me? Maybe he was right? Maybe he was meant to remain here? Or maybe there was still something we could do about it. Perhaps Deus was right about Barrett? I had no idea.

To my surprise Luke snapped to attention and looked towards the lift. I wondered what he had sensed, until I heard the little elevator come to life seconds later. I nervously observed its ascent. One floor. Two floors. It stopped. Level two or three? It hadn't reached the top floor, that much I could tell. Was Athanasia about to pay us a visit?

'Someone is coming,' I said, though it was obvious. I stood up and readied myself. There was no point getting melancholy about Luke. And certainly not now, when there were more pressing things to consider. Like whether or not I had rice. (I didn't.) I briefly considered leaving the mansion and going out into the night air of Spektor, but that would not really help things. At least inside I was protected by the mistress of the house, and her rule that I not be harmed. Protected *somewhat*. It wasn't a rule I particularly wanted to test.

I listened to the elevator descend, and soon it reappeared in the iron cage of the lobby, holding a solitary slim figure in a grey suit.

I relaxed.

It was the Fledgling Sanguine, Samantha.

'Hello, Pandora,' she said softly.

My predecessor at *Pandora* magazine didn't look so well. She'd grown paler since I'd last seen her, and her face was even more gaunt and angular. She was still wearing my old suit. Actually, it wasn't really that old. I'd bought it in Gretchenville at the finest fashion boutique in town in preparation for my exciting move to New York, but after experiencing the reaction it got from various fashion types (it clearly wasn't cool enough, to put it mildly), I couldn't wait to get rid of the thing. I'd given it to Samantha, who'd been bizarrely stripped of all her clothes and ID when I'd met her. (In truth it was less of a meeting than a derailed attempt at feeding.) It looked like she'd worn the suit day and night since I'd given it to her. It was quite filthy, and the hems of the pant legs were frayed over her dirty bare feet.

'Hi, Samantha. I haven't seen you for a couple of weeks. I was starting to get worried,' I said.

She shrugged in response.

'You're not with the others?'

She bit her lip and stared at her toes. She wiggled them and then looped a bit of greasy blonde hair around a finger. 'Athanasia doesn't like me hanging out with her,' she finally said.

'Why would you even want to?' I asked her.

'She is, you know . . . my mum.'

I sighed and shook my head. 'She's not your mum, Samantha.' We'd been through this before. I had that photo of her with her *real* mother in the drawer of my desk at work; a picture I couldn't bring myself to toss away. It pained me that her mother could never know what had happened to her. I didn't know if giving Samantha the picture would help matters. If she wandered off into greater New York to find her human mum, things could go very badly for all involved. No, it would not be wise to present this sad, Fledgling vampire with a photograph of her former life. It was better that she never saw her family again. When you became a bloodsucker all ties to your old, mortal, human life had to be severed. I had a lot to learn, but I did know that much.

'Is Athanasia here?' I asked, looking around suspiciously.

Samantha shook her head. 'They said something about her needing to go to ground.'

'The cemetery,' Luke explained to me in a low voice. 'To heal in the dark earth.'

*Yuck.*

'And what about the others?' I asked Samantha.

She shrugged weakly. 'Probably out feeding.'

*Double yuck.*

'What about you, Samantha? What have you been eating?'

'Rats.'

I suppressed a gag. 'Good,' I managed.

Samantha looked around the lobby, and shifted her weight. She seemed not to focus on anything. 'They say it makes you weak, but . . .'

'No, it's good,' I assured her. 'There's nothing wrong with rats.'

In truth, I didn't know if there *was* anything wrong with Sanguine eating rats, but it was a whole lot better than the alternative. I didn't want her hunting prey in Central Park, or roaming the subways of New York picking off passengers. Samantha did look pretty awful though. She was hollow faced and wan. I'd never seen her look particularly well, mind you, on account of the fact that she'd been confused, abandoned and freshly undead when I'd first crossed her path. She hadn't known if she was alive, or dead, and her cheekbones had been jutting out like knives. No one had taught her the basics. No one had told her she needed blood. Samantha had been nibbling the wooden railings of the third floor like a teething puppy before Celia came down with me, on my insistence, and helped feed her a couple of rats. I guess that had started her on the whole rodent diet.

(If Athanasia had been her mum, Child Protective Services would sure need a word with her.)

Lieutenant Luke watched Samantha cautiously. He knew we were friendly, or as friendly as you could be with someone who'd once tried to blindly rip your throat out, but her proximity to me clearly made him uneasy.

'I heard you talking to someone,' she said.

She could not see Luke. Spirits appear to very few of the living, and to even fewer of the undead. 'Yes. I have a friend here, Samantha,' I explained. 'I think I've told you about him before?'

'The dead soldier?'

I cringed.

'Samantha, I was wondering if you could help me with something. Have you seen any secret passages in the mansion? Hidden corridors, that kind of thing?'

She shrugged.

'Any skeletons . . . or coffins?'

Luke gave me a strange look.

Samantha nodded eagerly in reply. 'Oh yes. Quite a few.'

I gasped. 'Really? Where?'

'I can show you.' She seemed to perk up a little with the thought of being helpful.

We followed Samantha to the lift, and she pressed the round button for the second floor. When I explained that the architect of the building had conducted some odd experiments that may have involved human remains she seemed unfazed by the idea. That's what death did to you, I supposed.

'Maybe I should get something to, you know, take as a precaution,' I said, a bit leery of wandering around level two, which was where Athanasia and her gang hung out. I'd always stayed away from that particular floor. 'It might not be safe for me.'

'Why?' Samantha asked. 'They're not here.'

The lift began to ascend as Luke watched our exchange with his impressive jaw flexing tightly. In an instant he stepped sideways, straight out of the lift and was gone. My eyes grew wide and I opened my mouth to speak, but said nothing. Samantha did not notice his departure, nor did she seem to register my reaction. When we arrived on the second floor and the door slid open, Luke was already waiting for us. 'I believe there are no Sanguine on this floor right now,' he helpfully explained. 'Except the one standing next to you.' He tilted his chin down and gave Samantha a hard look. The young undead woman barely came up to his chest. He'd intervened once when I'd first met her. He hadn't trusted her since. Or rather, he appeared never to trust Sanguine. Which, come to think of it, was fair enough.

I nodded. 'Thank you,' I said quietly.

The second floor landing was much as I imagined. I'd seen it plenty of times as the lift had passed. Cobwebs. Damaged wall sconces. Dust. There was a set of large double doors, not unlike those on Celia's floor, except that these were scratched and unpainted. Samantha led us towards the doors, and when she hauled them open there was a screech of rusted hinges. I looked to Luke, saw his sober and concerned expression, and decided to follow Samantha anyway. We entered a large, dimly lit lounge room. The tall windows were boarded up from the inside with uneven sections of wood, effectively preventing sunlight from penetrating the space. A few gilded, Victorian-style couches were pushed up against the walls, along with an antique brass bed, loosely made up with dark, silky covers. I saw a few tall bottles on the ground – perhaps wine bottles – some were empty and had been kicked over. A full chandelier was sprawled out in the middle of the floor like a dusty crystal sculpture. The only source of light was a bare bulb hanging from the ceiling. I noticed sections of the old, ornate, stained wallpaper had peeled back in ribbons over the years, as if a clawed animal had shredded it, leaving strips of the walls bare.

'So, is this where you sleep?' I asked.

'No. Athanasia doesn't like me hanging out with her. But she lets me come down here to work, which is cool.'

*To work?*

'This way,' Samantha said.

She led us down an unfurnished hallway and stopped at a doorway. I realised that we were exactly two floors below the entrance to my room in Celia's penthouse. An uneasy chill formed in my stomach, and I had the feeling we might find something extraordinary beyond the door. I braced myself.

*Oh boy.*

Samantha turned the door handle.

Beyond the door was . . . a walk-in closet?

Racks of colourful designer clothes lined the walls from the floor to the ceiling. Shoes, boots and wooden trunks were lined up across the floor. Brightly coloured dresses and tops hung on coathangers. Jeans and leather pants were folded into stacks. Costume jewellery hung from hooks. Hats. Purses. Stilettos. Gloves.

*What the . . .?*

'What is this, Samantha?'

'Athanasia's room,' she replied, and I nearly choked. I studied her gloomy expression. She was not joking. Sanguine Samantha didn't know how to joke, I suspected. 'She sleeps in that one,' she said and pointed near my feet.

I noticed the edge of a shiny wooden casket, and I took a little leap sideways.

'And the others sleep in those three.'

What I had thought were trunks along the base of the walls were in fact coffins, partially camouflaged by the cascading wardrobe hanging above. I brought my hand to my mouth. I was speechless and, for a moment, I didn't move even to breathe. Despite all I'd seen since moving to Spektor I didn't anticipate that Sanguine slept in *actual* coffins. I'd thought it was just a Hammer Horror fantasy, as far from reality as Peter Cushing's crucifix-wielding Van Helsing and Christopher Lee's prosthetic fangs. How stupid that I hadn't even considered the possibility. These were not the remnants of Barrett's experiments, this was the place where my nemesis slept. (And dressed herself, apparently.) And Samantha had led me straight to it.

'Oh.' I bit my lip. *I shouldn't be here.*

'She lets me come in here to shine her casket. And hang her clothes.'

There were more wardrobe changes in that room than you'd expect to see backstage at a theatre, and yet, Samantha, the girl who used to work at *Pandora* fashion magazine, was dressed in my increasingly shabby polyblend suit because she'd been stripped of her clothes when she was turned. All so that Athanasia and her harpies could add to their wardrobe.

*Athanasia really is a total cow,* I thought.

Luke moved close. 'Sanguine often prefer to sleep fully covered by a lid so they are not more exposed,' he whispered in my ear. 'Many choose to sleep in coffins, for tradition. The caskets are considered a sign of status.'

'I see,' I said aloud.

'I don't have a casket though,' Samantha explained, as if I'd been responding to her. 'I sleep on the floor upstairs.'

I felt deeply sorry for Samantha, on so many levels and in so many ways that I just didn't know where to begin. 'Would you like me to find you a coffin, Samantha?' I found myself saying. 'Would that be more comfortable?'

*Where would I get a coffin from?*

She shrugged. 'Yeah, I guess,' she said, sounding pretty much like she didn't care either way.

It seemed there was nothing quite like the ennui of a depressed young vampire.

I backed out of the bedroom until I was just beyond the door. 'Where did you see the skeletons?' I dared to ask.

'What skeletons?'

I blinked. 'Thanks for showing me the, uh, coffins.' I looked at the clothes and then looked at Samantha. 'Why don't you just grab one of those outfits, Samantha? The Prada, maybe,' I said, stepping forward and ripping a coat off the rack. 'Or some of those pants?' I pointed at a stack. 'And some shoes. They don't need all this stuff.'

'I couldn't do that!' she exclaimed, completely shocked at the suggestion. 'She'd kill me.'

'She already did, Samantha. You've got to stop being Athanasia's slave.'

Lieutenant Luke had been silent all this time, waiting close at my back. I felt him become suddenly alert, and I turned just in time to see him disappear through the wall of clothes, as only he was able to do. He was gone for at least a minute, and I nervously awaited his return. What was it now?

'Samantha, you can't let them treat you this way. It's not right.'

I felt a coolness in the air as Luke's spirit returned. 'You have to go right now,' he said, re-materialising at my side. He took my hand firmly in his. *Right now.*'

'Athanasia's back?' I whispered to him. 'I thought she had to go to ground?'

'No. It's the others. And they're not alone.'

My throat tightened. I backed out of the room.

Samantha seemed confused. 'Do you want to look in her casket? It's real nice. It's lined and everything.'

'Oh, no. Thanks, Samantha,' I said. 'Um, the girls are coming back. I should really go.'

'Are they?' she said lazily, and carefully hung the Prada coat back in its spot and dusted it off. 'I guess I'd better go upstairs then. They don't really like me hanging around.'

*And I'm quite sure they won't like me hanging around.*

I turned and jogged back through the hallway and lounge room. We quickly reached the double doors, and when I opened them and looked across the landing I didn't need Luke's abilities to know that we were too late. The lift wasn't waiting for us. It was already on its way down to the lobby. Or even back up.

*Great.*

I ran back inside and shut the double doors with a squeak. 'Is there any other way out?' I asked breathlessly. 'Or a place I can hide? Where does that door lead?' I pointed at a nearby door, a few steps down a short hallway. Would it lead to an antechamber? An escape?

Samantha shrugged. 'Yeah, you could go in there,' she said.

By now I could hear footsteps approaching. They were close. How could they be so close? I opened the door and leapt blindly into the room. Hopefully it led to one of Barrett's secret passageways. 'There's no light. What is this place?' I whispered.

Samantha shrugged and closed the door, and everything went dark.

# CHAPTER
# THIRTEEN

I held my breath and listened. Beyond the dark, musty room where I hid I heard creaking double doors open. There were several sets of heeled footsteps, and a harsh, mirthless laughter that set me on edge.

'Finished scrubbing the coffins?' someone said in a mocking tone, presumably to Samantha.

*The fanged supermodels.*

I thought I recognised Blonde's voice. I didn't hear Samantha's response. Perhaps she simply shrugged, as was her way. She'd really embraced the whole passive undead thing. How could she let them treat her like that? Hopefully they would soon pile back into their measly Miu Miu camouflaged coffins and get some rest. I wasn't sure of the time, but if that awful trio were back, hopefully it was because they were packing it in for the night. Right?

*Please?*

The room I was in smelled stale and vaguely unpleasant. I couldn't see much. Lieutenant Luke had joined me inside; I could see his blue eyes glowing faintly in the darkness a few feet away, watching me with concern. Thankfully he wasn't the type to say 'I told you so', but I did feel a little foolish. I was sure Luke had seen this problem coming a mile away. I said nothing. Neither did he.

To the right of the door were the only other points of light, coming, it seemed, from small holes where rodents or water damage had eaten through the wall. I moved cautiously towards the light and kicked my foot into a box with a bang. I waited to see if anyone outside had heard, but their voices continued. I decided not to move further until my eyes adjusted properly. I was patient, and after a short wait I could begin to make out jumbled shapes, and more specific objects near the wall where the pinpricks of light filtered through. The place was packed with junk and there was hardly any floor space, from what I could tell. 'It's a closet, isn't it?' I lamented in a low voice. 'She's not led me to a hidden passageway. I'm in some kind of storage room.'

'Yes. I've not been in here before,' Luke said. After a moment he added, 'This is where they keep the things they have found.'

'Where Athanasia keeps things?'

'Someone before her.'

He could no doubt see objects in the room much more clearly than I could. There were some benefits to being dead, I supposed.

'Well, where would they have found this?' I asked, holding up what appeared to be a bent trumpet. I felt frustrated. Surely there would have been a passageway I could have taken, had Samantha led the way in time. Now I was stuck in a glorified storage closet. 'Oh, I can see them,' I whispered. I pushed my face up to the wall until my right eyeball was positioned over a small hole, following the faint light from the bare bulb in the lounge room beyond. I had a good view of the lounge. 'I guess I'll wait till they are out of view, and then make for the lift,' I reasoned aloud in a low voice. 'What a disaster.'

'There's something in here,' I heard Luke say in a voice that was strange and disconnected. I turned and looked at him, but I couldn't make out his expression.

'Are you okay?' I asked the faintly glowing eyes.

'Something . . .' he said ominously.

The voices in the lounge room drew my attention back to the peephole. Blonde, Brunette and Redhead were pestering Samantha, and now I saw that – just as Luke had said – they were not alone. They had a young, dark-haired man with them, possibly a fourth Sanguine. A Fledgling like the rest of them? So now I had to avoid four sets of fangs? *Fantastic.* The three women were dressed seductively and fashionably, as usual. Brunette wore a figure-hugging dress split to the thigh. Blonde wore fish-nets and a miniskirt that looked like it was made out of shiny plastic. Redhead wore tight leather pants and a corset. There was a lot of cleavage on display.

'Bring us a bottle,' Redhead demanded, and Samantha shuffled away to some unseen corner, and returned with what looked like liquor. Meanwhile, Blonde flicked a lighter over and over, as if in a trance.

'Give me that,' Brunette snapped, and grabbed the lighter. 'You are dismissed,' she told poor Samantha, who walked out of view, precisely in the direction I wished I had already headed. I figured she'd just wander out into the Spektor night, looking for her next rodent meal, or take the lift back to her empty lair upstairs on the third floor, to sit on the floor and stare into space.

*Poor thing.*

Brunette – who I began to suspect had designs on being the new group leader – had lit a six-pronged candelabra, and she slunk towards the man with it, swinging her hips.

Great. They were entertaining.

*I could be stuck in this closet for hours.*

Their guest was attractive, I noticed. He looked to be in his early twenties or late teens. He wore jeans and a heavy leather jacket and a scarf. The women were more scantily dressed, of course, as if they were experiencing a totally different season. And it was with that detail that it finally clicked. He wasn't like them. He wasn't a guest – he was a *victim.* I watched with a sinking feeling as the scene changed. I watched the predatory way the three model Sanguine began to move – like cats stalking their prey. The air itself seemed to shift. Their postures hunched forward slightly, and like creeping shadows they moved towards the man. He was clearly intoxicated but, even in that state, he seemed to sense the change around him. He stepped backwards and brought his hands up to his face. One foot hit the edge of the bed. Brunette pushed him with one slender, feminine arm. He fell back. Redhead pulled his coat down and Blonde began to undo his shirt. In seconds they had the man bare-chested. His skin was pale, but nowhere near as pale as Brunette's toned, bloodless thigh as she leaned over him seductively.

*He's a mortal. Oh no. He's a mortal . . .*

I heard Luke foraging for something in the junk behind me – I thought I heard something like a tambourine jangle – but I was too riveted to the scene unfolding beyond the wall to try to figure out what he was doing, or why.

The young man hadn't said anything – or at least nothing I could hear – but now he cried out in pain or fear. Brunette had one hand on his neck, and now she was on him, right at his throat, taking the first bite. She held his head to one side. Her long mane of hair fell over him. She took a moment to straddle him, and then went for the neck once more. She was clearly in rapture with her feeding, gripping his flesh with long fingers, and emitting sensual, animal sounds as she sucked. I wondered how long she would feed before handing him to the others. He didn't stand a chance.

I felt sick.

I turned away from the peephole, wanting to stop the horror. Surely I had to intervene? In minutes those three female creatures would drain this mortal stranger of every ounce of his blood. They would kill him right there on that bed and I would be an accomplice because I wouldn't have done a single thing to stop it!

'They're killing him, Luke . . .' I whispered. 'I can't let them!'

I heard a loud clang. Luke had turned something over, and beyond the wall, I heard a voice. I put my eye back to the peephole and saw that Brunette had raised her face from the prone body of the man and looked our way. Fresh blood flowed down her chin. My stomach did a little flip.

*Oh, no, she heard us.*

And then Luke's voice came loud and clear behind me. 'My sabre?' he said with astonishment.

'Shhhh. What?' I whispered with alarm. I whipped my head around.

I still could hardly make anything out in the cluttered room, but I was aware of Luke's excitement, almost as if it were my own. Something was happening. My ring let off a burst of heat that was stronger than before and it seemed almost to vibrate, and then Luke himself – not only his eyes but all of him – began to illuminate, from his cap right down to his leather boots. I could see more of our surroundings now with his light filling the room. The space was cluttered with old things. Broken musical instruments. Trunks. A cabinet on one side, broken. I could see that Lieutenant Luke, now glowing with increasing intensity, was standing over a trunk of sorts, and he had in his hand a long, gently curved sword in a silvery metal sheath. The handle was a bronze colour, with a large, elegant sweeping hand guard. He examined it closely, clearly awed by it.

'My sabre,' he repeated. There was emotion in his voice. He handled the sword with a kind of reverence and wonder, while I watched in dumbfounded silence. 'My initials. Those are my initials.'

'What's happening?' I asked in a low voice. 'You're glowing . . . You are becoming brighter . . .'

'I recognise every scar, every flaw,' he said, marvelling at what he'd found. 'I haven't seen this in one hundred and fifty years. I cannot conceive of what it is doing in this place.'

Slowly, Lieutenant Luke pulled the sword from its sheath.

A startling flash of heat passed from the obsidian ring, down my hand and through my entire body, straight to Luke. I gasped.

*What was that?*

And then, just like that, the light went out.

The room returned to total blackness. The heat and vibration of the ring ceased. I felt peculiarly drained and disoriented, and for a time I stood panting in the dark. I could not see a thing, not even Luke's glowing blue eyes. Gradually, as my sight adjusted, I could make out the cracks in the wall again. I could not tell where Luke was, if he was still there at all.

'Luke?' I whispered quietly.

'Miss Pandora.' By the sound of Luke's voice he was close now, but I still could not see him.

'Miss Pandora, touch me.'

I concentrated on his presence. Sometimes closing my eyes made him even more real to me, as was the case now. I felt him near, only inches away. I could almost make myself believe that he was a mortal, like me. I could almost feel the warmth of a corporeal body press gently against my side; I could almost believe that Luke was real and human, and present to me. Our hands brushed and then clasped tightly. In that moment he felt as tangible and human as anyone I'd been close to. I savoured the feeling. Despite the awkwardness of the small room, despite the danger, I found I didn't want that moment to end. I could forget where we were, could forget the bloodsuckers beyond the wall and their terrible feeding, and the dusty room that for the moment held me trapped. I sensed Luke lean in to me, and I raised my chin to him. Ever so gently he placed a kiss on my lips. Our lips parted just a touch and stayed there, pressing lightly together.

I kept expecting the mistiness, the melting feeling of his form beneath my lips, beneath my fingers. But it was different.

'Luke?'

He ran a hand softly over my hair. 'Miss Pandora, come,' he said, and I felt him guide me towards the door. Without caution he threw the door open and stepped into the hall where there was more light. By now I was only a foot or two from the view of those horrible women.

'Wait, there are too many of them,' I whispered and tried to turn back.

Then I looked at Luke, *really* looked at him, and all other thoughts left me.

He was different. Crisp. Real. He took a step back and looked down at himself. He had the sabre fixed on his leather belt now, and it looked like it belonged there. Sometimes things in the physical world looked out of place next to his non-corporeal form, but this was part of him. It was on the same plane. *He* was on the same plane.

'Luke? What's happened to you?' I said, and then cast a worried glance in the direction of the lounge room. They would soon see us, I felt sure.

'You can see it, too?' Luke asked and stretched a hand out in front of his face, flexing his fingers with a kind of awe, as if he had never seen them before.

'Is it . . . Are you?' I stuttered. I could resist no longer. I reached out and poked him hard with my finger. He felt solid. 'Luke!'

'I am *flesh*,' he confirmed.

Before I could really absorb the enormity of what he'd said, he strode into the lounge room. He walked straight up to the bed where the three women were perched like vultures over their still-breathing victim.

I followed him into the room, thinking myself quite mad. 'Leave that young man alone!' I demanded.

Brunette lifted her head. Her savagely beautiful face was glowing, her lips and chin slick with fresh blood. 'So it was you banging around back there. Why should we leave this strapping fellow alone? He likes it,' she said. She pointed at Luke with one talon. 'And who's *he*?'

The man on the bed was naked from the waist up, and his bloodied chest was moving up and down erratically. His breath sounded ragged. 'You're killing him,' I said.

'Nah, not tonight,' Blonde replied, her sick grin marred with red. She'd been nibbling on his wrist, I saw. 'He's worth a good drink or two. So stuff off.' She sneered at me, then regarded Luke with appreciation. 'You can leave him here, if you like though. He's cute.' She flashed him a lascivious, fanged smile.

*They could see him. They could really see him!* 'You've had enough for one night,' I said. 'We're taking this young man with us.'

Brunette, who had resumed her grim feeding, now raised her head, wiped her stained mouth and gave me a look that sent a chill down my spine. 'Reeeeeeally,' she said. 'Is that so?' And with an exaggerated sensuality, she placed her hands around the young man's bleeding throat and stroked it. She ran a tongue over his lips. Then she jerked the man's neck suddenly.

I heard a snap.

*No!*

The man's head lay at an angle. She'd broken his neck, just like that. I couldn't believe what I'd just seen.

'Ooopsy,' she said, and smiled at me with her fangs out, daring me to act.

I was speechless.

She stood up from the bed, all feminine curves and blood-smeared, undead beauty. 'Wanna fight about it? What we do here is our business,' she told me. 'You don't own this place, and just because your great-aunt does, doesn't mean you get to tell us what to do, little *morchilla*.'

Redhead and Blonde moved off the body, and I thought I detected some disappointment. Perhaps they hadn't had their fill. They weren't licking up what was left. The young man was left sprawling on the silky bed covers, half-naked, blood-smeared and limp, his dull eyes staring sightless at the ceiling. My mouth had been gaping in horror, but now I closed it and stood up tall.

'You are going to regret that,' I declared in a shaky voice. 'You're really going to regret it.'

Despite my words, I had no response to Brunette's senseless violence. I backed away, leaving the dead man surrounded by his attackers. In that moment it seemed that being the Seventh didn't mean much.

I had never felt less powerful.

# CHAPTER
# FOURTEEN

The clock said it was past three thirty as I sat on the edge of my bedspread with one hand gripping the bedpost. The knuckles of that hand were white with tension. My other hand was being held by a Civil War soldier who had died one hundred and fifty years ago, and apparently come back to life.

*I can't believe she did it! Right in front of us, just because she could.*

My stomach felt queasy. I was on the edge of tears. Despite all the death I'd experienced in my life so far − the many deaths I'd felt and foreseen, and all the ghosts I'd sensed and encountered − I'd never actually seen a human being killed. It was a terrible thing to witness. And Brunette's action had been so callous and deliberate. So unnecessary.

'They hadn't even planned on killing him, not yet anyway,' I continued venting. 'That's what the blonde one said. It was my fault that he died. She just . . . she snapped his neck like it was nothing, just to prove a point. And now he's dead.' I leaned my head towards the post and gently hit my fore-head on the wood.

Lieutenant Luke sat next to me, listening quietly. His chest rose and fell beneath his fitted uniform. For once, the weight of his human body made an indent in the bed covers.

'I handled it all wrong,' I said.

'The taking of a life is always terrible – whether it be murder or killing in the name of war,' he said. 'It is a difficult thing to witness.'

I wondered what he'd seen on the battlefield. I wondered how many Confederate soldiers he'd killed before he was slain.

'They would have drained that young man over a few days,' he reasoned. 'They might have turned him into one of their kind, as Athanasia did with your friend Miss Samantha, and then he would be a helpless slave like she is, or worse, he would be a predator just like them. How could you predict what they would do? They are killers. They are reckless. That's not your fault.'

I knew he was right, that they would have killed that young man sooner or later, but the idea brought me little solace. 'It's my fault he's dead right now.'

'No, Miss Pandora. No. He wasn't their first victim and he won't be their last. They would have killed him when they felt like it.'

He took my hands in his and furrowed his brow. 'It must be late. You should get some sleep, Miss Pandora.'

I let out a humourless laugh. 'Sleep? Not a chance. Not after that. And . . .' I cast my eyes his way. 'Look at you, Luke. I am not going to sleep, not with you right here.'

'I should leave you then,' he reasoned.

'No,' I said. I hadn't meant it like that, but Luke was already up and walking to the wall. He reached out one hand and rested it on the wallpaper, seeming to feel its solidity, or perhaps his own.

'You can't pass through it, can you?'

'I cannot.'

I felt my heart lift.

'Stay,' I found myself saying. I paused to find my words, my emotions running high. I felt on the edge of tears or laughter, or both. I thought I might soon go mad with all I'd seen. 'We have to talk about this. I don't know what happened, or why, but I can't be apart from you now. Not tonight. Luke, I want you to stay with me.'

He turned from the wall and we looked at each other.

'Will you . . .? Will you stay? I don't want to be alone.'

He hesitated.

'As you wish, Miss Pandora,' he finally agreed. 'I will stay if you do not wish to be alone. I will protect you, always.' He looked down at himself, unsure of what to do next. He couldn't very well stand around in his full uniform all night. Having decided to stay, he unbuckled the leather belt that held his sabre, and he placed it on the floor. Gently, he sat on the edge of the bed and removed his boots. With one hand he began to unbutton his frockcoat.

I felt a thrill course through my body. What if Luke was never human and real again? What if this was the only night we had? What was this miracle? Could I trust it?

I knelt on the bed covers behind him and helped him out of his stiff coat, and he stood and placed it over the small wooden chair by the Victorian writing desk, along with his cap. He quietly watched me, standing next to my bed in his uniform trousers and a cotton shirt he'd unbuttoned to the chest.

'I just want . . .' I began and stopped. What *did* I want? I lay back on my bed, slipped under the covers and folded my arms across my stomach. 'You are always gone too soon,' I said in a hushed voice. He pulled himself over and stretched out next to me. We lay on our backs, not quite touching, a living dead man and the Seventh.

I thought about that horrible spider woman. She'd known what I was. 'Luke, what exactly does it mean that I am the Seventh?' I asked. 'Please tell me.'

Luke rolled on to his side, propping himself up on one elbow. He looked at me with a troubled, sky-blue gaze. 'Miss Pandora, I can explain some things to you, but there are other things the dead cannot tell the living.'

*Supernatural rules.* Many of the rules were still a mystery to me. Why exactly did Sanguine have to be invited into a home, but not the lower floors of Celia's mansion? Why didn't New Yorkers 'see' Spektor, or remember it if they did catch a glimpse, as my date Jay briefly had? Why couldn't Luke explain where he was when he wasn't with me? Why hadn't anyone been able to explain the significance of the Seventh, beyond telling me that it was a gift and a responsibility and came with great powers?

'But why not? Why can't you tell me?'

Lieutenant Luke seemed hurt by my question, or perhaps my tone. He had mentioned this rule before and I had not forgotten. 'I can tell you some things, but not others,' he elaborated. 'It's like the door of the mansion. I may want to leave, but I can't. I am prevented.'

'But you're not dead anymore.'

His mouth opened, then closed again. For a while we were both silent.

He placed a hand on my bare shoulder, and I felt myself melt under his human touch. 'Miss Pandora, you are very powerful . . .'

'But?'

'But I hope you don't ever have to use your powers.'

His expression was grave. I wanted to press Luke for more, but the look on his face was too crushing. What could be so terrible about my powers?

'I don't feel very powerful,' I confessed and rolled on to my back again. I stared at the ceiling, frowning. I didn't have the heart to find out more. Not tonight, with all that had already happened. Not when the question was clearly so troubling, and when finally, for the very first time, I had him with me, as a man.

'Hold me,' I said. I had dreamed of his living embrace almost since I'd first met him. 'I want you to hold me tonight. Just hold me. Can we do that?'

Luke wrapped his warm, male, living arms around me, and I slid gratefully into his embrace. I rested my head on his broad, muscular chest and exhaled a deep breath that I felt from my toes to the top of my head. The fingers of my left hand gently gripped the opening of his shirt, brushing against the soft hairs there. He touched my hair, stroking it softly. His chest rose and fell with each miraculous breath he took.

It felt so good I never wanted him to leave again.

'You can trust me,' Lieutenant Luke whispered reassuringly, and kissed the top of my head as my heavy eyelids closed.

I'd never doubted it for a moment.

# CHAPTER
# FIFTEEN

*Luke . . .*

Faint light came in between the curtains, filtered by the fog of Spektor. It felt very late – or very early, and I peered at the clock with one squinting eye. It said it was seven. I'd barely slept. I rubbed my eyes.

Luke?

I sat up in a surge of panic. I was alone.

He'd disappeared with the light of day. Back to the mysterious spirit world that held him? Would he still have a solid form? Or had I dreamed that?

I swung my feet off the bed and breathed out a sad sigh. My bare toes hit something cold. It was Luke's sword, lying on the floor of my room. I stared at it. He'd been so pleased to have found it last night . . . why had he left it? Did it mean he was coming back soon? Or had something happened?

I heard movement in the kitchen and went to investigate. I found Great-Aunt Celia, perfectly made up and wearing her still-spotless red jacket and skirt, preparing tea. Her omnipresent

black widow's veil was in place. I wondered if she'd heard my
door open and put it on, or if she wore it constantly when I was
in the penthouse.

We exchanged nods, and she squeezed my wrist gently, but
said nothing. No doubt she sensed my desolate mood. It was
very unusual to see her in the morning, and I thought it likely
that she had not yet gone to bed. Perhaps she had even stayed
up to see me? I observed her for some time as she calmly made
the tea. I could feel her mind gently pressing against mine. She
was reading my thoughts. Somehow, it felt natural. If there was
anyone I was comfortable sharing my thoughts with, it was her.

She made my tea just how I liked it, and handed me a cup.
I thanked her.

'Something strange happened last night,' I said eventually.

'To your friend?'

'Yes.' It felt too surreal to comprehend, and now, in the
first light of day, I wondered if Luke had been flesh at all. My
mind continued to mull over the events of the day before –
the spider woman, Samantha, the trio of terrible Sanguine. I
thought of the poor man who'd been killed, and my stomach
lurched. 'The Sanguine from the second floor . . . they came
home while I was in their room with Samantha.'

'I see.'

'I tried to hide from them. We ended up – um, Lieutenant
Luke and I – ended up in a storage room of sorts.'

'Ended up? Wouldn't you say you were drawn there?'

I frowned. 'I wouldn't say that.' I hadn't been very happy
to be trapped in that room. I was drawn there? No . . . I
doubted that.

'Tell me what happened then,' my great-aunt suggested.

'Well, I guess Athanasia is recovering somewhere at the moment.' From having a face like pizza. 'And the other three brought this man back to their lair to feed. They . . . killed him.'

I felt a stab of guilt and renewed horror at the senselessness of the murder, but Celia only nodded. 'What else happened?'

'Well, the room we hid in was filled with a lot of stuff, trunks, a cabinet and trinkets, most of it junk.' She watched me as I spoke. 'There was a broken trumpet, for instance.'

'Séance props,' she said simply, and took a sip of her tea.

'Pardon?'

'Spiritualist séances were quite popular in Barrett's time. Séance means literally "a sitting", and in Victorian days it was popular to have a group join around a table for the purposes of contacting the dead. It was thought that the spirits might be called upon at will by a spirit medium, and that these spirits would show themselves to the room by making noises, playing with children's toys or musical instruments.'

The tambourine. The trumpet.

'Right.' I'd heard of séances, of course, but I'd heard time and time again that they were pure theatre, set up by charlatans looking to drain the bereaved of their dollars and sense. 'So séances were – are – real?'

'Some,' my wise great-aunt replied. 'Surely you wouldn't doubt that?'

Well, I had talked with an awful lot of dead people myself.

'There were frauds, of course – there will always be frauds – but there were some genuinely gifted mediums in those days,

as there are now, and some of the most prominent members
of society took part in legitimate séances. Spiritualism was not
so taboo as it is now.' She crossed her ankles and smoothed the
hem of her dress. 'Even Mary Lincoln organised numerous
séances at the White House.'

'With . . . *Abraham?*'

'Well, yes. Abraham Lincoln was very familiar with the
spirit world, and the undead for that matter. Remember, his
presidency was during a time of great spiritual uprising –
the agitation that occurs every one hundred and fifty years,
as I've mentioned. You've spoken to your friend about it?'
Celia said.

'A bit. I guess I became . . . distracted,' I admitted. Having
Lieutenant Luke as a man was quite a distraction, indeed.

'Your friend was mortal at the time of the last Seventh.
I suspect he may have great insight,' Celia said.

Luke had been a second lieutenant in the Lincoln Cavalry.
Lincoln himself was familiar with the undead? The last
Seventh had been alive during that time. Was it possible Luke
had known her?

My great-aunt watched me as I wrestled with those ideas.

'Pandora, the philosophers and thinkers of this age have
thrown out spiritualism with religion. They believe in chaos,
chance, happenstance. You would do well to unlearn those
ideas, and open yourself to the hidden meanings in events.
Very little happens by coincidence. The people you are drawn
to, the things you are drawn to . . . like that room filled with
significant objects. It may seem like chance, but is it really?'

I nodded. That was beginning to sink in.

'Tell me what happened next,' she said.

'Well, I was watching what was happening in the next room and Lieutenant Luke was doing something I couldn't see. He was drawn to a particular trunk in the room, I suppose, and he knew something was in there. And then I heard a noise and he began to glow. He was holding a sword. He said it was his sabre.' I thought about what happened next. 'And then it went dark again.'

'Just like that?'

'Just like that. Well, he took the sabre from its sheath, and there was a flash of heat, and it became dark.'

Celia gave me one of her significant looks.

'And this morning,' I said, 'he was gone but his sword remained. It's strange that he left it.'

'Perhaps he could not take it with him.'

'Okay, I'm totally confused now.'

'It seems likely his sabre has been imbued with some power, don't you think?'

I blinked. 'Like one big talisman?'

'Perhaps, in a manner of speaking. Metal conducts energy well. It sounds like this sabre of his was impregnated with something powerful, perhaps with the intention of communicating with or controlling the dead.'

*Necromancy.*

If Lieutenant Luke was buried with his sabre, it meant his remains *had* been disturbed. Perhaps Luke's uniform was in that trunk downstairs. Perhaps even his bones? Perhaps these were all props Barrett had used for séances, for his experiments, for attempts at communication with the spirit world. Dr Barrett had tried to communicate with Luke. He'd tried to tap into his spirit. Maybe he'd succeeded?

'Will Luke come back? Will he still be in corporeal form?'

'The moon may not be powerful enough tomorrow. But tonight . . . nearly anything will be possible tonight.'

'The . . . moon?'

She nodded. 'The moon is powerful, Pandora. Many powerful elements are at their peak at the full moon; things which are not possible at other times. Tonight is the Hunger Moon. When the moon is at its most full tonight, the power will be strongest.'

'I thought last night was the full moon?'

'The moon was strong and nearly full, but no. The Hunger Moon is tonight. Can't you feel it?'

I wasn't sure what I felt. 'What is a Hunger Moon?'

'The Hunger Moon, the Storm Moon . . . It comes this time every year in the winter. All moons have their own personality.'

'Hunger?'

'Hunger,' she confirmed.

I finished my cup of tea and contemplated what Morticia had said about crazies. Were there more crazies on the night of a Hunger Moon?

'You know,' I said, 'I was talking with my friend the receptionist the other day —'

'Morticia?'

'Yes. I found out she actually changed her name to Morticia. Isn't that funny?'

'Why?' Celia asked. She cocked her head, and sipped her tea, holding her cup with innate elegance.

'Why is that funny? You know . . . Morticia from *The Addams Family*? I mean it's kind of extra funny considering we live on Addams Avenue.'

'Well, it's hardly a coincidence,' Celia said and I blinked and put my cup down.

'Pardon?'

'Charles Addams has relatives here,' she told me.

I must have looked blank. *Charles?*

'*The Addams Family* creator. I think they named the street for his great-uncle. Or was it great-great-uncle? He orders magazines from Harold from time to time, I'm told. Really likes his reading. Shame I haven't run into him yet,' she mused. 'Those cartoons were quite droll.'

Charles Addams was in Spektor? Didn't he die years ago? *Oh.*

I was quiet for a moment. My wise Great-Aunt Celia finished her tea and placed it in the sink.

'Now, Pandora,' she said, bringing me back. 'When the moon reveals itself, call for your friend. Take his sword in your hand and call for him. After tonight I think you may find that your friend will be in spirit form until the next full moon nears.'

# CHAPTER
# SIXTEEN

A frigid wind picked up the edges of my hair, and blew ashen city dust into my eyes. I tucked a rogue strand of silky hair behind my ear and squinted at the little piece of crinkled paper again.

Arachne.

I had stopped on the corner of Seventh Avenue and 37th. The second address Pepper had given me led to a tall, 1920s brick building of faded, dusty brown, nestled among similar buildings of imposing height that towered over the sidewalks of the Garment District. It was a place for showrooms, workshops and sweatshops – not really the glamorous destination the moniker 'Fashion Avenue' evoked, I thought. The streets seemed fairly quiet for a Saturday.

I was dressed in my best jeans, a cream, silk, tie-top blouse Celia had designed in the fifties, my usual ballet flats and Celia's beautiful camel-coloured cashmere coat wrapped tight around me. The wind came up again and I pulled the collar up to my chin, studying the scrap of paper once more. In Pepper's small but legible scrawl, I could see the name 'Arachne' listed as the brand. After my discussion the evening before with

Great-Aunt Celia about the mythological origins of the name, I had to know if it was a coincidence. Coincidences did happen, didn't they? Regardless of what Celia, or Laurie Smith, believed. Arachne was a perfectly logical name for a knitwear brand, after all. Didn't Versace use Medusa as their logo? It hardly meant Medusa was real. Did it? Besides, I was too excited about the prospect of another night with Lieutenant Luke to be able to hang around Spektor till sundown, wondering if he would appear and what would happen between us. I also needed something to offer Pepper on Monday.

I stepped into the lobby of the building and scanned a large index of the building's businesses and occupants, set behind smudged glass.

ARACHNE. Twelfth floor.

Well, I seemed to have read Pepper's handwriting correctly.

I made my way to the lift and got in. Some of these old buildings still required an operator, but not this one. It had been refurbished sometime in the 1970s, I guessed. I pressed the round button for the twelfth floor, and it lit up in red. The doors closed with a series of squeaks and a dull thump, and the elevator began its ascent. When it stopped I got out and the doors rasped closed behind me. Stretched before me was a hallway of bland grey carpet and a series of doors marked with signage for an accountant and various importers. At the end was a white, rectangular sign that simply said:

ARACHNE

The hallway was still. Things were so quiet that I began to suspect the studio would not even be open.

I adjusted the leather satchel on my shoulder, walked up to the door and knocked. My fist sounded on the door with a hollow ring. Nothing looked out of the ordinary. When no one appeared, I took out my phone and dialled the number Pepper had given me. I pressed my ear to the door. It was dead quiet inside.

Strange.

It was then that I noticed a slip of handwritten paper on the floor at my feet. It looked like it had been taped to the door and had fallen off.

PICK UPS 13TH FLOOR

Hmm.

I strolled back to the elevator and pressed the button for level thirteen – I'd heard that some buildings, for superstitious reasons, didn't have a thirteenth floor, but this one obviously did. When the doors opened on level thirteen and I stepped out, I frowned. A cold, hard feeling formed in the base of my gut, though I could see no reason why. The single door ahead of me had no sign at all and I could hear the normal, muffled sounds of activity beyond it. From the sounds of footfalls and shuffling boxes it sounded like armies of staff were hard at work on this Saturday afternoon. So why was the sixth sense in my belly acting up?

Biting my lip, I took my cell phone out of my bag again, hit redial and listened. At first there was nothing, and then I heard a faint ring beyond the door. It rang once. Twice. Three times.

And stopped.

*Death.*

The cold feeling in my belly had me inching instinctively away from the door. Something had to be wrong. I would simply admit to Pepper that I hadn't made it on Friday afternoon after Smith & Co. I'd call for the quote instead, if she insisted. I had found the studio at least. It was indeed named after the mythological weaver. I was no longer sure I wanted to know more.

*Creeeeeeak.*

The door creaked open behind me and the sounds of bustling activity spilled into the quiet hallway.

With a lump in my throat I turned my head, half expecting to see the tall woman with the terrifying, freakish spider legs. But there was no one. Yet the door was open. Someone had opened it for me – or for someone else. I saw a flash of green as someone walked past the open door. Then another. The temptation was too great. I had come this far. I walked slowly up to the doorway and peered inside. The Arachne fashion house sure had dedicated workers. Two dozen men and women dressed in matching emerald green aprons emblazoned with the brand name walked back and forth carrying garments, packing and labelling parcels, stacking boxes. It was the factory for the brand.

*You have an overactive imagination, Pandora. You silly, silly girl.* I could hear my father's voice almost as if he were next to me.

I exhaled and shook my head, leaning on the doorframe with my satchel over my shoulder and my hands in my pockets. Such foolish panic. After a further moment of indecision I took the pad of paper and pen out of my bag.

I called out to no one in particular. 'Hello? Can I speak to the manager please? Or . . . the designer?'

Curiously, not one person answered me.

'Um, can I speak to whoever is in charge here?'

The workers ignored me as if I wasn't there at all. I coughed conspicuously, I waved, I asked again for assistance, but still the men and women walked back and forth like drones, set on their individual tasks.

Could they all be so rude?

The lack of sleep was really starting to show – what had I got? Three hours rest? Four? I blinked and rubbed my eyes, and when I opened them again the scene before me had morphed into something nightmarish. These workers were not people, they were spiders, swarming piles of spiders rising from the floor in the superficial shape of human beings, sculpted by an unseen hand, moving with a collective human-like gait, the green aprons suspended by a tide of tiny legs and bulbous arachnid bodies, the parcels transported by the gathering of hundreds of eight-legged creatures.

I opened my mouth to scream, but stopped. When I blinked again, I once again saw people walking back and forth. Normal, human people.

*What's happening to you?*

Disoriented, I shook my head. The eerie worker drones continued to ignore me. Unblinking and unwavering, they continued their tasks with the tireless focus of automatons.

I tried one more time. 'Excuse me? Can someone help me here?'

How odd. They still didn't answer me. I noticed they didn't talk to one another, either. They seemed not even to exchange eye contact. Hesitantly, I reached out one hand and touched the shoulder of a brown-haired woman as she walked past me pushing a rack of swinging garments sheathed in thin plastic sleeves. 'Excuse me —' I began. My fingers made contact with her shoulder, and her shoulder dissolved under my touch.

'My god!'

Like falling dominoes, once touched, the woman broke down, her form falling away like melting molasses until a puddle of writhing spiders was left on the floor where she'd stood. The rack of clothes she'd been pushing rolled to a halt. After a breathless moment, in which I found myself spellbound by the spectacle before me, the spiders climbed one upon another, beginning to reassemble themselves from the ground up, forming feet and ankles and legs . . .

No. Way.

My jaw dropped, and the pen and paper slipped from my hand and hit the concrete floor with a slap. With heightened horror I noticed that the other workers had stopped. Silence descended on the large space. In unison two dozen sets of eyes (or was it thousands of eyes?) trained on the interloper in their midst, bodies turning stiffly to face me. Racks stopped moving. Parcels were dropped. Tasks were abandoned. The expressionless creatures took one step towards me, then another.

Oh boy. Oh boy . . .

Time to go.

Finally I'd been noticed, but I wasn't so sure that was a good thing.

I turned to run out the door and down the hallway back towards the elevator that I prayed was still waiting on the thirteenth floor, but the exit had already been blocked by three of the drones. I backed away from the circling spider people, my eyes still deceiving me; one second showing my attackers as slack-faced humans, and the next revealing them to be thousands of tiny, unnaturally bound spiders that formed them. I reached around in my satchel, backing up, my mind ticking over furiously. A subway ticket, a hairbrush, lipstick, a book, a bag of rice. Darn it! The hairspray was gone, though it would take a whole lot more than that to take down so many aggressors. I didn't even have an umbrella to swipe at them. I slid the leather satchel from my shoulder and began to swing it around me in wide arcs like a shot-putter. The bag connected with one head, then another, taking them clean off. Once hit, the headless figures melted into the floor as the woman had done, but now, instead of reassembling in their human forms, they rushed towards me in a growing swarm on the ground.

Could these spiders behave in this way through minds of their own? No. They were being directed. But where was the puppeteer? Where was Arachne?

A mob of workers had circled me, and spiders were moving towards me steadily across the floor. There were too many. In minutes I would literally be covered in them from head to toe. The first had reached my shoes and begun moving up my jeans. I screamed and hopped and tried to kick them away, but for every one I flicked off, three more took their place.

It was only then that I spotted the emergency exit, and the fire hose folded behind glass beside it. I sprinted to it without hesitation, across the grim, seething carpet of arachnids, my ankles becoming ever heavier with their number. Before I even had time to think of what to do next I had pulled the fire alarm, smashed the glass, hauled the end of the fire hose out and turned it on.

The water came on in a powerful gush.

Too powerful.

Within seconds the emergency fire hose threw me off my feet with a violence I had not bargained for. I hit the concrete floor hard on my tailbone and screamed out, but by some miracle I still had hold of it. I gripped the wide head of the hose with white-knuckled determination and straddled it as it propelled me forward across the wet floor, pulling my shoes off, sliding sideways, wriggling and bucking, the projection of its spray hitting the tops of the standing creatures first, toppling their unnatural balance and dispersing them across the floor of the factory along with the racks of clothing and cardboard boxes blown sideways in the water blast.

For a confused minute I rode the fire hose like it was a giant, angry anaconda, and when I finally let go I was launched off it, stumbling to my knees before narrowly gaining my footing on the slippery floor. I sprinted barefoot across the factory floor as the hose arced wildly, all the time fearing the very real possibility that it would flick backwards and knock me out – or worse. In the confusion I had barely noticed the water coming from the sprinklers above me, and the ear-splitting sound of the alarm.

I threw the heavy fire exit door open and ran down the concrete stairs, flicking off ever fewer spiders from my jeans, my coat, my satchel. Thirteen floors later, I was water-soaked and oxygen deprived when I hit the open air at the alley behind the building.

I doubled over, held my knees and sucked in air.

My god. The spiders.

I ripped Celia's coat off, flipped it inside out and stomped on it on the ground, killing the last remaining creatures that clung to its outside. A final, poisonous black widow spider rode the edge of my jeans leg, and I flung it off with a yell and a full body shiver that would have seemed hysterical to anyone watching.

I was out. It was over.

From now on Pepper could get her own bloody quotes, I decided.

# CHAPTER
# SEVENTEEN

I looked like I'd been dragged under a subway car. Through a lake.

I emerged from the mouth of the narrow back alley on to 37th Street, barefoot and dishevelled, looking every bit like one of Manhattan's many homeless people. Celia's coat was damp and streaked with dirt and the remains of a lot of eight-legged dead things I didn't want to think about for the moment. I was red faced from exertion, and my mascara had run in smudged streaks. My bones ached. Especially my tailbone. My feet were soiled and wet.

I was not going to go back for my ballet flats.

I still had my satchel, though I doubted it would ever be the same. Two quarts of water had poured out of it. I'd shaken it out in the alley, so at least now there was no longer anything living inside it, which was a small blessing, though my subway ticket, too, appeared to have been killed in the excitement. I held the damp corner of it and scowled. Resigned to my fate, I bowed my head and began to make my way back towards the subway station with a kind of damp shuffle.

I could no longer say that I didn't kill spiders. My mother would not be pleased.

I wasn't even at the corner of Fashion Avenue before I had the distinct feeling I was being watched. No one watched homeless people in Manhattan, I knew. Homeless people were conveniently invisible. Yet someone was looking at me.

*Oh god. What now?*

I looked up to find an imposingly tall, pale man, dressed in a sharp suit and dark sunglasses, standing before the open door of a sleek black luxury car. He looked like someone's bodyguard.

*Vlad!*

I'd never in my life been so happy to see Celia's towering chauffeur. I was so relieved I almost wanted to kiss him. *Almost.*

'Oh, thank you,' I gasped and slid gratefully into the back with an embarrassing squeak across the leather seats. He closed the door behind me and I belted myself in. Nothing in Vlad's expression revealed shock at my appearance. Without a word he drove me back to Spektor. I didn't ask how he knew where I was. I knew he wouldn't answer anyway.

He never did.

I stepped out of Vlad's car on Addams Avenue, slightly more composed but soaked to the bone, just as the final moments of a violet purple sunset faded from the dark sky in the distance. The streets were eerily calm – in other words, just as I would expect. The familiar stillness was comforting.

I'd come to feel safer in this strange place than on the streets of New York where terrifying goddesses roamed free and factory workers could prove to be nothing more than clumps of amassed spiders, held together by some sinister spell. It said a lot for my new-found resilience that I didn't want to just go to my room and hide under the bed. Or check myself into a psychiatric hospital. Tonight was special. Soon the full moon would emerge. If Celia was right about its effects, I would be able to call Luke. After all I'd been through, the thought of his warm embrace kept me going.

I thanked Vlad, and instead of walking straight to the door of the mansion I took a quick detour to Harold's Grocer. The bell chimed when I entered.

'Hi Harold,' I called out. 'It's me.'

The store was no less musty than last I'd seen it. The glass-fronted fridge hummed in the back of the shop. I walked to it and grabbed myself some fresh milk and cheddar cheese. I'd become absolutely ravenous. I was just placing these items on the counter next to the old-fashioned cash register when Harold made his entrance.

'Well, hello there, Pandora English,' he said, emerging from the back in his plaid shirt and belted work pants, smiling and trailing debris. At the sight of me, his expression came over shocked. 'You look like you've had a big day.'

I nodded. 'I sure have, Harold.' I tucked my wet hair behind my ears and stuck close to the counter self-consciously so he didn't notice my bare feet.

'Here,' he said, and pulled a clean-looking rag out from behind the counter. 'Sorry, I don't have a towel.'

'Oh, thanks,' I said gratefully. I dried myself off a bit more, but of course I was still damp, and worst of all, Celia's cashmere coat looked like it had been stomped on. Which of course it had. I didn't look forward to showing her.

'How is that great-aunt of yours? Such a lovely lady . . .'

'She's well, Harold. She's very well. It's the Hunger Moon tonight, she says.'

'Ah yes. The Hunger Moon. Could be eventful,' he replied with a wink.

I thought of Luke and smiled. 'Yes, I think it will be eventful. Harold, if you were entertaining, say, a soldier from the early Civil War, what do you think he might like in the way of . . . I don't know . . . a welcome drink?'

Harold gave me a jovial nod. 'Have a friend, do we? Very good then. Very good. Well, I've met a few fellows from that war. They all seem to like Asses' Milk.'

'I beg your pardon?'

'My apologies, Miss Pandora. I don't mean to shock you, but that's what they called it. It's only rum and lemonade. 'Twas quite popular.'

'Goodness,' I remarked, making a face.

'You could always give him a Splitting Headache. Rum, lime juice, cinnamon, ginger, nutmeg.'

I thought about that. 'Sounds a bit complicated for me. I don't think I'd make a very good bartender. You see, I don't drink,' I explained and bit my lip.

'Of course not, Miss Pandora. Of course not.' He brought a finger to his green-tinged mouth.

'What about something simple?' I pressed.

'Well, perhaps he'd like a nice glass of apple cider?'

'Apple cider? That sounds more like it,' I said, relieved. 'That might make a nice welcome drink.'

'Very well then, Miss Pandora.'

He disappeared for a moment and I heard boxes being moved and mysterious clanging sounds from the back of the shop. Soon Harold returned to the counter with a tall bottle. It had one of those glass stoppers at the top and it didn't have a label. 'Homemade apple cider,' he announced.

'You made this?'

'One of the fellas here in Spektor makes it. It's top notch. Maybe heat it up in a mug. Your friend might like that. It's nice in winter. Hot apple cider was a treat for the boys in the battlefield, I believe.'

'Thanks Harold. Good thinking.' I hoped Luke would like it, or appreciate the thought at least. 'Great-Aunt Celia mentioned you sometimes get the papers. I suppose I can get some in town tomorrow, or when I head in to work on Monday, but you wouldn't happen to have anything here?'

'Wanting to keep up on the news?'

'Well, yes. I've had a little trouble lately,' I admitted.

He rubbed his chin. 'Mmmm, yes. With Arachne.'

My eyes widened. 'You've heard?'

'There's a bit of a grapevine here in Spektor. I'd heard she was in town. Some of the residents are a bit nervous, to be honest.'

I felt my chest tighten. 'Oh dear.'

'I imagine you'll want to watch yourself.'

*No kidding.*

Harold ducked under the counter, giving me a striking view of the green swaying tufts of hair on his head. I heard papers rustle just beyond my view. 'We used to have a weekly in Spektor.' Harold's voice sounded slightly muffled. 'A community newsletter of sorts – you know, all the events and things. The lady who produced it moved on. Regrettably, there's not been anything since.'

I thought about the quiet streets of Spektor and wondered what events there could possibly be to announce in a weekly newsletter. And, more importantly, where does one go when one 'moves on' from Spektor?

Harold stood up, looking a little more dishevelled than before, and placed a broadsheet on the counter. He tried to straighten his collar and it let off a puff of dust.

I sneezed.

'Sorry 'bout that, Miss Pandora. Best I can do for you is yesterday's *New York Times*. That of any interest to you?'

'No, that's okay, Harold. Thanks anyway.' There hadn't been much on the missing designers in Friday's paper, and I suspected the incident with Laurie Smith would go completely unreported, anyway. I resolved to call him on Monday to see if he was okay.

'Sorry I couldn't be of more help,' Harold said.

'You were of great help,' I assured him, holding the bottle of apple cider aloft. Harold bagged my groceries, put it all on Celia's tab (which she still insisted upon, despite my protestations) and I headed towards the mansion.

I walked through the gathering dark, thinking of Luke and wondering what would happen tonight under the Hunger

Moon. Would Luke appear? Could he enlighten me about the spider goddess and her minions and what I could do about her? Could we leave the mansion together? Could we walk down this same stretch of road, and beyond?

*Could I crawl into his arms and never leave?*

I was several metres from the mansion when the front door opened.

I hoped for Celia.

What I saw was Brunette, Blonde and Redhead.

*No.*

The fearsome trio spilled out of the mansion in tight tops and thigh-high splits, ready for another night of hunting. Blonde stepped over something on the doorstep, and stopped. She picked it up.

'Pretty,' I heard her say.

'Give me that.' Brunette snatched it away.

It was only then that they noticed me. I had paused on the sidewalk, holding my groceries.

'Well, if it isn't meddling Miss Country.'

'That's not even clever, you know,' I said. I'd stopped in my tracks.

Blonde observed my dishevelled state and let out a sharp, amused chuckle. 'Wet-look hair is so early nineties. And your coat —'

'Leave me alone.'

They began to approach me and I found myself wishing Vlad hadn't already driven off.

'You didn't seem to want to be left alone last night. Actually you seemed to be trespassing,' Redhead said.

I opened my mouth to explain what had happened, and that's when I saw the pretty thing in Brunette's hands. I paused. 'Um, what's that you're holding?'

Brunette held up the beautiful jet black and emerald green package, satin bows shining. 'What's it to you?'

One of the parcels. Just like the one at Victor Mal's. Just like the one Laurie Smith opened. The boxes at Arachne's studio were probably packed with these pretty parcels.

*Oh god. The spider goddess sends them to her enemies. And now she has sent one to me. She knows where I live.*

'Whom is it addressed to?'

'Me,' she said, and gave a smug grin. Blonde and Redhead giggled.

I took a step forward. 'Listen to me, you really don't want to open that. Trust me,' I said. Slowly, I lowered my groceries to the pavement.

'Is that so?'

'Yes. That's so.'

'Watch me.'

I held my hands up. 'Don't,' I pleaded. 'Don't open it. Trust me.'

She tore the bow off the top in a show of defiance, and ripped the box open. The parcel and its wrapping fluttered to the ground, leaving her holding what looked like a large, beautiful, cream-coloured pashmina shawl.

'Nice.' Brunette flicked her fingers and it unfolded. She looked at the tag. 'A-r-a-c-h-n-e. I haven't heard of that label.'

*Arachne.* 'Oh god, put it down!'

Instead, she slung it around her shoulders. It wrapped around her elegantly, and she did a little spin. 'Jealous?' she said, as I stood with my hands out in front of me, bracing myself.

Blonde fondled the wrap. 'Mmmm, soft and silky. I want it.'

'Well, you can't have it,' Brunette teased. 'When Athanasia's not here, I'm the head of the gang, and I say it's mine. Mine, mine, mine . . .'

And then the wrap moved.

I noticed it before she did. The edge of it furled around Brunette's shoulder, and it might not have seemed strange, except that there was no wind to push it there.

And then things moved quickly. The fabric sprang outwards and grew, suddenly opening around her like the mouth of a giant Venus flytrap, and in a flash it folded back on itself, enveloping the brunette Sanguine from head to toe. I barely heard her scream, muffled as it was by the constricting fabric. Her friends stepped backwards, confused.

'Do something! She'll suffocate!' I yelled.

But the two vampires just stared with their mouths open as their friend was enveloped in the silky cocoon. She began to struggle inside it, doubling over, and soon the whole mass began to vibrate and shake as I'd seen it do at the Smith & Co workshop. The spiders. It was filled with spiders.

'What *is* it?' Redhead cried.

Brunette had callously killed someone right in front of me only the night before, yet I couldn't just stand there. I had to do something. I left my position on the sidewalk and ran forward. 'I'll get you out!' I yelled. 'Try and hold still.' Blonde and Redhead cowered at the door of the mansion, uncharacteristically silent. 'Help me hold her still.'

But I couldn't get her out. Without the sharp point of scissors or a knife there was no way to penetrate the silky web. The webbing was sticky, soft and slightly translucent, but somehow as strong as piano wire. My struggles were useless, and my fingertips became raw with the effort. I drew blood.

'Someone! Quick!' I yelled to the open street, but there was no one to help. What could anyone have done anyway?

There was no time left.

In minutes the cocoon deflated on the sidewalk, shrivelling up as if it did not hold the brunette Sanguine at all. And indeed, it didn't. It was empty, sucked clean, apart from the hundreds of spiders that spilled from its spent husk and filed away into the gutter.

# CHAPTER
# EIGHTEEN

I knocked, let myself into the penthouse and placed my groceries on the counter. I leaned there for a while with my head down, reeling.

*The spider goddess knows where I live.*

It was only a matter of time before I encountered her again. She and her horrible spider people. And now I was sure what had happened to the missing designers.

They wouldn't be coming back.

I was desperate to tell Celia what had happened, and to ask for her help, but she appeared to be out. The lights had been off when I came in. Her fox stole was gone from the Edwardian hatstand. The penthouse was quiet. I stood in the kitchen for a while, wondering what to do. The curtains were open in the lounge room and the moon was full. The Hunger Moon. Beams of moonlight were creating shadows with the furniture in the lounge room, and with all those strange objects that Celia had collected over the years. Inanimate shapes seemed alive. The butterflies appeared to move. I could feel the pull of the moon, just as Celia had suggested.

It seemed likely I did indeed have a big night ahead of me. I hoped I would not be spending it alone.

In times of trouble and anxiety, rituals could be comforting. I took my time in the claw-foot bathtub as I washed my hair with a sweet-scented shampoo, and luxuriated in the soapy water, trying my best to focus on Lieutenant Luke and not the shocking visions with which I had been confronted. To Luke's credit, I found it wasn't as hard as I'd thought. I recalled our kiss in the storage room and the way it had made me feel; the sensation of his warm, human embrace, the way his chest rose and fell with each breath. I was so focused on my romantic recollections that I almost didn't notice the tender bruises coming up on my knees and the ache of my tailbone. I carefully shaved my legs and towelled myself off, taking my time drying my hair. I walked out to the kitchen around seven, feeling excited about the evening ahead. I lit the stove and heated up some of the apple cider in a pot, and filled a couple of mugs with it. I looked at the mugs and cocked my head. What did one serve with hot apple cider? I took a couple of biscuits from the cupboard and laid them out on a plate, and then returned to my room to arrange it all on the Victorian writing desk. I brushed my long hair once more, and adjusted my top in the mirror. I changed once. Twice. And finally I put the same white blouse back on with my second favourite jeans. My favourite jeans were rather the worse for wear after the fire hose incident. I didn't want to look like I was trying too hard to impress Luke. Even though clearly I was.

*Oh, this is silly.*

*Here goes.* I threw open the curtains of my room and looked at the fat, full moon glowing in the sky over Manhattan. I picked up Lieutenant Luke's sabre, feeling the cool grip in my hand. The obsidian ring began to warm on my finger as soon as I touched it.

I held the sabre aloft. 'Luke,' I said aloud. 'Lieutenant Luke.'

I waited.

There was nothing. The sabre was heavier than I'd thought. My slim arm began to shake and I felt my heart shrink a little in my chest. *Please?*

I closed my eyes and tried again. I held the sabre with all my strength. 'Lieutenant Luke,' I said, gripping the sabre firmly. 'Come to me.'

After a brief moment that seemed like an eternity, I felt a cool mist descend at my side. Just as Luke's form began to materialise, there was a shocking flash of heat, and he appeared in full human form, clutching the sabre, his two large, masculine hands over my one small hand. We both seemed shocked to find ourselves together so suddenly, and for a time, we stood with our hands layered over the grip of his cavalry sword. Our eyes engaged. The bright blue of his eyes had not faded one bit. They didn't seem to glow, exactly – not tonight – but they were so bright I felt I could see my own reflection. Finally we both let our arms relax, and I let go. My arm was tingling. Luke held up his sabre, and we watched it glint in the moonlight. He returned it to the metal sheath hanging from the leather belt around his waist. He seemed to wear it permanently now.

'Welcome,' I said, as my body thrilled at his closeness.

He smiled at me with his eyes and I exhaled.

I moved to the desk and grabbed a cup. 'I'm not sure if . . . you know . . . you can drink . . . but h-here is . . .' I stuttered. 'I made this for you,' I finally managed to explain.

He took the cup and examined it for a moment. A smile spread across his handsome, clean-shaven face. He raised the hot apple cider to his lips and took a cautious sip. A long sigh of pleasure escaped from him. A century and a half was quite a long time between drinks, I supposed.

'Thank you, Miss Pandora.' He reached for the other cup and placed it in my hand. The handle felt warm. I brought it to my lips, and he raised his cup again.

We drank.

'Oh, goodness,' I said. Apple cider tasted stronger than I'd expected. Much stronger.

'That tastes . . . Heavens that tastes good,' Luke remarked.

'Doesn't it?' I gulped mine down eagerly. 'I'll get us some more. Don't go anywhere,' I said, and then found myself laughing.

'I promise I won't go anywhere, Miss Pandora.'

I stopped in the doorway. 'Good.'

We talked and talked. It seemed almost as if I could not stop the torrent of words that poured out of me.

I told Lieutenant Luke all about what had happened with the parcel on the steps of the mansion and the spider workers I'd seen at Arachne's factory warehouse. There was little doubt in my mind that I had the poor, trapped souls of the Triangle Shirtwaist fire to thank for my escape. Factories were never the same after that landmark tragedy, and the safety measures that had been put in place since had saved my life. Even if no one had designed fire hoses to combat hordes of spider people. I told him how Vlad had mysteriously found me and driven me home, and how I'd hoped so badly that Celia was right about the full moon, and how worried I'd been when I'd woken up with only his sword. Luke was relieved I was okay, and once again he earnestly vowed to protect me. I downed cup after cup of Harold's apple cider and the horrors I'd seen slowly began to feel distant. I found I felt a bit strange. My body was very relaxed, and my brain even more so. But that didn't stop me from asking ever more touchy questions.

'Luke,' I said, leaning into his chest. 'Do you think your uniform is downstairs in that trunk? Or even your . . . remains?'

I hated to use the word, and as soon as I did, I had a horrible visual of what the word meant. Whether I liked it or not, Luke was a dead man, and somewhere in the world was a rotted and bare skeleton that belonged to him. Maybe it was buried in a grave, or perhaps it was waiting to be discovered in Barrett's things. Either way, Luke had a discarded human body. And it wasn't the lovely one I was looking at. It was a horrible thought.

'That trunk held my sabre, but nothing else that belonged to me. Of that I am certain,' he said, taking a deep breath – a wonderfully human-like, living breath.

I wasn't sure how he could be certain, but I trusted that he was, and frankly I was relieved to hear it.

'Okay,' I said. 'I have to ask something else, too.' I took another sip of apple cider. I thought of the look on his face when I'd asked about my powers. 'My great-aunt said you would know something about the significance of the Seventh. Or what happened one hundred and fifty years ago?'

He appeared hesitant.

When he didn't speak, I felt an uncharacteristic surge of impatience. 'Luke, maybe you are trying to protect me, or trying not to scare me, but the fact is I was nearly torn apart by a woman with spider legs. A woman who can control thousands of spiders like a conductor can an orchestra. *She* knows what I am. I need to know. Tell me what I am, Luke.'

Lieutenant Luke nodded stiffly and I felt the intimacy between us fade. He took a step back. 'It is known that every one hundred and fifty years the forces of the Underworld rise up.'

*It is known?* 'The Underworld. You mean Hell? I can tell you, the press may talk about the end of the world every once in a while, but they certainly never talk about Hell rising up!'

'Not Hell,' he corrected me. 'Not as they taught it when I was mortal.'

'What is the Underworld then? Is it like with Persephone and Hades and Pluto and all that?'

Luke shook his head. 'Not exactly.' He frowned and looked down at his drink. 'I want to articulate it . . . but I can't. I am prevented from speaking of some of these things.'

'You are? Still?'

'Yes.'

'Even though you are human right now?'

'I am still bound by the rules of the dead.'

Those darned supernatural rules. It was so unfair. I stuck my lower lip out, and then took another sip of the cider.

'You may want to slow down with that,' Luke said quietly, and looked at me with concern.

'What are you talking about?' I replied, and took another large sip. 'Do you know what my powers are?' I demanded.

Luke closed his eyes, and when he spoke, he sounded far away. 'Every one hundred and fifty years there is a Seventh. She is the mediator between the living and the dead. She is a powerful agent for rebalance —'

'A powerful agent? It makes me sound like some kind of cleaning product.'

Luke didn't laugh. He looked at me strangely. 'There will be an agitation,' he explained.

Celia had used that word, I remembered. 'The agitation has already started, hasn't it?'

He nodded soberly. 'Yes. Dark forces are gathering. Beings, once content in the shadows, are starting to show themselves.'

*The Blood Countess. The spider goddess. And whom else?*

'Then comes the revolution. The Seventh has a very important role to play in the revolution.'

'What revolution, exactly?'

Luke looked down. The air between us seemed to be growing colder. My head felt strange. I had become a touch combative, but I couldn't seem to help it. Was it the full moon? The topic? The lack of sleep?

'It is the revolution of the dead. The rising up of the Underworld. The Seventh must stand between mankind and their destruction. But . . . it will never come to that,' he said, still averting his eyes.

'They won't rise up?'

He straightened his head and looked at me steadily. 'It is not certain that . . .'

'It's not certain that what?' I demanded. 'What is it that you don't want to tell me?'

'I . . . I can't,' he said. 'I want to. But that is all I can say.'

I thought of all the spirits I'd encountered or spoken to, and all the pain it had caused my parents. The child psychologists. The strange looks from the neighbours. Why hadn't my mother told me that she understood? That she knew what it was about? I'd heard my mum and dad fight over me so many times when I was a child. Maybe if they were still alive they would have finally accepted the things that made me different? Maybe my mother would have eventually opened up about what she was – what *I* was. How much had she known? Had she known what my future held? Had she known about this prophecy?

*You will stand between mankind and their destruction . . .*

'Miss Pandora?'

I had been quiet for a long time. I felt distant and over-whelmed. 'This prophecy . . . will it come true?' I finally asked.

'No one knows if it will come to pass. But there are believers.'

I watched Luke's handsome face carefully. 'What about you? Are you a believer?'

Deep lines of tension appeared across his square jaw and sculpted cheekbones. 'Miss Pandora, the dead and the living are opposing forces. Do you not see? The dead make way for the living to inhabit this world, and eventually some of the dead will want their old world back.'

I blinked. 'Is that what *you* want?'

'No,' he said firmly. 'No, I do not. It is not the proper way of things.' He shook his head. 'No, the earthly plane is for the living, and there should be peace for the dead when living is over.'

But Luke didn't have peace, did he?

'There are those who covet the living realm,' he explained. 'There are those who will try to conquer the living. The revolution came one hundred and fifty years ago and failed. The living who witnessed it are now gone.'

'Dead.'

'Yes.'

'You were one of them,' I guessed.

He was still, but his gaze was steady.

So Luke *was* there when the last Seventh was alive. Celia was right about that.

*Did that mean . . . ?*

'The Civil War. Are you saying that the Civil War was a revolution of the dead?'

He did not answer, but I could see from his face that I had hit on the truth.

'That's . . . that's not possible. No!' I protested. I backed away from him until my back was at the wall.

'History books can be rewritten, Miss Pandora. Memories can be erased.'

I knew that too well. I brought a shaking hand to my mouth. My eyes welled up. 'No. You're lying. It's not true. It's not!'

I went to sit on the edge of the bed, trembling. Lieutenant Luke walked over to me and placed a strong, human hand on my shoulder. I shook it off.

'I can see you are upset,' he said. 'I am sorry, Miss Pandora. These revelations must be troubling. You will need some time.' He returned his cup to the Victorian writing desk and looked around uncertainly. 'Thank you for the cider. And thank you for this,' he said, looking down at his physical body. 'However temporary it may be. I am in your debt.'

Lieutenant Luke bowed his head to me, his cap held in his hands. And then I watched him walk out of my bedroom.

I didn't stop him.

*You will stand between mankind and their destruction,* I thought, and felt my stomach roil and heave.

# CHAPTER
# NINETEEN

*The designers. This is what happened to them.*

I found myself back in Arachne's factory, though I didn't know how I'd got there. The walls and floor were white concrete, and beyond the stacks of boxes and racks of clothes I could see Arachne herself weaving great tapestries with giant black spider legs that reached to the ceiling. Her spider people were at work all around me, their deceptively human faces slack and expressionless. I recognised the face of Victor Mal among them. *The designers. She turned them into her spiders. This is what happened to them,* I thought. Brunette was there too, also a drone. Now that I knew what lay beneath the illusion of that superficial skin and bone I watched the creatures with trepidation as they moved back and forth, back and forth, some passing only inches from me, carrying the awful black and emerald parcels, destined for victims unknown.

I had to get out before I was discovered. Before Arachne did the same to me. Before I became one of these awful, mindless creatures.

*What do I do?*

The fire exit was still there, but there was no fire hose. I didn't have my satchel to knock them down. When they noticed me, I would be in terrible danger. Motionless and terrified, I stood stock-still amongst them, breathing quietly, as silent and invisible as I could manage. Slowly, I tilted my head and looked down at myself. I too was wearing one of the green aprons.

*No!*

A thunderous knocking came from the fire exit, and in seconds the heavy door swung open and Second Lieutenant Luke Thomas stepped through – Luke, my friend, my would-be boyfriend, the beautiful Civil War hero come to rescue me. I felt a rush of relief, and I tried to step towards him but my legs would not budge.

*What's wrong with me?*

'Luke!' I dared to yell across the warehouse floor, no longer fearing the drones, no longer fearing Arachne in his presence.

Lieutenant Luke valiantly held his unsheathed sword aloft, a heroic vision, and the spider people stopped what they were doing and cowered, as if answering a silent command.

'Luke! Help me! I can't move!' I called out to him. 'I can't move my legs!'

And then he looked at me across the warehouse floor.

It was then I saw his pallid complexion, the blood around his mouth, the awful, ropey blue veins that wove across deathly white skin. His uniform was tattered and blood stained, and worst of all, his eyes . . . his beautiful, bright blue eyes were beautiful no more. They bulged round in their sockets, bloodshot and terrifying. He had no eyelids.

My pleas froze on my lips.

The creature that was Luke marched towards me, parting the spider people like water with the end of his bloodied sword. Arachne's workers fell to pieces around him, melting into pools of seething spiders, and I worried fleetingly that I might do the same at his deadly touch. He opened his mouth to speak and I realised with horror that Luke's teeth were pointed and stained. How had I never noticed his sharp teeth? His lidless eyes? The menace of his glowing red glare?

'Which do you choose, Pandora?' he demanded in a booming voice. 'Will you be one of them, or one of *us*?'

And I saw his army. Behind him, wave after wave of bloody revenants appeared; a grisly army of dead Civil War soldiers gathering at his back in perfect, deadly formation.

*The Revolution of the Dead.*

I looked down and saw that my hands were made of spiders.

I screamed.

# CHAPTER
# TWENTY

'Miss Pandora, wake up!'

I sat up, rubbed my tired eyes and looked at the room through a foggy filter of sleep. I was in my delicate white linen nightie in my four-poster bed in Celia's penthouse. My legs were caught in a bundle of sheets so I kicked them free. I'd been having an awful nightmare – something about spiders and dead soldiers – and I could see I'd been tossing and turning. Lace-edged pillows were scattered on the floor. It was still dark out but moonlight was streaming in from the half-open curtains of my bedroom windows.

The Hunger Moon.

'Luke?'

'Pandora, wake up. Hurry!'

I shook myself into a more wakeful consciousness. Luke stood by the edge of my bed, extending a hand to me. I took it in mine, feeling the blissful realness of it. Yes, he was still flesh. It felt good to hold his hand.

'I tried knocking on your door but you didn't answer,' he said, sounding tense. Even with his brow furrowed he looked handsome in his blue uniform, his leather riding boots gleaming, his frockcoat open and shirt unbuttoned casually to reveal a glimpse of tanned chest.

*The Civil War.*

I recalled the horrible truths he'd told me. And how badly I'd reacted. 'I'm sorry about last night, Luke. I don't know what came over me. I guess I was a little overwhelmed.'

Despite my words, Luke continued to look deeply concerned. And distracted. His jaw was set tight, and his eyes were troubled beneath pinched brows. 'Miss Pandora, you must get up now. Quickly.'

At his urging I finally slid out from between the sheets and let him guide me to the window. The hardwood floor felt cool under my bare toes. My body seemed to take longer than usual to get moving. My head ached dully. And now I remembered the apple cider I'd got from Harold's Grocer. Had it made me a bit . . . tipsy?

'Look,' Lieutenant Luke said.

He peered down the street and I followed his intense gaze. Something was different, very different, about the main street of Spektor. It took my eyes a moment to adjust under the cool light of the full moon.

*The street!*

The street was moving.

When I saw what was causing the illusion, I gasped. Any remnants of sleep fell off me at once. My adrenaline kicked in.

A seething army of eight-legged creatures moved down the pavement of Spektor, they rushed across the road and along the sidewalks, and poured over the street lamps, moving towards Number One Addams Avenue, towards *us*. I squinted and made out the shapes of thousands and thousands of spiders – black widows and wolf spiders, orb-weavers and tarantulas. They were all different sizes, some black and some with tiny markings, and they were all headed our way. Some were already climbing the lamp post outside my window, while others were climbing the buildings.

Unfortunately, this was not all.

'*There*,' Luke said under his breath, and pointed. At the north end of the street the mass of spiders was at its greatest height. It rose a full, horrifying two storeys. Atop this seething blanket of arachnids was a robed figure. The spider goddess herself rode the wave of eight-legged horror, her hands held aloft, fingers splayed, as if she were a conductor.

Arachne.

I covered my gaping mouth with my hand, speechless.

'I fear she is coming for you, Miss Pandora. You can't stay here.'

Luke was right. I looked around the room, my legs were tingling with adrenaline and fear. She was after me and I couldn't just wait for her to get me. I had to do something. But what . . .? How could I escape a two-storey wave of spiders?

It was then I heard the strange scratching on the glass of my bedroom windows. A multitude of legs scratching to get in. The first wave of spiders had reached our penthouse floor. Thousands more were behind them. 'Quick!' I cried, as the bottom corners of the windowpanes began to fill with spiders. Luke swiftly closed the one partially open window to keep them out, and stomped on a small swarm on the floor that had already infiltrated my room.

'No! Don't kill them!' I protested.

Luke stopped to look at me.

'On second thought,' I said, 'do what you have to.'

'Miss Pandora, the windows will not hold. We need to get you out of here.'

He was right.

I ran into the main lounge room and checked that the windows were shut tight. It might give us more time, at the very least.

'Look! Webbing!' I cried.

The spiders were weaving a giant web across the windows so I couldn't escape. Soon, Luke was at my side with his frockcoat done up, his belt tight and his sword in place. Wordlessly, we ran from the apartment to the elevator outside.

We peered down.

'I think they are building a web to cocoon the whole building,' I said. Would they . . . *swallow up* the whole building? Could they? As they had done with Brunette? As they tried to do with Laurie?

The lights were on in the lobby downstairs and what we saw there made my heart sink even further. Already many hundreds of spiders had squeezed through the small gaps in the front door and were moving steadily across the tiles of the lobby, blackening the floor like spilled ink. There was little doubt where they were headed. They would soon climb the lacework on the lift and swarm the penthouse. The laws of the Sanguine did not limit them. These spiders needed no invitation; their mistress's orders were enough to see them enter our top-floor sanctuary.

*Celia. Where was Celia?*

I raced back inside the penthouse and pounded on Celia's door. 'Celia!' I used the key she'd given me and stepped inside the antechamber. The only light came from three lit candles – one white, one red and one black – sitting on the low carved table. The red candle was larger than the others, and its flame danced high above the wick.

'The pentacle,' Luke observed, noticing the carving.

I nodded.

'I thought she was out, but . . .' I rushed to the first of the doors in the antechamber. 'I have to make sure she is not sleeping.'

'I cannot pass through the walls,' Luke said with regret. 'I can't check if she is here.'

'Celia? Are you in there?' I said, banging on the door.

I heard nothing from the other side. I tried the door handle, and found it locked. The key she'd given me did not work. I tried each of the other doors, again knocking and calling for my great-aunt.

Luke placed a hand on my shoulder. 'The spiders are climbing the inside of the building.' He looked back towards the lounge room. 'The windows won't hold.'

I turned back to the door. 'Great-Aunt Celia!' I cried again. 'Celia, wake up!'

'Her fox stole was not by the door,' Luke remarked.

'Celia?'

There was still no answer. Despite the glowing candles, I had to assume she was not home.

Strange how the red candle danced like that.

I walked blindly to the corner where I'd seen the coffin, and when my toes found it I bent and opened the lid. A faint flicker of light glowed from within. 'Luke, close the door behind us. Quick, into the coffin.' Despite the absurdity of my statement, he did as I said. I pulled the lid fully open and crawled inside, and Luke followed. It shut above us with a dull thud. I prayed that my great-aunt was somewhere safe.

*Wow.*

The staircase beneath the open bottom of the casket led down to a darkened hallway of old stone. There was a flickering candle in a rusted wall sconce. Beneath it was a pile of white wax, rising up like a melted snowman. The place smelled slightly of sulfur. In the candle's light I could see that the stone walls were stained with age exactly like the exterior of the mansion. There was no furniture here, no wallpaper, carpeting or hardwood floors.

'It's a secret entrance, I think. Deus uses it,' I told Luke. In one direction the stairs led down. In the other direction they went up. I paused for a moment, pondering the best course of action. I found myself instinctively headed for the descending staircase.

But Luke took me suddenly by the elbow. 'I don't think you want to go that way,' he told me firmly.

I felt a rush of unexpected annoyance and stiffened, wanting to shake off his grip. For an awkward moment we stood that way in the corridor, my body urging me down the dark staircase and Luke holding me fast. I became aware of an unnatural pull, and an odd, faintly sulfurous smell coming up the stairs towards me. Something about it was distantly familiar. And then I remembered what Celia had said:

*If you discover a passage that leads underground, do not take it. Do you hear me? Not even with your guide.*

'Here. This way leads to the roof,' Luke suggested, gently pulling me back from my thoughts, and from the strange pull I had felt. Of course he knew about these passages. He had been present in this building for many years. He probably knew every nook and cranny in the place. 'Come with me, Miss Pandora.'

He let go of my elbow and offered his hand. I took it.

I turned on my heel, and from the corner of my eye caught a glimpse of the most horrifying sight.

'Spiders. Look!' They were coming up the stone staircase, crawling over the walls in a steady stream, like a dark wave rolling up the corridor. The mansion was slowly drowning in spiders.

'Up! We must go up!' I said. 'Quick!' I grabbed the candle and protected the flame in my palm. It lit the way for us as we ascended the cold, damp steps that soon began to change direction and pull into a tight circle.

'We are in one of the turrets, aren't we?' I said, and Luke nodded.

We soon emerged from the turret on to the roof of the mansion. Ahead of us was a dramatically sloping roof flanked by carved gargoyles. The view was spectacular, if deadly. The night-time winter air was bracing, and I shivered in my thin nightie; I'd neglected to dress properly in my haste.

The Hunger Moon illuminated the dramatic angles and curves of the rooftop, as well as the sheer drop to street level. The streets of Spektor seemed a long way down. I felt a sudden vertigo overcome me and I swayed a little.

'I've got you,' Lieutenant Luke said, and I felt his arms around me.

I had not imagined myself to be scared of heights, but the view was dizzying.

We heard glass crashing below us.

'The spiders. They're coming in the windows.' The house would be teeming with them now. I wondered where Arachne was. Would she come in through the front door? Or . . .? I looked for a way across to another roof. Perhaps we could hide somewhere. Or make it into another building? Where was Arachne?

My question was answered far too soon.

I couldn't hide. I wasn't going anywhere.

The spider goddess appeared just beyond the edge of the sloping roof in front of us. She was rising slowly as if she were floating. Her arms were extended, and she let out a strange, high-pitched scream. She launched a web at me. I turned back to the turret but the web hit and wrapped around my lower leg, like a rope of fine, silk fishing line. I struggled to free myself, but then another shot of web hit me and knocked me over. My footing on the roof was lost, I slid down the shingles at heart-stopping speed towards the spiders and the long, steep drop to the street below. I managed to grab at a large gargoyle at the far edge of the roof and bring myself to a halt. I lost my candle and I watched it plummet over the edge and smash on the street below.

'Luke!' I called, but got no answer. I'd lost sight of him. I couldn't get the web off me, I was stuck.

Arachne rose up before me – close, so close. She was riding the mountain of spiders as though they were a living, breathing, frozen wave. Others poured up on to the roof of the mansion, across the sloped roofs and over the turrets and gargoyles. They were coming towards me.

I was trapped like a fly against the shingles, captive beneath the stars and the full glowing moon.

'Pandora English,' Arachne spat. She moved towards me and I could see the outline of her spidery legs moving beneath her clothes. 'You dare go to my factory and destroy it! And my workers! You dare try and stop me from exacting my justice?'

'Justice?' I said.

'Those designers had to pay for their boasts.'

'Like you paid, you mean? When you boasted you were the best?'

'I paid dearly, but I shall pay no more. I've lived in the shadows of this world long enough. If this world will not accept me, I will make this world mine. I will make the world my web, and my children will inhabit every inch of the Earth.' She gestured to the thousands of spiders behind her, and I wondered whether my dream had been real. Whether beneath the eight-legged bodies were real people consumed by her pride. She moved closer, until her pointed spider legs touched the edge of the roof. I could see them, long and thin, and dangerous. She leaned over me. 'And I can't have the likes of you around to get in my way . . .'

Arachne smiled, and revealed a set of fangs – horrible,

dark fangs. They lengthened with sickening speed until they were bigger than the fangs of any vampire.

*What is it with everyone and fangs?*

She was on the roof now, more sure-footed than I could ever have been on my bare human feet. In one movement she hunkered down on all six of her horrible legs, and crouched forward, her human neck stretched at a gut-wrenching angle, eyes staring at me. She came towards me, and crept *over* me, her large, spider belly bulging over my hips and thighs, her strong, thin spider legs flexing. She straddled me and I couldn't even move. My legs were still caught in the webbing, which was probably all that kept me from falling off the sloped roof and down on to the street below.

My arms were still free though. I swung a fist at her delicate jaw, but she caught it in one try, and squeezed my fist in hers with disturbing strength.

'You are so powerless, little mortal. Don't you see?'

Using two human arms and two spider legs, she forced my arms back on to the shingles and bit into my shoulder. I felt the spider fangs go in, piercing my skin and immediately setting my body on fire with an acid sting. When she pulled back I could see her fangs dripped with an unearthly green fluid. She wiped her mouth with one black sleeve of her robe, and the hideous fangs slipped away again, as if that small dark mouth were almost human.

*No!*

I could feel the paralysis of her spider kiss almost instantly.

Soon I was completely paralysed, and wrapped in her web

of sticky thread. I could no longer even struggle against the silk binds.

'*The Seventh?* Look at you. Such a reputation, and yet look at how pathetic you are. You'll be my little treat tonight. One tiny triumph before I take on bigger things. Normally I prefer to devour men, but you will do fine, little girl. You should be honoured to be at my table.' She tilted her warped face and examined me closely. 'Yes . . .'

I would have shivered, or perhaps even vomited, but I could not move a thing except my eyes, which I held wide open. Then my eyes blinked. And blinked again. I felt a poisonous sleep pull at me, urging me to fall away into nothing. Anything was better than this paralysis, this helplessness . . . *no*, I had to stay awake, had to find a way to escape this. My head spun and, though I urged my body into action, I could not wiggle even my toes. Only my eyes could still move, though it seemed increasingly hard to keep them open. And now my eyes detected movement.

A glint of steel.

A blur of uniform.

Luke!

Lieutenant Luke Thomas appeared from behind the gargoyle, perched over the statue, holding tight, his cavalry sword in his hand, the tip pointing right at Arachne.

'Back away! Back away from her now!' he shouted.

Arachne paused over me, and looked up at him, straining her unnaturally bent neck. 'Ah, you're more like it,' she said. 'I like a man in uniform. But wait your turn while I deal with this one. Apparently she's special . . .'

Quickly the spider goddess reared up and threw a web at

Luke. He dodged it, but temporarily lost his footing. My heart skipped as he swung precariously to one side. His cap slipped off his head and tumbled through the air, disappearing over the edge of the building. *No!* As a ghost he might be safe, but his new, human body could not survive a five-storey fall to the street below.

I saw the sabre fall from his hand. I watched it as if in slow motion.

*The Kumokirimaru*, I thought. *The spider killer.*

And then to my amazement it wasn't falling at all. I could *feel* it. With my mind. And in my mind I held it, making it fly towards us, spinning, the blade flashing in the moonlight.

Arachne shrieked.

She pulled her robes back and grasped the hilt of the sabre. Somehow it had gone right through her belly. 'No! My babies. No!' she screamed, gasping and squirming. The tip of the sword poked right through the robe at her back. There was a hole in her, and now the skulls of her victims began to tumble out of her distended belly – skulls and baby spiders. She screeched again and again, and all around us, her spiders began to screech. It was a terrifying, unnatural sound, high-pitched but louder than thunder – the sound of thousands of nails on a giant chalkboard. The spiders that surrounded me began to jerk and shrivel as they screamed, curling up like burning paper, and with them, the webbing across the building began to shrivel.

As did the webbing that held me to the roof.

I felt myself start to slip. One inch. Two. I had no voice to cry out, no limbs to stop myself from tumbling away.

*Oh god . . .*

My bare feet could not find a grip on the steep shingles. I only had inches to the edge, and in seconds I found myself sliding right past the screaming goddess that held me.

I hit the edge of the roof and plummeted over.

Paralysed and motionless, I nonetheless thought I heard something as I fell – a voice. Not mine, not Luke's. 'Deus, would you mind?' I thought I heard someone say. *Was that Celia?*

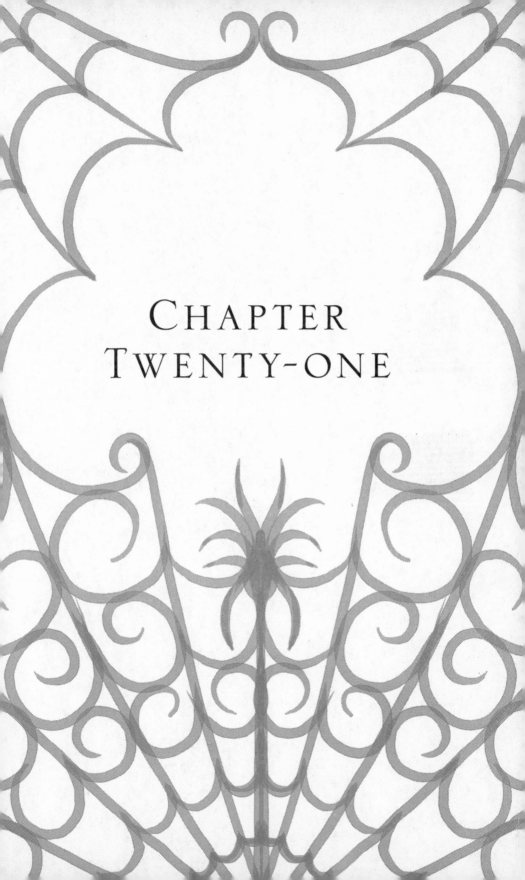

# CHAPTER
# TWENTY-ONE

I woke in Celia's antechamber.

I felt like I'd been coming in and out of consciousness for a while, and when my eyes finally fixed and focused on something, it was on the bright flame over a red candle. It seemed to flicker and dance an inch or two above the top of the wick.

'Celia?'

The sounds of the room around me came in and out. I recognised Celia's voice, and Luke's. Though I tried, I could not form words. Someone was telling me to drink some more, and I realised that I had been drinking something that still clung to my mouth. I licked my lips.

*Strange. Sticky.*

'It's safe now. We saved her,' I heard Great-Aunt Celia say, and she seemed to be talking to me. Her face appeared above me, white and serene beneath her widow's veil. 'Don't fret darling, I made sure she didn't die.'

'Didn't . . . die?'

I sat up on my elbows with some effort, and felt Luke's warm arms around me. 'Miss Pandora, you're all right. I'm so sorry I let you fall.'

I took in the dimly lit room around me. I was on the velvet chaise lounge. The three candles still burned on the low, carved table. There was a glass of red wine, and a jar on the table – a small glass jar.

'If we keep her in there much longer we'll have to poke some holes in the lid so she can breathe,' Celia said.

'Are you saying —'

'That is Arachne. Yes.'

It seemed only a moment ago that Arachne was destined to destroy all of Spektor, and now my great-aunt was concerned that she be kept alive? That she got enough oxygen? The surprise must have shown on my face, because Celia added, 'As you well know, I couldn't let her die. There would be ecological ramifications.'

*You shall live to swing, to live now and forever, even to the last hanging creature of your kind.*

'If she dies then spiders will become extinct?' I asked.

Celia only gave a quick nod. 'She is the goddess of all spiders.'

I swung my rubbery legs off the lounge and leaned forward to look at the jar. The woman – the *goddess* – who had been intent on devouring me piece by piece now looked impossibly small and vulnerable trapped in that tiny glass jar. Her expressive human face was pure spider now, her half-human torso had morphed into a plump, round shiny black body marked with the distinctive red hourglass of the black widow, the bright red marking just where Luke's sword had cut her open – as if all black widow spiders had been created to show that piece of present history on their bodies. Where once Arachne had slender, human arms above six monstrous limbs, she now had eight tapering spider legs. She was perhaps ten millimetres long. There was nothing about this little spider to indicate she was the immortal weaver, the goddess of the ancient tale.

'You saved me, Luke. It was so close. I thought you'd dropped your sword but you got her. You are amazing. She would have eaten me.'

'But that was you, young Pandora. You took hold of that sword.' It was Celia who spoke.

'But, I couldn't move.' Then I remembered the strange feeling I'd had. The feeling I was controlling the sword. Had that been real?

'It's true, Miss Pandora,' Lieutenant Luke said.

My great-aunt smiled. 'You didn't know, did you? You have the gift of Mind Movement, just like Madame Aurora.'

*Mind Movement?*

'Telekinesis. Once you learn to harness it, it will come in quite handy, I should think. And just imagine what else you can do. This is just the beginning.'

I blinked. Was it possible? Telekinesis. I opened my mouth to protest, but fell silent. I thought of how the jar with the tarantula in it had been shaken from my bag, and yet it had ended up in my hand before anyone could see.

*Imagine what else you can do . . .*

'How are you feeling?' It was a male voice, not Luke. I scanned the antechamber until my eyes fell upon a third person. Well, not a person.

*Deus.*

'Good evening, young lady,' he said, stepping into the pool of light thrown by the candles, and grinning his magnetic Kathakano grin. I felt myself lurch forward. 'Take it easy now. The first drink is the strongest,' he said.

First drink? My eyes moved to the glass of red wine and I squinted. I brought my hand to my lips and then gazed at it. There was blood on my fingers.

*No!*

'Don't worry. I only gave you enough to kill Arachne's poison. Celia's strict instructions, you understand.' He crossed his heart.

I was speechless.

'Remember to be grateful, Pandora,' Celia told me in a low voice. 'If Deus was not so talented at flight, he wouldn't have got to you in time. A lesser Sanguine could not have done it.'

He could fly. I remembered the shadow I'd seen fly past my window that night, just before our second meeting. And now I'd been drinking his blood . . .

'I have to get up,' I said. 'Now.' I pushed myself forward and felt my ankles wobble.

'Your legs may not be strong enough yet,' my great-aunt warned. 'The poison was quite toxic.'

Just like that, Lieutenant Luke scooped me up off the chaise lounge and into his arms. With effort I linked my arms around his neck.

*I hate the whole damsel-in-distress look, but heck, it's awfully nice up here.* I found myself smiling as full feeling returned to my face.

'I'll take care of her tonight,' Luke said.

My great-aunt gave me a wink. 'He's keen, isn't he?' she said.

'Well, I should be going.' Deus gave a courteous bow. 'I do so hope you won't let my blood go to waste?' He eyed the wine glass.

'Darling, are you kidding?' Celia said. She and Deus brushed lips, and she whispered something in his ear. He bid us goodnight, walked to the casket on the floor, opened it and disappeared inside. He'd no doubt exit via the roof.

Celia opened the door to the penthouse and Luke walked me over the threshold. I felt weirdly like a bride. A bride in the arms of a dead, yet not dead, Civil War soldier. He carried me down the hallway to the lounge room and Celia followed after us with the jar. She carried it very carefully, I noticed.

Celia placed the jar on her shelf and turned. Beneath her veil I watched her take in Lieutenant Luke, from his leather boots to his handsome, chiselled face and back down again. The corners of her perfectly painted mouth turned up ever so slightly, I noticed, but she said nothing. Luke did not notice her appraisal. He was too busy watching me attentively.

'Your legs will be fine in a few minutes. How about I fix us some tea, to help wash things down,' Celia suggested.

I swallowed. 'Yes please.' The less I thought about what I'd been drinking, the better.

I indicated Celia's hassock, and Luke gently placed me there. 'I'm so glad you are okay, Miss Pandora,' he said, and kissed my hand. I tried to run through what had happened since he'd woken me. The sight of Spektor under siege. The race to the roof. The confrontation.

Celia soon returned with perfectly prepared cups of tea on her silver tray. 'I was so worried about you, Great-Aunt Celia,' I told her. 'When I entered the antechamber I saw the candles glowing, and I thought you might be somewhere inside.'

'Ah, the offering to the Triple Goddess.' She handed the tray around and we each took a cup. 'The Mother was powerful tonight, was she not?' she said, and disappeared back into the kitchen.

'The . . . Triple Goddess?'

I thought of the red candle. I had woken staring at it. And the low table. And then it finally occurred to me that there might be a word for what my great-aunt was. I'd at one time worried fleetingly that she was a vampire − or Sanguine. But a *witch*? It hadn't crossed my mind until now, though looking back, perhaps it should have. There were signs I might have picked up on, had I not been blinded by Hollywood's Wicked Witch of the West with her pointy hat and green warty skin. The witch was always depicted as the embodiment of female ugliness and evil; polar opposites of the attributes my great-aunt possessed.

Celia returned to lean on the leather arm of her reading chair. 'Ah, *The Wizard of Oz*,' she lamented, and sighed. It seemed Celia knew precisely what I was thinking. The thought made me blush. 'You didn't think we all ride broomsticks, did you?'

'Sorry,' I muttered awkwardly. After my childhood exposure to history and mythology, I knew better, and yet the cliché had popped into my head in all its neon-green Halloween hideousness.

*Great Aunt-Celia – telepathic, half-Sanguine witch?*

But of course, my great-aunt was never one for labels. True to form, she changed the subject. 'Now darling, our guest requires rather a better home, don't you think?'

I turned to Luke, who stood just next to me, politely sipping his tea as if it might still be 1860, and he'd been taken home to meet the folks.

'Not him,' Celia said. 'Her.'

*Arachne.* The jar was on her shelf.

'But where did all the other spiders go? The web they were creating around the building?' I asked.

'The spiders were extensions of her, and when her powers vanished, so did they.' Celia looked around the lounge room and frowned. 'Though the shattered windows remain. Shame.'

It was quite a mess.

'So they weren't real spiders?'

'It depends what you mean by real. They certainly weren't imaginary, were they?'

'No wonder it wouldn't eat,' I remarked of the spider I'd brought home.

'The tarantula. Yes.'

It had spied on me. It had led her straight to me.

Celia walked across to her bookshelf and took down the spider's vivarium. 'Now, help me put her in here,' she instructed, and pointed at the jar. 'Your legs should be fine now.'

I stood up slowly and circled my ankles and wrists. The poison did seem to have worn off. I exchanged glances with Luke, who carefully watched what Celia was doing.

I walked up to the jar, and looked in. Arachne scuttled along the round base of her glass prison. The tiny hairs on the back of my neck stood on end. What if she became the spider goddess once more and tried to devour me?

'And when she's in the vivarium, um . . . assuming we get her in there . . . what if the spell you cast wears off and —'

'Have you no trust in me yet, Pandora?' Celia calmly asked.

I blushed. Of course I trusted her. She had only ever helped me, despite my naivety and, at times, my resistance. And now she had used her powers and her connections to well and truly save my life.

I raised the glass jar and marvelled at the moment – here I was with my unnaturally youthful, stereotype-defying witchy great-aunt, holding a spider that used to be a woman and a goddess, and talking about spells wearing off. Oh how my life had changed since leaving Gretchenville.

'She is in stasis. Neither dying, nor transforming back into her original human self.'

'How did you do that? I mean, transform her?'

'Well, she was already half-transformed, and like I've said many times, I'm not so powerless. Besides, magick works well on magick, especially when the timing is right.' Celia had laid the vivarium on the floor. 'The same magick that allowed her rather showy entrance into our little neighbourhood also helped transform her into what we see now. The moon is full and the magick is high tonight. The Mother is at her most powerful. Thankfully she picked our side. This time.'

We both gazed at the little jar, and the spider trapped within it.

'Go on. It is for you to do,' Celia told me.

I unlocked the top of the beautiful castle, placed the lid on the floor of the lounge room and, holding my breath, unscrewed the top of the little jar. I placed it inside and tilted it, and the spider slid into her new home. I quickly retracted my hand, placed the lid back on top, and locked it. When it was done I breathed a deep sigh.

'See, it's perfect for her.'

Thousands of years ago, the spider had been a mortal woman, then an immortal goddess, and now she looked like nothing more than a common black widow spider. Was she self-aware? I wondered. Did this little spider know who she had been? I suppressed a shiver at the thought of being trapped in another creature's body. My experience of being paralysed in her web was bad enough. I felt a rush of sympathy, until I remembered that she'd aimed to eat me.

My wise and beautiful great-aunt placed the little castle back on the shelf in her lounge room, alongside her other curios. I found myself looking at each item – the small vase, the tiny figurine carved of bone, the art deco nymph, the Venus flytrap plant – and I wondered what or *who* they were.

'Great-Aunt Celia?'

'Yes, darling?'

'Are there any other goddesses here in your lounge room?'

She only smiled.

'Now, I have a certain someone to catch up with,' Celia said, and I knew she meant Deus. 'Don't you two do anything I wouldn't,' she told us. She turned on her elegant heel and left Luke and I alone.

I looked at my companion. The Hunger Moon was still full, shining through the broken windows behind him, silhouetting his frame.

We had tonight. I knew that much. We had tonight.

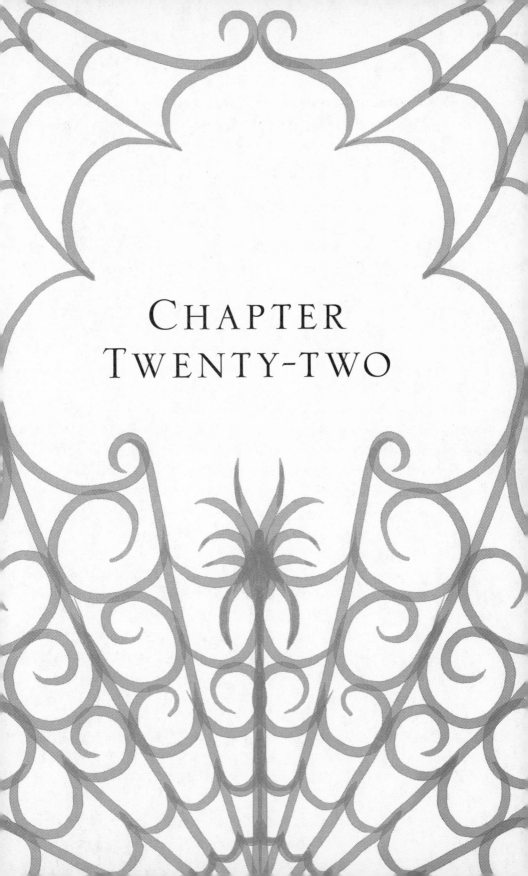

# CHAPTER
# TWENTY-TWO

On Monday I arrived at work to find a gorgeous white orchid on my desk, wrapped in a large, red bow. I assumed at first that the beautiful flower was for my boss, Skye, but to my surprise, I found that the card had my name on it.

PANDORA ENGLISH

Can ghosts send flowers? I wondered at once. The morning after the Hunger Moon I'd woken alone, with Luke's sword on the floor of my room. I hoped he would be back. I hoped . . .

*It can't be from Luke.*

I opened the card to find I was right. It wasn't from my soldier friend. It was a thankyou card from Laurie Smith, of Smith & Co. After a lifetime of being underappreciated in the real world, I was unprepared for this show of thanks. My surprise, of course, didn't match the bafflement of my deputy editor, who stood over me as I opened the card.

'Laurie Smith? Why would he send you an orchid?' Pepper said.

'We got on pretty well,' I answered.

I wondered how much he remembered.

'Oh.' She seemed thrown by the attention I'd received.

'What information did you get?' she asked, and put out her hand.

'Just the basics, like you asked for,' I told her. 'But I didn't get anything from the other studio,' I said. 'No one was there.'

*No one human, anyway.*

'And I wasn't able to get anyone on the phone,' I added.

'Oh. I'll check it out. The Smith & Co quote is probably more important anyway. Thanks.' She walked back to her desk with the notes I had transcribed.

This time I was the one thrown. I was impressed, hearing that six-letter word from her.

The knitwear piece was going to print, and there would not be one single mention of the missing designers, whom I knew perfectly well were never coming back. The cover and fashion spread would feature fashions by Victor Mal, Richard Helmsworth, Sandy Chow, Smith & Co and a lesser-known knitwear company called Arachne, which I was sure didn't have much of a future.

I had the feeling Smith & Co were about to corner the market.

At twenty minutes past five, hours after the latest issue of *Pandora* magazine was put to bed, I stared intently at an ordinary ballpoint pen on my desk.

*Come on, Pandora.*

*Come on . . .*

'Nothing,' I muttered with disappointment when it was clear the pen was not going to move. Mind Movement? Could

I really do it? Maybe if I started with something smaller? A paperclip?

I was distracted from my failed attempts at telekinesis by a chime at the door. To my surprise, Skye DeVille walked in. I'd written her off for the day, and was ready to start packing it in myself, but in a way I was kind of glad she was finally making an appearance. I'd snuck the stolen Chanel jewellery back into her office, and I wondered what she would say when she found it. And I was even more curious about how she would be after a weekend off from Athanasia's parasitic attentions.

*That woman has a lot to thank me for, not that she will ever know . . .*

Skye sauntered past reception in a trailing outfit of black and maroon, chin in the air like nothing was amiss, and made her way straight towards her little office without a word. And all the time as she approached, I found myself staring. My stomach grew colder, and colder. With some effort I tore my eyes from the pallor of her skin, her change of dress, the way she seemed so indefinably separate from the rest of the office.

I took a glance at the window. Twenty past five. That was very late. The winter sun was low.

Oh boy.

Pepper saw her boss hide away in her office, and she marched straight over and knocked on the door. I heard the doorknob turn. On instinct, I grabbed my things and stood up, as if to greet her and bid her farewell for the day. When Skye opened the door I pretended to drop my satchel.

'Oops!'

I picked up the bag clumsily, letting some things spill.

'What are you doing?' Skye demanded in a shrill voice.

The little bag I always carried with me had fallen out, and a handful of rice grains were spread out across the floor at Skye's feet. My face turned a deep crimson, despite the purposefulness of my act.

'I, uh, dropped my leftovers from lunch,' I said lamely.

'You eat uncooked rice?' Pepper asked.

I knelt on the floor, and watched Skye for a reaction. Nothing. There was no reaction from her but an obvious and predictable disdain for me. She didn't begin counting grains. This was good news because it probably meant she wasn't on her way to becoming a Fledgling vampire. It was bad news because she now thought me even worse of an idiot than before.

'What on earth is wrong with that girl?' I heard Pepper say under her breath as she stepped inside the door of Skye's office.

What indeed.

And then the worst possible thing happened. Skye DeVille followed Pepper inside, and then paused. She turned and cocked her head, looking at the ground where I knelt.

I saw her lips move. One, two, three . . .

My god, she's counting.

# ACKNOWLEDGEMENTS

This is the bit where I gush about how fortunate I am to have amazing people in my life.

I need to firstly thank Rod Morrison, who came to me years ago with the idea that I ought to branch into a new series. Thanks for coming around on the supernatural, and for letting me build Spektor. I'll always treasure the sight of you in plastic fangs. You are missed. A special thanks to Cate, Claire, Joel, Caitlin and the team at Pan Macmillan for your support and hard work, and for believing in Pandora.

I count myself truly lucky to have friend/literary agent/fairy godmother/Great-Aunt Celia inspiration Selwa Anthony in my life. You and Brian are family. Thanks also to the support of the Foxtel family, 13th Street and CI Network. It's been an awesome year.

I am blessed to have the most wonderful friends, including the Gothmother Alison, Aunty Hels, Mindi, Sarah, Caroline, Amelia and Desi, Misty, Kelly and Mick, Jacinta, Lizzy, Lauren and Josh, Tessa and Shane, Martin, Josh, Nige and Brig, Penelope and Karim, Jody and Simon, Jack and Venetia, Charlotte, Jenny and Linda (Forever Miss J). Whether there are trees falling at my doorstep, my crazy house needs warming or I need a word of encouragement, you are always there. And to my precious family Dad and Lou, Dorothy and Nik, Maureen, Jacquelyn and Annelies, I love you. Mum, I never forget you. To my beautiful husband Berndt and our girl Sapphira Jane, thank you for making me such a happy woman. This year has been the best of my life.

Thank you Wiccan goddess Fiona Horne for the obsidian. And thank you to Charles Addams, and of course *The Spider Goddess* herself for the inspiration.

We all have a hidden Spektor.